That damned noise again!

I'm not imagining it, Smith thought. But what the hell could it be? Leeches falling off the ferns? Some kind of jungle cat? Vietcong looking for me? VC!

He heard the noise again. Definitely VC!

Smith moved his sweaty hand forward along the dirt-encrusted stock of the Garand M-1 with agonizing slowness. His entire left arm felt as if it were made of lead. When his fingers finally reached the trigger guard, he had to push a leech out of the way before he could ease the safety off. He barely had the strength to do it, but the adrenaline was pumping again. Not much, but enough. He'd manage somehow. They weren't going to take him without a fight. His other hand found the fore end of the rifle, steadying the heavy weapon against his shoulder. The humidity in the jungle was oppressive. Just another enemy.

All right, I'm ready for you sons of bitches, Smith thought. I'm not going to die in Vietnam.

Also available by Eric Helm:

VIETNAM: GROUND ZERO

VIETNAM: GROUND ZERO
P.O.W.

ERIC HELM

A GOLD EAGLE BOOK FROM
W☉RLDWIDE

TORONTO • NEW YORK • LONDON • PARIS
AMSTERDAM • STOCKHOLM • HAMBURG
ATHENS • MILAN • TOKYO • SYDNEY

To Captain Humbert Rocque Versace
and Sergeant Kenneth M. Roraback,
who resisted to the end.

And to Ellie, who waited patiently
through the long months.

First edition October 1986

ISBN 0-373-62702-5

Printed in Canada

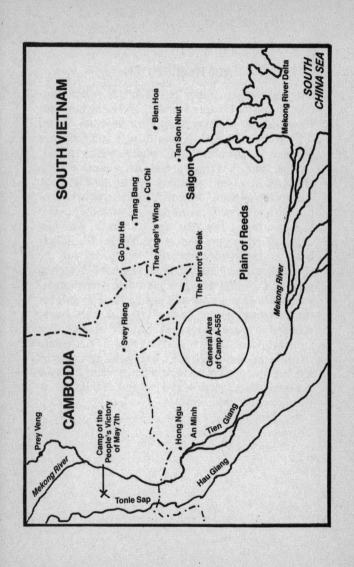

AUTHOR'S NOTE:

On or about September 25, 1965, U.S. Army Captain Humbert Rocque Versace, an Intelligence advisor with the Military Assistance Advisory Group (MAAG) at Ca Mau (Quan Long), and Sergeant Kenneth M. Roraback, a communications specialist with the U.S. Army Special Forces camp at Hiep Hoa (Ap Tan Hoa) were executed by the Vietcong. According to Radio Hanoi, Versace, who was captured while accompanying a patrol from the Special Forces camp at Tan Phu, and Roraback, who was captured during the Vietcong attack on Hiep Hoa, both in 1963, were executed in reprisal for the shooting in Da Nang of three suspected Vietcong prisoners by the South Vietnamese government. Roraback's name evidently caused some trouble for the Vietcong, as the Radio Hanoi announcement referred to him as Sergeant Coraback, apparently a contraction of his first and last names. According to the radio announcement, both men were shot by a firing squad at ten o'clock in the morning. The exact date, time, location and method of their executions remains unknown.

VIETNAM: GROUND ZERO
P.O.W.

PROLOGUE

CAMP OF THE PEOPLE'S
VICTORY OF MAY 7TH,
CAMBODIA

The camp sat about a dozen kilometers inside Cambodia, some forty-odd kilometers east of Takeo and a bit farther south by southwest of Prey Veng. It was situated between the Tonle Sap Thaot and Mekong River, almost due north of the point where they crossed the border into South Vietnam and became the Song Hau Giang and the Song Tien Giang. Despite the official ''neutrality'' of the Sathearnak Roath Khmer and the Sihanouk government in Phnom Penh, the camp was a Vietcong operation and training camp.

Major Vo Dinh Tien stared out the doorway of the tin-roofed grass hut that was his office, his bedroom and the center of his life and tried to penetrate the late-afternoon rain that looked like a curtain as it fell just beyond the overhang of the tiny bamboo porch. It was a wasted effort. He couldn't see more than half a meter beyond the porch, and for one insane moment he wondered vaguely whether the camp was still there.

Perhaps it has all been washed away by the rain, thought Vo. Perhaps it is all gone now: the radio shack that houses the old French radio that never works, the longhouses or barracks of bamboo where the men sleep, even the kitchen where the miserable excuse of a cook prepares indigestible meals. Perhaps all these things are no more forever.

And then Vo carried the dream one step further. Perhaps not only were these things no longer there, but maybe they had never been there at all.

Suddenly Vo was no longer standing in a hut in the middle of the Cambodian jungle. He was back once more in his home in Hue, listening to the rain beat upon the tin roof and watching the people outside scurrying by the window, struggling to stay dry beneath their parasols. The vivid colors of the parasols reflecting brightly but without shape on the wet asphalt, the effect reminding Vo of an artist's watercolor.

Vo could hear his young wife, Tam, singing softly as she prepared an early supper for them in the tiny kitchen of their three-room flat. Both were students at the Imperial College for Administration, she majoring in classical Chinese literature, he in the political history of Western Europe. They had met one day by accident while both were walking along the bank of the Song Huong, the Perfume River. It had been love at first sight, love such as Vo had believed occurred only in storybooks. But their love had been real. It had lasted almost three years now and seemed to grow greater every day.

They had married at the end of the first year despite some misgivings of their parents. But there were advantages in coming from financially secure families with good connections other than being able to attend college. Tam's father was a dentist in Hue, Vo's father a career bureaucrat in the French Colonial government in Hanoi. Both had become exposed to Western ideas through the influence of the French in Indochina. Had they been Vietnamese traditionalists, marriage while still in college would have been impossible. But then, had they both been Vietnamese traditionalists, college itself would have been out of the question.

Vo laid aside the book he had been reading, a history of the French Revolution, pushed back his chair and stood. Two short steps carried him to the window, and he looked down the street toward the bus stop where a young French soldier dressed in khaki and a blue overseas cap was attempting to offer his trench coat to a Vietnamese woman who looked to be about thirty. The soldier's offer was not being very graciously received. The rain had ruined the woman's parasol and her expensive French hairdo. It had also soaked through her white silk dress and plastered it to her body in such a fashion that, even from where Vo stood, it was obvious that the woman had gone out without wearing a bra. This startling revelation had attracted the attention of several onlookers, to the woman's obvious embarrassment, and the young soldier, in a show of French chivalry, was apparently offering her his coat to spare her further embarrassment. The woman evidently had misinterpreted the offer, however, and an argument ensued that ended when she struck the soldier with her parasol and strode off down the street. The young soldier stared after the woman for a few moments, then shrugged in Gallic fashion and struggled back into his coat before walking in the opposite direction.

Vo laughed out loud at the spectacle because it was good.

One week later it all came to an end. At two o'clock in the morning, a peremptory knocking heralded the arrival of a half-dozen French paratroopers dressed in camouflage fatigues and carrying MAT-49 submachine guns. Before he could even ask what it was about, Vo was punched, kicked, handcuffed and thrown into the back of a French army truck. His only clear memory of the arrest was hearing the screams of his young wife coming from the bedroom before he was dragged outside.

For nearly two weeks Vo was a guest of the French military authorities. During that time he was seldom fed, frequently beaten and endlessly questioned. The French interrogator, a lieutenant with the unlikely name of Krause, was very polite. Never once did he threaten Vo or strike him. Lieutenant Krause left that unpleasant chore to other soldiers, who were only too willing to oblige. Lieutenant Krause merely asked the questions. He was, after all, trying to help Vo out of a serious predicament, the good lieutenant explained. But there was little he could do for him if Vo did not cooperate and answer the questions.

On the fourth or fifth day Lieutenant Krause greeted Vo with his usual pleasant smile at the start of their session. He even offered Vo a cup of coffee and a cigarette, a Galois. Lieutenant Krause explained to Vo that he was in a good mood that day. During the night, Krause further explained, Vo's wife had admitted being a Vietminh agent and was now cooperating fully with the French in their investigation of the Communist terrorist organization. Lieutenant Krause even hinted that Vo's wife would be released as soon as she had finished making her statement.

Perhaps, the lieutenant theorized, she would be released as soon as that afternoon and be home in time for supper. Now, surely, the lieutenant suggested, Vo would also want to cooperate with the French in their investigation, especially since his wife was being so cooperative.

Vo told Lieutenant Krause that he was very pleased to hear that his wife was going to be allowed to go home and that he would like very much to cooperate with him, especially if it meant that he would not be beaten again. But there was really nothing he could tell the lieutenant since he did not know anyone who was a Vietminh. Vo told the lieutenant for the thousandth time that of course he had heard of the Vietminh and the Vietnam Cong San. But he did not know anyone who was a Vietnamese Communist. He was only a student, and his father was a loyal employee of the French Colonial government in Hanoi.

"You say that you do not know any Vietcong," said Lieutenant Krause. "But your wife is a Vietcong. She had told us that she is a Vietminh agent. Surely you do not expect us to believe you do not know your own wife?" Lieutenant Krause looked at Vo from behind his desk, and his smile grew even wider.

Vo replied that he could only repeat what he had already told the lieutenant.

"I see," the lieutenant said pleasantly. Then he got up from his chair and walked around to the front of his desk. He took the cigarette from Vo's mouth and dropped it into Vo's coffee. Then he set the coffee cup carefully upon the desk and, still smiling, nodded slightly to the two soldiers who were standing on either side of Vo, holding hard rubber truncheons.

The remainder of Vo's stay with the French military authorities was a blur of more beatings, most questioning and an illuminating introduction to what a field telephone could be used for other than communication.

And then one day the French grew tired of the game and let him go. They did not bother to officially release him; they couldn't since he had never been officially arrested or charged. They simply let him go.

A guard came and unlocked the steel door of Vo's cell and left it open. Vo, suspecting a trick of some kind, remained where he was for over an hour. When it finally became obvious to Vo that no one was coming to get him or to relock the door, he got up from the floor of his cell and shuffled slowly to the doorway. He cautiously looked outside.

The long hallway was empty. Vo walked slowly toward the concrete stairs, past the other cells. Most of the steel doors were locked. A few, like his own, stood open, but the cells were empty, waiting for the arrival of new guests.

At the top of the stairs, Vo stumbled along a hallway painted a sickly yellow-brown whose only remarkable features were a series of wooden office doors set on either side. Vo did not try to open any of those doors. When he got to the end of the hallway, he tried the door he found there, which opened easily and let him out into the booking room of the military police station. Timidly Vo approached the bored-looking sergeant sitting behind the high desk.

"What is happening?" Vo asked.

"You may leave," said the sergeant.

"I am free? You are releasing me?" Vo asked incredulously.

"You may leave," the sergeant repeated. He said it in a tone that indicated to Vo it would be better if he did not ask any more questions.

Vo walked unsteadily to the door, fully expecting at any moment to be seized by soldiers and dragged back to his cell, but nothing of the sort happened. He pushed open the heavy doors and made his way shakily down the steps. It was late afternoon, and the street was alive with bicycles, motor scooters and lambrettas. No one paid him the slightest attention.

Sure that there would be a sudden cry of alarm behind him or that he would be struck down by a bullet in the back, he walked along the sidewalk away from the military police station. Vo went several blocks before he realized that no one was going to come running after him and walked a few more blocks before he realized where he was and that he was going in the wrong direction.

He was shirtless and barefoot, and his pants were torn and filthy. Except for a few mildly curious glances from passersby, however, nobody seemed particularly interested in Vo Dinh Tien or where he had spent the past twelve-and-a-half days.

Vo walked several blocks out of his way to make sure that he stayed well clear of the military police station, and then he went home to the apartment near the Imperial College. He had no money for a pedicab or the bus, and the trip took him nearly an hour and a half. When he arrived, there was a padlock on the door.

Another hour's walk brought him to the house of his father-in-law. There was no padlock this time, but the door was still locked, and no one answered his knock. Vo was in despair. He had no money, no place to go and no hope. He paced aimlessly in front of the house for some minutes, then finally sat down on the step and began to weep softly.

After a while a neighbor woman whom Vo had met once or twice approached him cautiously, looking about nervously as she crossed the street. She invited him in and gave him some food and one of her husband's old shirts and a pair of sandals that were too small for Vo's feet. She explained that Dr. Cao and his wife had gone to stay with relatives in Da Nang because the French suspected them of being Communist sympathizers. They had left her an address in Da Nang and some money should she see him. They were not staying at the address, but he could get a message to them there. Did he wish the money and the address?

"Yes," said Vo. "I will take them. Have you any news of my wife?"

"Only rumor," said the neighbor woman.

"What do the rumors say?" asked Vo.

"They say that your wife is dead," said the woman.

Strangely, Vo found himself unsurprised to hear the news. Too much had already happened. His system was already numb with shock.

"Do you know how she died?" he asked quietly.

The woman did not answer him.

"How did my wife die?" he shouted at the woman.

"They say she was tortured to death by French paratroopers of the counterterrorist unit," she answered. "Now, take your money and your address and go. Please. You must go before the French come and find you in my house."

Vo took the money and the address and left. But he did not go to Da Nang, nor did he go to his father's home in Hanoi. He went instead back to the Imperial College and began asking questions of his friends. Most of them were reluctant to talk to him and eager to see him leave. But eventually he found one who introduced him to a classmate who might know someone else who could possibly introduce him to a man that could tell Vo what he wanted to know.

When Vo was finally introduced to the man that could answer his questions, Vo realized with a shock that Lieutenant Krause had been at least partially right. Vo did know someone who was a Vietcong. The man was Vo's history professor.

Three months later Vo was with a Vietminh guerrilla patrol in the Iron Triangle northwest of Saigon when it ambushed a small column of French soldiers. When the shooting stopped, the guerrillas walked out onto the road and bayoneted the survivors before stripping them of all their weapons, equipment and clothing. It was the first time Vo had killed anyone. Afterward he laughed because it was good.

Years had passed, and Vo had become a battalion commander of a main force unit of the Vietcong Army of Liberation of the National Liberation Front. The French soldiers were gone, replaced by the Americans, to whom the French had transferred both the task of propping up the Saigon government and the penchant for wearing berets and to whom Vo had transferred his consummate hatred of the French. By hating the Americans, Vo continued to hate the French by proxy. His hatred was the one thing that continued to give meaning to his life.

Almost reluctantly Vo turned away from the rain and peered into the dimness of his hut. Dau, the political commissar, and Major Ngoi, the NVA advisor, were staring at him expectantly, but Vo ignored their stares and looked past them at the Chinese advisor who stood apart, quietly smoking a filter-tipped American cigarette.

"All right, Comrade Major," said Vo, addressing the Chinese officer, "tell me. What is this brilliant new advice that the People's Liberation Army is so anxious to impart to me? What is this great new idea that judging by the look on their faces, has already been discussed with and met with the approval of my faithful advisor from the North and his political expert?"

It was a serious insult to all three men, but only the two North Vietnamese frowned, and Vo did not greatly care if they were insulted. They were seldom helpful and always putting on airs, as though being a part of the NVA made them somehow better than the Vietcong. Vo, having been born in Hanoi himself, was un-impressed with their smugly superior attitude.

The Chinese officer remained unruffled, however. He puffed briefly on his cigarette, then held it out in one hand and studied the glowing tip as he spoke.

"It is really very simple, Major Vo," he said, intentionally avoiding the Party-approved use of the title Comrade. He knew that Vo had become a Party member largely for convenience rather than conviction, much the same as he himself had done. They were both professional soldiers and ignored politics as much as the Party would allow them to do. "What I have in mind is a plan that will permit us to destroy the U.S. Army Special Forces Camp A-555 and regain domination over our entire operational region."

Vo emitted a derisive snort. "May I remind you, Comrade Major, that that has already been tried on numerous occasions, ever since the Americans built their cursed camp across the border, and the results have been uniformly disastrous."

"You may remind me if you feel it is necessary, Major Vo. But I am already well aware of these facts. Please do not forget that I was the area advisor here for a long time before you became the area commander."

"Yes. And as such you helped plan many of the previously mentioned disasters, no doubt. Why should this time be any different?"

The Chinese officer remained unperturbed. Despite Vo's abrasive manner, the Chinese had a secret liking for the man. Vo was a real fighter, unlike many of the VC and NVA he had worked with; he was an unorthodox tactician and leader. Further, Vo harbored a hatred for the common enemy that was personal rather than political, and that, in the Chinese officer's mind, made him far more reliable than any card saying he was a member in good standing of the Communist Party.

The Chinese major drew languidly on his cigarette before answering. "This time is different, Major Vo," he said, "because this time we shall not attack the body of the dragon. This time we shall cut off its head."

"You speak to me in Chinese puzzles," said Vo sourly. "Can you not tell me what you are talking about in language that a poor, dumb Vietnamese peasant can understand?"

The PLA advisor could not suppress a thin-lipped smile. He knew that Vo was not dumb and had never been a peasant.

"Certainly, Major Vo," said the Chinese. "As I said before, it is really very simple. I have devised a plan that will deliver into our hands the twelve members of Captain MacKenzie K. Gerber's U.S. Army Special Forces A-Team. How would you like to have twelve Green Berets as your guests for an extended period of time?"

There was a lengthy moment when the only sound was the hammering of the rain on the tin roof of the hut, and then, slowly, Major Vo returned the Chinese major's smile.

"Yes," said Vo. "Yes, I believe I would like that. I believe that I would find having these twelve Americans as my guests very entertaining indeed. I think, Comrade Major, that I would like to hear this plan of yours. Tell it to me."

Without further preamble the Chinese advisor unfolded his maps and began outlining his plan. He talked for forty-five minutes without interruption, and when he had finished, he carefully refolded his maps and lighted another cigarette.

"Well, Major Vo," he said at last, "does the plan meet with your approval?"

Vo got up silently from his chair and walked back to the doorway to stare once again at the rain. Then he threw back his head and laughed a deep, throaty laugh. He laughed for a very long time. He laughed because it was good.

1

THE MARKET OF
AN MINH, REPUBLIC
OF VIETNAM

Sergeant First Class Derek Kepler of the United States Army's Special Forces Detachment A-555 stood in the mud at the edge of the squalid hamlet and stared hard at the three old women, one old man and six very small children who had suddenly seemed to find one of the tiny settlement's communal cooking fires the most interesting thing in the entire world.

Kepler's fatigues were soaked with sweat and slimed with patches of rust-colored mud, which was already beginning to crust over in the heat of the midmorning sun. When he shifted his balance slightly as he transferred the heavy M-14 rifle from his left hand to his right, his feet squished softly in his jungle boots, where his toes were awash in the excrement-laden water from the rice fields to the northwest of the village. A couple of flies buzzed noisily about his head, and one of them picked Kepler's right cheekbone for a landing zone. Kepler hardly noticed. Slowly he raised his left arm to about the height of his pistol belt and, with a butterfly motion of his hand, waved his troops into the village.

The old women and the man studied the fire even more intently. They were trying very hard not to see Kepler or any of the dozen Tai strikers who had accompanied Washington and him on the patrol. Even the children were absorbed by the fire, except for one naked toddler who twisted around in the arms of the woman holding him to see what everyone else was so carefully ignoring. He stared at the soldiers in open curiosity until the woman hissed at him, and then he started to cry.

The Tai slid wordlessly past Kepler, going about the routine business of war in Indochina, the two with BARs taking up covering positions on either flank while the other ten moved down the rows of thatched bamboo huts lining either side of the red mud trail that was the hamlet's only street. With the same wordless efficiency they searched each hootch in turn, two soldiers to each hootch, one covering while the other looked for any sign of weapons, contraband or recent visitation by the Vietcong. When they got to the end of the street, they left two soldiers with grease guns at the edge of the hamlet and the other eight worked their way back toward Kepler, this time moving more slowly and checking more thoroughly, looking under grass sleeping mats for tunnel entrances, checking beneath woven blankets and iron kettles for trapdoors to spider holes, moving carefully the odd bit of strangely positioned crockery or earthenware jug that might conceal a hiding place or be wired to a booby trap.

Kepler watched the scene unfold with stoic detachment. He'd seen the same scene played out at least a hundred times before in at least half a hundred hamlets and villages, any of a dozen of which might have been this very same hamlet or at least its twin. Kepler knew that the two soldiers with submachine guns at the end of the street were unnecessary. There were another six men in the high grass out along the paddy field dike, and they had a .30 caliber Model 1919 Browning machine gun with them. The assumption was that the villagers didn't know they were out there, however, and Kepler intended to keep it that way. Things that the villagers knew about, the Vietcong had an unpleasant habit of finding out.

Kepler couldn't decide if the scene was good or not. When you went into a village and the people were going about their business and then stopped at your approach to come forward to be friendly and chatty, that was a good sign. That sort of thing didn't happen often in this part of South Vietnam. The Vietcong had a way of making those kinds of villages disappear. It was when you went into a village and everybody was just a little bit too friendly and polite that you had to be really careful. That was when you started feeling relaxed and got careless and stupid and got your ass zapped. But you could usually spot those situations by the absence of the children, who the villagers would have hidden someplace relatively safe from bullets and shrapnel. One like this was hard to figure. It could mean the men of fighting age had all slipped away to escape recruitment by the Vietcong, or they were off a klick or so up or down the trail, industriously preparing an ambush for you to walk into.

"Well, what do you think?" a voice said at last from somewhere behind Kepler. It was Washington. Kepler shot a quick glance in his direction.

Staff Sergeant Thomas Jefferson Washington, T.J. to his friends, was a large black man with a wistful smile that all by itself managed somehow to convey the impression that he would have been happier playing fullback at a Big Ten university than he was practicing medicine without a license amid the jungles, swamps and hills of Southeast Asia. He was the A-Detachment's junior medical specialist.

"Hell, I don't know," replied Kepler. "There aren't any men, and there are too few women, but they haven't hidden the kids. It ought to be all right, but one never knows . . ."

"No, my man, one never does. Which is what keeps life interesting and McMillan and me in the doctor business. Let's go see what ails these folks today, shall we?" As he spoke, he slung his rifle and opened his medical bag.

The two Americans walked slowly toward the Vietnamese, who continued to ignore them, even when the Americans were standing next to the fire.

Kepler looked down and noticed that one of the women had an angry red welt on the back of her hand, extending up her arm until it was hidden by the sleeve of her coarse white blouse. Kepler knelt, staring at the welt until finally the woman turned her head enough to look at him out of the corner of her eye. When she did so, Kepler gave her his best see-what-a-swell-guy-I-am grin. After a moment the woman grinned back, showing crooked teeth stained a deep blackish brown from chewing betel nuts. Kepler categorized it as an excellent example of see-I'm-friendly-too-you-bastard-so-what-the-fuck-do-you-want grin. It was a beginning, though, and he switched to a warmer, softer smile.

"Chao ba. Chung toi la ban. Dung so, chung toi muon giup cac ong," said Kepler, pointing to the woman's arm.

She gave him a look that said she didn't entirely believe him.

"T.J., do you want to take a look at this?" asked Kepler. "Looks like this woman has a pretty bad burn on her arm."

Washington crouched near the woman but made no move to touch her. Flashing a mouthful of bright teeth, he indicated her arm and said, "How about letting me take a look at that, ma'am. I think maybe I can do something about that burn." When the woman didn't move or speak, Washington tried his own limited Vietnamese. *"Dung so. Chung toi muon giup cac ong."* He still got no response. Finally, in exasperation, he pointed to himself and said, *"Bac si,"* then reached out and carefully took hold of her arm. The woman flinched, but didn't pull away.

Washington held the woman's arm gently as he examined it. It was a boney arm, the skin almost paper-thin yet tough and leathery. Washington pushed the sleeve up to the woman's shoulder and examined the burn. It appeared to continue onto her back. Finally he nodded and said, "Uh-huh."

"Uh-huh what?" asked Kepler impatiently.

"Uh-huh, she's got a bad burn, that's what. And I don't think it was an accident."

"Are you saying somebody did that to her on purpose?" asked Kepler.

"People burn people on purpose all the time, man. Especially in war. We do it to Charlie with napalm and foogas. He does it right back with white phosphorus and Molotov cocktails. Sometimes to us, sometimes to these people here. Although in this woman's case, I'd say somebody heated up an iron rod until it was good and hot and ran it along the poor lady's arm. If you're asking if it was Charlie or an irate husband who caught her with another man, I don't know the answer to that one." He considered the woman's appearance for a moment. "Well, okay, probably not an irate husband."

"Can you do anything for her?" asked Kepler.

"For her? No, man. The arm maybe I can fix. Half these people have got tuberculosis or plague or dengue fever. The other half have got all three. The kids we might be able to save if we could get 'em out of this stinkin' country, but out here, by the time you hit forty, you're livin' on borrowed time.''

''We're all living on borrowed time out here,'' said Kepler. ''What about the arm?''

Washington shrugged. ''The burn itself isn't all that bad. What makes it a bad one is that it covers so much area and it's about three days old. If I could have caught it just after it happened, I could have wrapped it up in plastic, given her some antibiotics and not been too worried about it. Now about all I can do is put a topical antiseptic and a clean dressing on it, have you tell her to keep it clean and hope for the best. Infection? Who knows? If it's gonna get infected, it probably already is. If it is, she'll probably lose the arm. Hell, Derek, out here she'll probably die.''

''What's this about wrapping it in plastic?'' asked Kepler.

''Little trick I learned from McMillan,'' said Washington, rummaging in his kit. ''Doc says it goes against protocol, but it works. With a bad burn the body loses fluid, mostly blood plasma, out of the injured tissues. Because the integument is damaged, it also lets bacteria get into the wound and cause infection. It's the fluid loss and the air getting to the raw nerves that causes the pain. If the burn's bad enough, the nerves will be burned completely away, and it won't hurt at all until the tissue starts to grow back, but the fluid loss can be a real killer. Gets you before you even have to start thinking about infection. The plastic keeps the fluid in and the germs out. Oh, here it is.'' Washington fished a small tube of ointment out of his medical kit and dabbed some of it on the burn, carefully spreading it around the injury. Then he took a couple of sterile dressings and covered the burn, wrapping the entire arm with a gauze bandage to hold the dressing in place.

''What's an integument?'' asked Kepler.

''Skin, man. Just skin. An integument is a covering. We medical professionals like to use big words. Keeps you laymen on your toes.'' He tied the ends of the bandage. ''Ask her if there's anything else, will you?''

Kepler spoke briefly in Vietnamese to the woman and she rattled off a long speech, smiling as she spoke and pointing at the black medical sergeant. Kepler decided the smile was genuine this time.

''What did she say?'' asked Washington.

"She said to tell you thank you for your kindness. That her arm felt suddenly cool. She wants to know if there is anything she can do to repay you."

"Just tell her to try to keep that bandage on and keep those dressings clean. Tell her that will be repayment enough." Washington smiled at her again, then got up and moved over to see if there was anything he could do for the old man.

For a moment Kepler didn't move, just continued kneeling there on one knee, watching the old woman stir the pot of boiling liquid. Finally he said, "Where is everyone? *Nguoi lang o dau?*"

The woman threw him a furtive glance and went back to stirring the liquid. It was a minute or two before she spoke. "Tending the fields," she said in Vietnamese. "They're all out tending the fields. No one's here but us."

"I don't think so, Mama-san," said Kepler softly. "I think they're hiding somewhere, but I don't think they're hiding from us." Kepler continued to press the woman. "Where is the head man of the village? *Lang truong o dau?*"

"Tending the fields," the woman insisted.

Okay, fine, thought Kepler. If that's the way you want to play it, we'll let you take us to them. *"Xin chi doung den cho do."*

The woman glanced at him again, and Kepler saw either fear or apprehension in her eyes. He gave her his best winning smile and said in Vietnamese, "Look, now, we've tried to help you. How about being honest with us? We both know the men are not in the fields. They're hiding somewhere. I don't even care where they are if you don't want to tell me, but at least tell me why they are hiding. Are they afraid of us?"

It took the better part of another five minutes, but Kepler finally extracted from the woman that all the young men and women of the village had gone into hiding in the distant hills because a Vietcong recruiting platoon was expected to come through looking for fresh converts to the cause of Marxist-Leninist world revolutionary struggle. A small Vietcong squad had been through the hamlet three days earlier and had boasted of their alleged recent victories over the puppet ARVN troops and their running dog American allies. They had also told the villagers of the recruiting patrol and warned them that An Minh, like all other villages, was expected to contribute both food and fighters to the cause. After the VC squad had left, the young people had all gone to the hills to hide. They would hide for at least a week, she explained, since no one was sure when the Vietcong were coming.

Kepler did his best not to appear excited by the news. He asked the woman how she had burned her arm. She looked at the ground, but did not speak. She had, however, stopped stirring.

"Please tell me," Kepler persisted in Vietnamese. "I really would like to know what happened."

The woman was silent for a moment longer, then she said, "VC." She spat the words out and spat on the ground after them.

Kepler had half expected the answer but hadn't really thought it would be given. "Why?" he asked at last.

The woman did not look at him. "They wanted to take my daughter with them," she said. "She did not want to go, and I did not want her to go. First they did this." She moved the burned arm slightly. "Afterward my daughter went with them." The old woman spat on the ground once more. "VC," she said and spat again.

When the Tai had finished their fruitless search of the hamlet and Washington had completed his MEDCAP visit, Kepler moved the patrol out of An Minh, first walking south but turning to the northwest once they were out of sight of the huts. After walking about half a klick in that direction, Kepler halted the patrol to await the rendezvous with the machine gun squad that had remained in concealment along the paddy dike to cover the patrol's withdrawal from the hamlet. While they waited, Kepler used the PRC-10 to contact Camp A-555, or Triple Nickel as the men liked to call it, to file a request for airlift support back to the camp. Since the request had to pass through Big Green, the logistics and support command in Saigon, it was denied as usual. Kepler sighed and ran down the antenna on the heavy backpack radio. The stupidity and pettiness of the Saigon command used to disgust him. Now he had grown so used to the routine denials of support and supplies that he found them more amusing than anything else. The airlift denial was typical. He'd have been surprised if Big Green had okayed it. As soon as the machine gun squad had joined them, Kepler got the patrol moving again. It was a long walk back to the camp, nearly eight klicks over miserable terrain. It wasn't really all uphill, Kepler knew. It only seemed that way. You can't walk uphill for eight klicks when it's nearly all swampland, he thought, at least they'd have good walking for the first three-quarters of a klick. Kepler's feet squished softly in his boots as they moved off through the scrub.

AS THE AMERICAN AND TAI PATROL moved out, it was watched through binoculars by four Vietnamese clad in camouflage uniforms of the type normally issued only to Red Chinese snipers. One of them was, in fact, a very good sniper. His name was Sergeant Doan, and he had fifty-six confirmed kills to his credit. Nearly twice that many probables. He had been trained by some of the top marksmen in North Vietnam and China and had been a student of a famous Russian woman sniper, herself a hero of the defense of Stalingrad. But Sergeant Doan and his security team were not there today to kill Americans or Tai, although Doan had little doubt that he could kill both Americans easily. Today Sergeant Doan was there merely to observe. His orders had been quite explicit on that point.

"It is time to leave," Doan said simply to his men after the Americans and Tai had moved out of sight. "We know what we wanted to know. They know."

KEPLER PACED BACK AND FORTH in Captain Mack Gerber's tiny office. There wasn't much room for pacing amid the makeshift furniture, the ammunition-box filing cabinets and the metal cot with the wafer-thin mattress, but Kepler was too excited to sit down despite his aching feet. First Kepler stared out the open doorway, past the sandbagged redoubt and the fire control tower toward the helipad that lay beneath the sun like a huge black wrestling mat with a large yellow H painted on it. A sandbag on each corner held the net down. Beyond the helipad was the worse than useless pediprimed runway. Kepler then stared at the map tacked to the wall of Gerber's hootch and finally back at his thirty-year-old commanding officer.

The captain appeared unimpressed with Kepler's information. He was sitting back in his folding steel chair with his hands behind his head and his feet up on the small desk he'd hammered together from old ammo crates and scrap lumber. Finally he spoke.

"I just don't know about this, Derek. It sounds just a little bit flaky to me. The old woman, for instance. Just how sure are you that she was telling you the truth?"

"Christ, Captain, I saw the burn. T.J. treated it. Why would she lie after they'd done something like that to her? If it was an act, it was an awfully good one, and I just don't see where she'd have any percentage in telling us a tale like that if it wasn't true. It's the first hard intelligence we've gotten in the last month on VC movement in the area. If you'll pardon my saying so, sir, I don't understand your reluctance to pursue the matter."

Gerber gave no indication of being annoyed by the last remark.

"Come on, Derek, it's not hard intelligence, and you know it," said Gerber. "It's a good beginning, but that's all. We've heard nothing else about a recruiting platoon from any of the other villages and nothing from your network of agents. Right now all we've got is some old woman's story that may be nothing more than the boasting of some VC soldier's overactive imagination. The whole thing just seems a bit thin to me."

"Captain, it could be that the information is so new that none of the other villages have heard about it. Besides, Charlie doesn't normally send out engraved invitations announcing an upcoming recruiting drive."

"My point exactly, Derek. Doesn't it strike you as just a little bit funny that this time he's giving advance notification?"

"It wasn't advance notification, Captain. The guy was bragging and he screwed up. The old woman said that one of the other VC got all over his case for mentioning it," Kepler insisted.

Gerber let his feet drop to the floor and leaned forward. "I still don't like it. Maybe we should just pass the information on to Nha Trang and let it go at that. Let them decide what they want to do with it. You know, we're getting awfully damned short here to be going off on something half-baked."

Kepler quit pacing and stopped in front of Gerber's desk. "Just because we're getting short doesn't mean that we've stopped being soldiers, does it?" he asked bitterly.

"Of course not, Derek. You know me better than that. It just means things have changed a little. We don't have the time left in-country to follow through on everything. It also means that now is not the time to start getting stupid. We've got one old woman's say-so about a VC recruiting platoon that might not even exist, and her story is unsubstantiated by any other intelligence source. That's pretty thin stuff to justify putting an operation into the field, maybe having one member of the team run out of luck, step on a mine and go home minus a foot or worse.''

''What's to follow through on?'' Kepler persisted. ''We know where they're going to be, and we've a pretty good idea of when. We even know the approximate strength of the enemy unit. It'll only take a couple of hours to put together the operation and get some people into the field. By tomorrow or Wednesday it could all be over.''

''I still don't like it,'' insisted Gerber. ''There's something about it that just doesn't feel right. I still think we should just pass this on to Intel in Nha Trang and let them deal with it. If they think it's good, they can get up a special operation to deal with it. Maybe make some use of the Mike Force.''

''Captain,'' Kepler pleaded, ''we haven't gotten anything like this information in a long time. It would be a good way to go out, sir. A sort of final parting victory. What have we got to lose? Really, sir, I just don't understand your reluctance to take these guys!''

Gerber rubbed his chin. Kepler was getting hot, and Gerber knew he had to cool him down. ''I don't really understand it, either, Derek. I've just got a bad feeling about this one. I must be getting short-timer's jitters.'' He was silent for an instant, then said, ''Find Lieutenant Bromhead and Master Sergeant Fetterman and come back here. We'll talk it over and see what they have to say about it.''

Now Kepler grinned. Bromhead, the team's young executive officer, was fast becoming a real tiger. Kepler knew that Bromhead would be in favor of any mission that might make contact with the enemy. And Fetterman, the team sergeant, was a real old pro. The man had been fighting in a war someplace or other ever since he lied about his age and shipped out to France back in the Deuce. Once the captain said to find them, Kepler knew the mission was on.

''Yes, sir,'' said Kepler. ''I'll have them here in ten minutes.'' He went out the door of Gerber's hootch whistling a merry little tune.

By the time everyone was gathered, Gerber had already roughed out a working plan. Bromhead sat on the folding cot shoved against the wall, Fetterman collapsed into one of the lawn chairs and Kepler sat on one of the stray ammo crates arranged haphazardly about the dirty plywood floor. Gerber reached into the bottom drawer of his desk and pulled out a bottle of Beam's Choice. "Before we begin, why not a touch of Beam's?"

"Why not, indeed," grunted Fetterman.

Gerber took a long pull, then passed the bottle around. When it got back to him, Gerber took another pull, swallowed and put a finger to his lips. "Smooth as ever." As he put the bottle away, he said, "Derek has some interesting information he'd like to share with us about enemy troop movements. Derek?"

Kepler took the floor and briefed them about the VC recruiting platoon. When he'd finished, Gerber picked up the thread of the conversation without waiting for anyone else to say anything.

"I would think that we'll need about a company for the op," said Gerber. "An ambush platoon, two platoons for a blocking force and one for a ready reserve and field HQ."

Fetterman, who had fought as a teenager in France and Germany and later as a slightly older and much wiser man in Korea, immediately saw what the captain had in mind. "The object of the ambush platoon is not to annihilate the enemy but to force him to withdraw along a specific route so that he runs smack into the blocking force."

"Brilliant," said Bromhead. "A classic military maneuver."

"If they stand and fight," continued Gerber, "their forces and the ambush platoon should be about evenly matched in manpower, although the ambush team should have an edge in automatic weapons and the advantage of surprise. This, of course, assumes that the old woman was telling the truth about the VC unit being platoon strength and that she knows what a platoon really is."

"Captain," interrupted Kepler, "I don't think the recruiting squad will really be up to platoon strength. It's much more likely to be a squad or two at most. My hunch would be one or two political cadre, a couple of noncoms to keep the new recruits in line and a small security detachment—probably won't be more than ten or fifteen VC in all, unless this turns out to be the tail end of their recruiting trip. In that case, they might have a pretty good bunch of conscripts with them, not all of whom will be exactly crazy about the idea. I would think that most of the conscripts would break and run as soon as the shooting starts. Besides, the VC's table of organization and equipment is structured for slightly smaller platoons than ours are, and we're talking about a recruiting team, not a combat patrol Any way you look at it, we should have them outgunned."

Gerber nodded and moved to his map. "If the information the old woman gave Sergeant Kepler is correct, we can expect that the VC will move through the area tomorrow or Wednesday. We'll figure on keeping the troops in the field until Saturday morning to allow for the VC being late. If we don't have contact by then, we'll give it up as a lost cause. I don't think the Vietcong are going to wait more than a few days after letting the information slip to the villagers, and that was three days ago. I also think it unlikely that the VC who broke security about the recruiting trip to the old woman would have picked up that kind of scuttlebutt much more than a week in advance of the recruiting team's visit so, if we haven't turned up anything by market day, we'll take our marbles and go home. Understood?"

There were nods from the group of men.

"Now, an ambush set up here," Gerber went on, pointing to a spot on the map, "will allow for limited options by the enemy. If he stands and fights, we'll be able to reinforce quickly, either from the blocking force, or the reserve force, putting the squeeze on the Cong from both ends. If Charlie decides that discretion is the better part of valor, the only real avenue for withdrawal will be along this thin tree line, which will dump him right into the laps of the blocking force. By moving through this area of swamp, the blocking force should be able to sneak into position without tipping our hand. It's going to be a really crummy job, trying to cross this swamp and get into position unobserved, the blocking force is going to get very wet, very muddy and undoubtedly develop a close relationship with a wide variety of interesting fauna, mostly leeches." Gerber looked pointedly at Bromhead.

Bromhead smiled wryly and said, "Sounds just peachy. Why, I'd be delighted to volunteer to lead the blocking force through a leech-infested swamp, Captain. Can't think of anything in the whole wide world I'd rather do than lead a blocking force through a leech-infested swamp. You know how fond I am of leeches, sir."

Gerber smiled back. "That's nice, Lieutenant. I was hoping you'd feel that way about it."

"Captain, who's going to lead the ambush platoon?" asked Fetterman.

"I'd sort of figured that would be the kind of assignment you'd be interested in, Master Sergeant. Who do you want to take with you?"

"I'd like a platoon of Lieutenant Bao's strikers, sir," said Fetterman. "They have better fire discipline than the PFs do in an ambush situation. Maybe Sergeant Krung as senior Tai NCO. His English is getting pretty good, and I think he'd probably enjoy the opportunity to add to his trophy collection."

"Christ!" said Bromhead. "I'm beginning to think you're spending too much time with Krung. I suppose next you'll start keeping one of those damned disgusting trophy boards yourself."

Like all the other Americans, Bromhead was aware of Sergeant Krung's "trophy collection," as the man called it. Two years earlier the Tai NCO's family had been murdered in a particularly brutal fashion by the Vietcong. They had been impaled on sharpened bamboo stakes. It had taken three days for Krung's older brother to die. The Vietcong had killed all of Krung's family except his youngest sister. The VC had been content with merely raping her. In fact, forty or fifty of them had been content with merely raping her. Later the humiliation had driven her to commit suicide. The ugly lesson had been intended by the Vietcong to be a demonstration of what happened to families who supported the Saigon government. The Vietcong had made one serious mistake, however. They had missed killing Krung. Krung's people were Nung Tai, and among them there was a fierce sense of honor that demanded a blood code. Krung had carried that tradition one step further and vowed not to rest until he had killed ten VC for each member of his family. He kept score by cutting off the genitals of the male enemy soldiers he had personally killed and nailing them to a plywood board in his hootch. Krung had had a large family.

"Why, Lieutenant," said Fetterman earnestly, apparently offended by Bromhead's suggestion, "you know I would never do anything like that, sir. I'm a professional soldier. Besides, I probably couldn't fit a board that big in my quarters."

Everyone laughed, but Bromhead had the uneasy feeling that Fetterman wasn't joking about the size of the board. Especially when you considered that the man had been in the Second World War and Korea. Fetterman had already done two tours in Vietnam, as well as some side work for the CIA in Laos before being assigned to A-Detachment 555 as a replacement for the unit's original sergeant, Bill Schattschneider, who had been killed within a month of his arrival in South Vietnam. And Fetterman had accrued thirty-two confirmed kills in the short time that Bromhead had known him. That number represented only the number of confirmed personal kills. It didn't consider the probables and the assists, and it didn't count any of the master sergeant's previous tours or previous wars.

For a moment Bromhead had difficulty reconciling that image with the picture of the short, thin, balding man with the gentle face who sat in a brightly colored lawn chair near the door of Gerber's hootch. A face that belonged to a man who was kind to small children and stray dogs and had, in fact, initiated the paperwork that would allow Fetterman and his wife to adopt a Vietnamese orphan boy. Fetterman was one of the gentlest men Bromhead had ever known and the most deadly.

Bromhead felt a momentary uneasiness, then remembered his own record. Eleven kills and seventeen probables, a pretty damned good record for a first tour. A pretty good record? thought Bromhead. Christ! He felt an inward shudder. Mixed with it was a curious sense of guilt and pride.

"All right," Gerber was saying, "that leaves the reserve force."

"Captain, if it's all right with you, I'd like to head that one," said Kepler.

Gerber considered for a moment, then shook his head. "Sorry, Derek. I know it seems like a dirty trick, since the whole thing was your idea, but I'll want you here to coordinate this thing from our end. Besides, you're going to be busy the next couple of days trying to confirm the information from other sources and helping me convince Nha Trang that we're doing the right thing.

Anyway, I can't have all my best people running around out in the field.''

"How about Sergeant Kittredge, then?" offered Bromhead. "He's been complaining that he never gets a chance to go out on patrol. Says all he ever gets to do is sit up there in the fire control tower, and correct other people's mistakes. Besides, sir, he is cross trained in demolitions and medicine."

"Steve's been complaining we aren't working him hard enough, has he?" Gerber smiled. "Okay, I guess we can spare him for this one. I wouldn't want him to think we don't appreciate his efforts. He might drop a short round on the latrine or something. I'll brief him myself in a few minutes. Anything else anybody can think of?"

"Only when do we leave?" said Fetterman.

Gerber looked at the map again. "Lieutenant Bromhead has the longest distance to go over the worst terrain. Johnny, I think you should plan to move out within the next hour. Tony you go out as soon as it's good and dark. I'll send Kittredge along about an hour and a half after that. Any further questions?"

"Sir, what about the Vietnamese?" asked Bromhead. In the excitement of planning the operation, the issue had almost been overlooked.

"I'll take care of that," said Gerber. "I'll have to tell Captain Minh, but given some of the problems we've had with security among the PFs lately, I think he'll be willing to keep this an all-Tai operation. Anything else?"

Each man silently shook his head.

"Okay, then," said Gerber, "that's all. I'll see each of you before you go out."

They all stood up, and Gerber reached for the bottle of Beam's again. "A last drink, to the success of the mission." Even as he said it, Gerber couldn't shake the feeling that he was making a mistake.

2

**THE SOUTH GATE,
U.S. ARMY SPECIAL
FORCES CAMP A-555,
SOUTH OF THE
PARROT'S BEAK,
RVN**

Dusk had come and gone and with it Bromhead's platoon. They had exited the south gate of the camp as the sun kissed the horizon in flaming oranges and reds, and Fetterman and Tyme began coordinating their patrol. Now that it was night, the oppressive heat of late afternoon had broken slightly but the humidity remained high, making it impossible for the soldier's sweat-dampened uniforms to dry. It was nearly pitch-black because of low-hanging clouds and all the lights in the camp were hidden behind thick, heavy curtains. Gerber wouldn't even let the men smoke outside when the night was this dark.

Gerber found Fetterman by process of collision when he nearly walked into the small master sergeant. "You ready, Tony?"

"Of course, Captain. Did the lieutenant get out on time?"

"More or less. He's now ass deep in that swamp but claims to be making good progress."

"You going to provide any cover fire for us?"

"Don't think it will do any good, Tony. Besides, even if you're observed leaving, the VC aren't going to know exactly what you're doing."

Sergeant First Class Tyme quietly stepped up behind them. He was a young man in his mid-twenties with sandy hair and a passion for weapons. Even though he was the light weapons specialist, he was as knowledgeable about howitzers as he was about pistols. He said, "The equipment is check complete. We're ready to go when you are."

"You going on this boondoggle, too, Justin?" asked Gerber.

"Yes, sir. Wouldn't miss it for the world."

Fetterman, pointing at the strangely shaped pistol that was just barely visible in the darkness, said, "Now what in the hell is that, Boom-Boom?"

"Second World War flare gun called a Very pistol. Got it off an Air Force pilot down in Saigon. Fires a twelve-gauge shotgun shell, although I do have a couple of flares that came with it."

"You've replaced your Remington hand howitzer with that?" asked Fetterman, somewhat aghast.

"Only for this mission. It's a little more versatile, given what we're planning. My shotgun won't fire flares."

Gerber shook his head slowly. "I just got a directive from Saigon about unauthorized weapons, and that is about as unauthorized as anything I've seen. How safe is it?"

"For whom?" responded Tyme. "For me, it's no problem. I've tested it a couple of times, and it works quite well. Accuracy after about three feet goes all to hell, but in the jungle I won't be shooting at anyone very far away."

"And your backup weapon?" asked Gerber.

Tyme automatically glanced down at his rifle. It was made of high-impact black plastic with a lightweight barrel that was a dull, dark gray. The weapon had a rear sight that looked like a carrying handle. "I've got one of these new M-16s. I'm not really happy with it, but I think it'll be okay. It's got field problems that come from the efforts to step down the cyclic rate of fire, causing it to jam."

Gerber turned his attention back to Fetterman. "How many of your people are carrying M-16s?"

"Only a couple."

"Doesn't that increase the amount of ammo you have to take? You've got 7.62 for the M-14s and M-60s, plus other ammo for the M-1s and the .45 caliber rounds for the pistols. Now there's the 5.56 for the M-16s," Gerber said. "Hell, we're supposed to be soldiers, not munitions suppliers to the Third World."

"We're not going to be out too long," Fetterman replied. "And we've stripped the packs down to the bare essentials, such as a couple of C-ration meals, and left out spare socks, ponchos and the like. Besides everyone is carrying some of the ammo for the M-60s. The advantage of the M-16 is that the ammo and weapon weighs less than the M-14. We can carry more rounds."

"Okay, okay," said Gerber. "You can move out whenever you're ready. I'll send Kittredge out in about an hour."

"Thank you, Captain," said Fetterman. "See you Wednesday or Thursday."

"Good luck, Tony. You too, Justin. Be careful and remember we're all getting pretty short."

"Yes, sir," said Tyme. "Can't get involved in any long conversations. No time left to finish them."

"Yeah, yeah," answered Gerber. "I've heard them all. Can't check books out of the library because you're too short. Anyway, good luck."

"Justin, take the point and get us out of here," Fetterman said. "Stop in about fifteen minutes and we'll regroup."

With that the patrol, consisting of nearly fifty men from the First Tai Strike Company, left through the flimsy gate in the south wall and began to wind its way out of the camp through the six wire barriers. They headed south through the tall, dry elephant grass that made travel difficult toward a large clump of palm and coconut trees that they often used as a staging point. Once there they regrouped, checked the maps and then moved out to the northwest, walking along the rice field dikes and skirting the swamp that now shielded Bromhead and about eighty other strikers.

GERBER STOPPED by the team house for a cup of coffee. Sitting down at one of the tables, he dumped sugar into the brew without realizing what he was doing. He was very worried. For nearly a year they had been extremely lucky. He had lost only a few of his men, and one of those had been with the unit only a short time. He had pulled off a couple of victories that had amazed the people in Saigon. He had gotten out of trouble a couple of times by being prepared with the proper answers. Brigadier General Billy Joe Crinshaw, an officer who had managed to insert himself into the chain of command, had tried to convict two of his men for murder and had failed when Gerber had shown up with evidence proving they were ordered to violate the Cambodian border. It was a constant war with the brass hats in Saigon, but he had always felt confident. Now it was different.

He tried to tell himself that it was because they were short. In just a few weeks they would be going home, and because that goal was now within reach, he was getting jumpy. He had almost moved his cot into the commo bunker for the added protection of the heavy sandbags and beams that would stop mortar rounds, but decided against it when he found both Smith and Kittredge had already moved in. The whole team had talked about extending for six months, which would give them a month's leave in The World, but they hadn't begun the paperwork yet. A couple of clerks in Saigon had told Gerber it was too late, but he knew that if he and his team really wanted to extend, the clerks and the Army would find a way to make it happen. No one was about to turn down a volunteer's offer to stay in Vietnam.

Idly Gerber stirred his coffee and looked around the team house. It wasn't much, but it had been home for nearly a year. There were several tables with four chairs at each in the building that doubled duty as a mess hall and dayroom. Near the door was an old refrigerator that labored to keep its contents slightly below room temperature. Next to it was a coffeepot that was kept busy twenty-four hours a day. Across one end of the room was a counter, and behind that was a galley used by a Vietnamese woman to cook the meals. On one of the plywood walls someone had drawn a fireplace in a sudden burst of Christmas spirit. A ceiling fan suspended from the rafters at least put the heat in motion. Over everything was the film of red dust that became synonymous with Vietnam in the mind of every American soldier.

He looked up when he heard a noise. Robin Morrow, a journalist that Crinshaw had saddled him with, stood in the doorway. She knew her job, had learned a great deal about Special Forces tactics since she had arrived weeks earlier and had even helped save Fetterman and Tyme from the hangman. She was a tall, slender woman with long blond hair cut in bangs that brushed her bright green eyes. She was dressed in khaki pants and a partially unbuttoned khaki shirt. Her hair was damp with sweat.

"You looking for some coffee?" asked Gerber.

Morrow sat down next to him, fanning herself with her hand. "What I'd really like is a cold beer. That is, if you have one around."

"We always have beer. What I don't know is if I can give you a cold one. The refrigerator is acting up again."

Morrow stared at him as if she wanted to kill. "For this I gave up my air-conditioned room in Saigon that had hot and cold running water, indoor plumbing and room service."

Heading for the refrigerator, Gerber said, "The room service I can provide, if all you want is a beer. I could also provide air-conditioning of a sort, but that's about it."

Morrow accepted the beer that Gerber handed her. She pulled a church key hanging on a chain around her neck from under her shirt and opened the beer. After drinking deeply, she sat back with a sigh. "Warm. Maybe cool. But definitely not cold. Now what about the air-conditioning?"

Gerber picked a magazine off the table and fanned her with it. The slight breeze didn't stir her wet hair.

"How come the heat doesn't bother you?" she demanded.

"I'm used to it by now. Haven't had the opportunity to sit in air-conditioned rooms ruining my acclimatization. After three or four months you just get used to having your clothes wet all the time." ·

"Great. Just the encouragement I needed to hear."

"I can whistle up a chopper for you anytime you want. You can be back in Saigon by noon tomorrow, sitting in a tub washing off the dirt, while room service sends up a seven-course meal."

"Nice try, Captain," she said, draining the beer quickly. "But I saw those patrols go out, and it looks like an interesting mission. Thought I'd hang around long enough to find out what it's all about."

"To be honest with you, I'm afraid that it's not such a big deal. More or less routine." But her remark bothered Gerber. If a reporter who hadn't been in Vietnam very long could see the significance of the size of the units sent out, surely the VC would understand. One more thing for him to worry about.

"I have learned," said Morrow, getting up so that she could get another beer, "that, any time someone starts a sentence with 'to be honest,' they are usually less than honest."

"It really is routine," protested Gerber. "With luck we might pull off something interesting. I doubt that it will be interesting to the press because we're hunting an enemy unit of fewer than forty men, but if we find them, we strengthen our hold in the area."

Morrow collapsed into her chair and rubbed the can against her forehead. She pulled the front of her shirt away from her chest so that she could blow down it. Sweat was beaded on her upper lip and dripped down the side of her face. Finally she said, "If it wasn't for the humidity, I could take this heat a lot easier."

"Only advice I have," said Gerber, "is to take a shower. Wash off the sweat. Makes you a little more comfortable. I'll even stand guard for you."

She smiled for the first time. "Stand guard, huh? And who'll guard you?"

"I could call Anderson over. Or maybe Doc McMillan. Or maybe even Kepler."

"And who will guard them?"

For some reason Gerber was suddenly annoyed. "We'll all keep our backs turned," he snapped.

But Morrow kept on smiling. "And what if I don't want you to keep your back turned?" she asked, almost innocently.

Gerber remembered a night in Saigon they had spent together just after he had met her. A night she engineered so that they would have to be together. He had let it take its natural course, but he sometimes wanted to let it stand as a night with no past and no future. He just wasn't sure that he wanted anything to do with Morrow because of her sister, Karen, who had once been a good friend, a lover and who had never mentioned that she had a husband. Now he sat across from Robin and found himself staring at the beads of sweat that formed between her breasts and wished that he was on patrol with Bromhead or Fetterman.

Morrow tried to prod him. "Well?"

He knew that he had to say something fast, but Gerber felt as slow as an Iowa summer. He turned and looked at her carefully. "Your timing in incredibly bad," he said.

Not sure what he meant, she asked, "My timing is bad?"

"I've got nearly a hundred men in the field with a real possibility that they'll be in contact within a couple of hours. I need to stay loose."

"Then the patrol is not routine."

"Yes, it is routine, but the situation is fluid. You understand, don't you?" He badly wanted her to understand.

She reached out and touched his hand. "I really do understand," said Morrow, realizing that the patrol had very little to do with Gerber's agitated state. "But I'll still need someone to guard me while I take my shower."

Gerber pushed his chair back and stood. "I'll give it a try, but if I yell for you to grab your towel it's because I'm going to desert my post."

"You've got a deal."

BEFORE HEADING to the makeshift shower situated near the team house and Gerber's hootch, he walked to the south gate where Sergeant First Class Steven Kittredge and Sully Smith, the stocky Italian-American who, at twenty-two, already had one complete tour in Vietnam, were waiting. Smith was the senior demolitions expert. Kittredge, although older than Smith and with more Army service time, was only now completing his first tour in Vietnam, as were most of the members of the A-Team.

Gerber found them ready to move out, their weapons and equipment checks complete. He gave them the same speech he had given Fetterman and Tyme. In the back of his mind, he still felt uneasy about the mission and the timing, but tried to write it off as a short-timer's nerves.

"Don't worry, Captain," Smith said. "I'm not about to do anything stupid out there. Not after spending so much time here already."

"Steve, you know the route. You're there to support Fetterman if he needs it. He might also call on you to provide a blocking force. Remain flexible."

"No problem, sir."

"Okay. Good luck. See you when you get back in."

As Kittredge left the compound, he turned his troops to the northwest, parallel to Fetterman's trail. They moved slowly through the elephant grass, with Kittredge breaking the trail by twisting his foot as it touched the ground. That broke the elephant grass and pushed it aside so that the man following found the walking easier. But even with the sun gone, it was still hot, humid and tiring.

They moved into the tree line on the western side of the camp, and Kittredge thought that he detected movement ahead of him. He signaled everyone to drop and then crawled forward slowly, watching the trees and brush in front of him. Within a minute Sully Smith was beside him.

Kittredge pointed to the right and made a flanking motion with his hand. Smith nodded his understanding and began easing off in that direction. As he moved, he slipped off the safety on his M-14.

Kittredge held his position and looked off to one side, trying to pick up movement with his peripheral vision. For a long time nothing moved. There was no sound except the distant popping of artillery as it shelled someone somewhere.

Smith crept toward a large teak tree and then peeked around it. At first he, too, saw nothing. He felt the breath rasp in his throat and the sweat trickle down his sides as he watched and listened. Then he heard a faint rattling and turned toward the noise. There was the briefest motion, as a bush blowing in a light breeze. Only there was no wind, and in the shadows Smith could now see a human shape.

Smith wasn't sure what to do. He didn't want to tip his hand, but he didn't want to leave a known enemy on his lines of communication. He didn't think that one man would present much of a problem, but where there was one enemy soldier, there usually were more.

Of course, if the enemy knew that he had been spotted but not engaged, it might make the VC more cautious. Smith's only course of action was to kill the soldier. Smith set his rifle aside, then thought better of it. He didn't know for sure that there was only one of them, and he didn't want to get caught in the open without his main weapon. He safetied and slung it, and pulled his Randall combat knife. The blade's dull surface wouldn't reflect light.

Quietly he moved around the tree, keeping to the available cover, never taking his eyes off the enemy soldier. And then Smith let his gaze wander, suddenly afraid that his staring would somehow warn the VC that he was near. Smith wasn't sure that he believed in ESP, but he figured that there was no sense in taking chances. He glanced back at the Vietcong to make sure that he hadn't moved, but he no longer stared.

The enemy never heard him. Smith cupped a hand under the VC's chin and over his mouth and nose. With a whisper like silk being cut, Smith drew his knife along the Vietcong's throat as he jammed his knee into the soldier's back. Then he pulled back, dragging the body and wrapping his legs around the VC so that the man would not have a chance to make a noise. He sliced at the throat again with so much force that the enemy's head broke away from his trunk, and there was a spurt of blood that splashed over Smith, soaking him.

Just as he rolled free from the dead soldier, dropping the head, another man rose out of the darkness, walking straight toward him. From his attitude Smith didn't think that the man knew what was happening, but Smith couldn't take the chance. He thrust out with his knife, driving it deep into the man's chest just under the breastbone. Smith twisted the blade, trying to rupture the heart and penetrate the lungs. He felt warm blood wash over his hand as the VC's heart burst.

As the enemy soldier died, he fell backward in a spasm, wrenching the knife from Smith's grasp. The VC fell with a thud that sounded like an elephant crashing through dried grass, drumming his heels on the soft, moist earth of the tree line. There was a shout in Vietnamese, followed by a burst of gunfire that raked the trees above Smith's head with emerald tracers.

With all the noise Smith dropped flat, covering his eyes momentarily to avoid ruining his night vision by looking into the muzzle flashes of the enemy weapons.

"Sully!" shouted Kittredge. "You all right?"

Smith, unsure of the locations of either the strikers or the enemy, didn't want to reveal his position so he didn't answer. He rolled to the left, unslinging his rifle, wishing that he could find his knife. It had cost him too much money to lose now, not to mention all the time that he had put into customizing it.

From the rear came a sustained burst from an M-60. The ruby tracers lanced through the night, skipped on the ground and bounced into the sky. There were a couple of answering shots from an AK and an explosion from one grenade, the flash lighting the area like the strobe of a camera, and then Kittredge was kneeling beside him.

"You okay, Sully?"

Smith got to his knees and tried to brush the dirt from the front of his jungle fatigues. There was blood caked on his jacket and staining his web gear. He realized just how wet he was and knew that not all of it was from enemy blood. Part of it was the sweat brought on by the fright and his nerves. He took a deep breath and said, "I'm fine. I killed two of them, but the last one or two eluded me."

One of the Tai strikers came up then. "We find one body, one weapon."

"Maybe we got them all," whispered Kittredge.

"Either that," responded Smith, "or the survivors didn't get the chance to pick up the weapons before they split."

Kittredge moved off to the RTO, calling the base to report the brief encounter and to say that he had no casualties. Smith crawled off in search of his knife. They would proceed from there.

3

**THE SWAMPS
SOUTHEAST OF U.S.
ARMY SPECIAL FORCES
CAMP A-555**

Bromhead was unhappy. Unhappy, wet, tired, and the splashing by the Tai as they moved through the swamp seemed to be enough to wake the dead. For three hours they had been stumbling through water that was at times chest high. There had been no place to take a break since he had found the high ground earlier. That had been a series of small islands of mud that allowed them to get out of the water. There had been no real cover on the islands, just some grass that masked the deep holes and the wreckage of a South Vietnamese plane that helicopter crews used for target practice during the day.

After twenty minutes in which they used Army issue insect repellent to coax some of the leeches to drop off, Bromhead had reluctantly ordered his men back into the swamp that looked like a giant grassy plain. The hidden swamp water quickly soaked through everything, and in the heat of the afternoon that might have provided some welcome relief, but now, long after midnight, it was merely cool, clammy and uncomfortable. It filled a man's boots, weighing him down and sucking at his feet, sapping the strength of his legs. It slowed the platoon and stole their energy. It made them sloppy. They stumbled, splashing each other and adding to their misery.

The grass was no help. Sometimes it was only waist-high, other times it reached higher than the heads of the men. They lost sight of one another and tripped over hidden logs and stumps. They soaked their equipment and lost some of it. If that wasn't dried quickly, they knew that there would be rust by late afternoon the next day.

Bromhead could hear his men breathing hard with the effort of moving through water that was ankle-deep, knee-deep or waist-deep, depending on the rise and fall of the land. There was rattling of equipment as the men grew tired, but there was no way that they could rest while they were in the swamp. Then, in the distance, not more than a couple of hundred meters away, he could see a tree line that suggested they would soon be able to take a rest break.

He turned to look at the men and saw that they had begun to bunch up again. He was going to order them to spread out when he heard the telltale pop of a mortar being fired. He waved an arm and yelled, "Scatter! Scatter!"

Bromhead was going to dive for cover, but in the swamp there was no cover. Only water and grass. He slumped to one knee, the water lapping at his chin as he held his rifle over his head and studied the trees. He saw the flash of the mortar tubes and heard shouting in Vietnamese as the mortar rounds rained down on them. But the mortars weren't very effective against troops in a swamp. They didn't explode on the surface but dropped through the water to detonate on contact with the mud. The water absorbed most of the shrapnel.

The mortars were followed by concentrated fire from several RPD machine guns. Bromhead heard the rapid chattering and watched the green tracers flash by. He saw fountains of white where the bullets hit the swamp. Some of his men slumped into the water, floating in spreading stains of red barely visible against the darkness of the water.

Still Bromhead hesitated. He thought about charging the enemy position, just as the infantry manual directed, but he would have to move his men nearly half a klick without the benefit of cover. The machine guns would cut them to ribbons, and if anyone survived the assault, they would be in no condition to engage the enemy. An enemy who had mortars and machine guns and assault rifles.

There was a sporadic return from the weapons of the strikers, but it was ineffective and only served to identify by the muzzle flashes their locations for the VC gunners. About three hundred meters to the left, there appeared to be some high ground and cover. No enemy fire originated from that location and it would allow them a chance to regroup and to assess the situation.

"Cease fire!" ordered Bromhead. "Follow me. Let's move it."

Most of the men turned with Bromhead, happy to have someone in charge with some kind of plan. Bromhead wasn't happy because he felt that he was maneuvering into a trap. He was moving to the only high ground and cover available, but he was certain that the VC would have thought of that, too. It seemed highly improbable that the Vietcong would not see the advantage of putting another ambush on that ground. He hoped that he could get close enough before they opened fire so that he could mount a successful attack.

The firing from the tree line increased as AKs and SKSs joined the machine guns, their white tracers joining the green. Bromhead let some of the men get in front of him and then tried to urge the others to run. He screamed at them to hurry, which was difficult in the waist-deep water. He pushed at the backs of some and grabbed the web gear of others, trying to force them forward. He knew that, if he could get them moving with a goal in mind, he would be able to keep them moving in that direction, even if the enemy had taken the high ground. Once a man was running a certain way, he tended to keep running that way. If he was walking without a goal, it would be easy to turn him—to chase him back into the swamp where he could be killed.

Bromhead fell back with a couple of the grenadiers and attempted to lob grenades into the ambush to slow down the murderous fire. The water all around them was kicked up into a white froth, and the white-and-green tracers from the enemy weapons laced the night sky. Streams of red flashed back into the trees from his own men, the paths of the bullets crisscrossing in the dark.

The explosions of the grenades, like brilliant yellow fireworks among the trees, caused some of the VC to back off, and the fire from the tree line tapered off slightly. The surge through the swamp had carried the American force within a hundred feet of the high ground. It was then that the second ambush was sprung.

The first five or six men disappeared into the water. A couple dived out of the way, letting the water close over them for a few seconds. Bromhead instinctively ducked and then fell to one knee, bringing his rifle to bear on the enemy soldiers. A few others did the same.

Bromhead realized that he had let his advance falter and that could be disastrous. He grabbed one man by the shoulder straps of his pack and tried to push him forward. He screamed at them, "Get the fuck moving! Let's go!"

This time he led the charge himself, firing from the hips, burning through his magazine. He ejected it into the swamp and slammed another home. The Tai, seeing the big American forcing his way toward the high ground, joined him in the charge, shooting and yelling and cursing. There was an increase of enemy fire, but it was poorly directed, passing overhead. It seemed to irritate the Tai, and they yelled louder, fired faster and ran harder.

Suddenly the water dropped away, and Bromhead found himself standing on land. Around him were a dozen or so of the Tai. He saw where the enemy was dug in and turned toward their position, running in a crouch, firing his weapon from his hip. He didn't call to the Tai or give orders. He simply expected them to follow him. He didn't realize that he was screaming like a Sioux warrior.

All at once, as he leaped a small stone wall that marked the perimeter of a Vietnamese peasant's graveyard, Bromhead found himself standing among the enemy. There were three VC squatting behind gravestones. One of them stood to meet Bromhead, brandishing a bayonet attached to his AK-47. Bromhead used his rifle barrel to push aside the bayonet and then swung the M-14 butt upward, hitting the VC under the chin and flipping him backward. He heard the snapping of the man's jawbone and the shattering of his teeth.

Bromhead kicked outward, knocked the second VC to the soft earth and then dropped to one knee on the man's chest, pinning him to the ground. As the third turned, Bromhead shot him three times in the chest, the bullets ripping into the man just below the collarbone and blowing out his back. He dropped without a sound. Bromhead then turned his rifle on the VC he held down and shot him in the head as the man tried to reach the combat knife strapped to his thigh.

All around Bromhead the Tai were engaging other VC in hand-to-hand combat. Pistol shots punctuated the melee, and men were screaming in anger and pain. From the far tree line the VC machine guns continued to fire into the swamp and mortars continued to explode among the Tai trying to reach land. Bromhead attempted to rally his men so that he could consolidate his position and take stock of how things stood. But then there was an enemy counterattack, launched from the trees about fifty yards away.

The Tai grenadiers had been well trained. They didn't allow themselves to be engaged in the hand-to-hand fight but stayed back. When they saw the enemy charge, they began lobbing 40 mm rounds as fast as they could reload their weapons. The explosions, accompanied by fountains of sparks mushrooming among the rear elements of the VC attack, cut down the enemy enough to break the first assault. The VC fled to the safety of the trees.

About that time the Cong who had been part of the ambush on the high ground tried to break contact and retreat. There was a sudden increase in the firing as the two sides separated.

Bromhead crawled to the rear, looking for one of the Tai officers or NCOs and trying to find a radio. He found a second lieutenant, pointed to the left and shouted, "Get the men there set. Have them deploy to receive an attack from the trees. Get the machine guns emplaced. Use the gravestones for protection. You understand all that?"

The Tai nodded in response.

"You seen any of the radio operators?" Bromhead added.

"No. No see a one," the Tai replied as he moved.

Next Bromhead found a Tai sergeant who had been grazed by a bullet. His shirt was badly ripped, and there was blood dripping down his arm. One of the Tai was wrapping a bandage around the wounded man's chest.

"You okay?" Bromhead asked.

"Yeah," the sergeant said as he looked up at Bromhead. "It looks worse than it is."

"I want you to find a radio. We need to make contact with the camp. And I want a head count. I have to know how many men we lost in the fight."

As the Tai sergeant was helped to his feet, Bromhead started to place the men he could find so that they could support the machine guns. He put a couple of men behind them as a rear guard and equipped them with the grenade launchers. He didn't expect the VC to try to cross the open swamp. If they attacked again, he figured it would be from the trees. Once all of that was done, he checked on the injured. The men who had been hit were only slightly injured; the ones who had been seriously hurt had been left in the swamp where they had probably drowned.

FETTERMAN WAS DRAWING close to his ambush point when he heard distant firing. At first it was just the crump of mortars and then machine gun bursts and finally a thunderous swelling of automatic weapons. He knew that it was Bromhead. Kittredge and his men would be to the east and north of where the shooting was coming from.

Fetterman halted and listened, wanting desperately to know exactly what was happening. As long as there was shooting, Bromhead and his force were still alive. At least that was something.

Finally he moved back to the radio operator and called the camp. Nothing had been reported and they had heard no shooting. As far as they knew, the plan was proceeding according to the timetable.

ON THE HIGH GROUND Bromhead had organized his force into a circular perimeter, anchoring it on one side with the gravestones of the Vietnamese cemetery. The machine guns could cover anything and could be moved to the area of the strongest attack with a minimum of effort. The wounded were being cared for in the center of the perimeter.

Once he was set, he crawled around the perimeter, encouraging the men and looking for a radio since the Tai sergeant had been unable to locate one. Apparently neither of the radio operators had made it out of the swamp. He had lost all communication with the camp.

He was about to ask a couple of Tai if they would help him go out to look for the radios, although he thought they would probably be waterlogged, when firing broke out. Bromhead turned and saw about fifty men leave the trees and run across the open ground. A bugle sounded behind them, and a shout rose among them.

Bromhead didn't have to give command to fire. The Tai began to shoot as soon as they saw the enemy. The red tracers of the M-60 machine guns crisscrossed the green of the VC's tracers.

Bromhead thought that the attack would break before it reached his lines, but suddenly the Vietcong were there, overrunning the machine guns to engage the men behind them. Again Bromhead used his rifle butt on an enemy's head, hearing it split like a ripe melon.

Another VC came at him with a machete held high, as if he wanted to chop Bromhead into pieces. Bromhead didn't even blink. He put two bullets into the man's stomach, and as the enemy doubled over, he put a third into the top of his head. As Bromhead turned, a VC loomed out of the dark, swinging a machete as if it were a baseball bat. Bromhead grabbed the barrel and the butt of his rifle and blocked the blow. He stepped close to the enemy, moving inside, and shoved, knocking him to the ground. The man rolled and lunged with his blade, trying to impale Bromhead. The young lieutenant sidestepped the VC and kicked at his arm, snapping his elbow. The VC howled in pain as his machete went spinning into the dark. He grabbed Bromhead around the ankle with his hand, but Bromhead stomped down, smashing the bones of the man's forearm. As the enemy continued to scream, Bromhead swung his rifle butt, hitting the man in the head and ending his wailing.

Around him the fight raged. He saw another VC with a machete lop the head from one of the Tai. Then the VC was bayoneted from behind by another Tai. A third shot the VC seven or eight times.

Someone fired a flare, and it burst into the brightness overhead, throwing a yellowish light on everything. Bromhead could see the individual fights in the shifting shimmering shadows of the eerie half-light. Men struggled with men until one or both fell to the muddy earth. He heard calls for help, cries of pain. The firing was sporadic in the clash of rifle barrel against machete and bayonet. Bromhead ducked like a quarterback dodging a blitzing linebacker as a VC tried to knock him to the ground. He whirled and shot the man in the back, the impact slamming the enemy into the mud. Ragged firing came from the perimeter, and a couple of flashing grenades almost blinded the combatants in the semidarkness. A bugle sounded, was answered by another and was joined by a whistle. Bromhead expected another assault, but the VC who were still standing slowly tried to disengage, falling back until they could turn and run for the safety of the trees.

With the close of the fight, Bromhead made a quick check of the men. More than half his force had been killed or was missing. Another quarter had been wounded, a couple of those seriously. He made the check again, as if he couldn't believe how badly his force had been mauled by the VC. There was no way he could complete his mission. Worse, he couldn't contact the camp to tell them, and they would be unable to warn Fetterman, who would operate under the assumption that Bromhead had a Tai strike force close at hand.

AT THE CAMP Gerber was standing next to the tiny shower, staring into the night sky. Behind him he could hear the water splashing. It was ridiculous, he thought. A woman in the camp caused all kinds of extra problems. They'd had to build a separate latrine and then screen it. Whenever she wanted to take a shower, one of the men had to stand by to make sure that no one walked in on her. Not that he was worried about his men taking advantage of the situation. Sure, they'd peek if they could, but they wouldn't go out of their way to see, especially when, without much difficulty they could get a night in Saigon to visit the various strip clubs, massage parlors or bordellos.

Gerber was surprised that Morrow was still with them. She had tricked Crinshaw into letting her into the field in the beginning, with the request for a reporter to view U.S. Army Special Forces Camp A-555 made by R. Morrow. Crinshaw had naturally assumed that the request had been made by a man. Of course, when Crinshaw had realized his mistake, he had let it stand. When she'd said that she wanted to stay, Crinshaw didn't object.

"Captain!" said Anderson as he rushed up, breaking into Gerber's thoughts. "I just received a call from Sergeant Fetterman saying he heard some shooting in the vicinity of Lieutenant Bromhead's patrol. We tried to raise the lieutenant but couldn't get a response."

"Okay, I'll be with you in a minute." He turned, looking over his shoulder, and said, "That's it, Robin. I'm going to desert my post."

"Wait a second!" she said frantically. "I'm covered with soap."

"Hurry it up," he ordered.

A moment later Morrow appeared, an OD towel wrapped around her body, her wet hair hanging in her face. One hand swiped at her hair while the other tried halfheartedly to keep the towel in place. "You're a lousy guard."

"Sorry. Duty calls. See you in the morning." He watched her walk away, the towel not quite covering her rear. For just a moment he wished that he didn't have to go to the commo bunker.

In the commo bunker Gerber saw Bocker behind the plywood counter hunched over one of the radios. He was speaking into a hand-held microphone and twisting the gain knob on the front panel of the Fox Mike. He turned at the sound behind him and shrugged.

"You think there's a problem?" Gerber asked.

"Don't really know, Captain. Haven't been able to raise Lieutenant Bromhead, but you know the trouble we've had with the radios, especially when we're operating near water."

"Just what exactly did Sergeant Fetterman say?" asked Gerber.

"He used our standard code to say that he had heard some firing in the area where the lieutenant was supposed to be operating. Said that it sounded like a sustained firefight. I haven't been able to reach the lieutenant, although I did make contact with Kittredge and his people."

Gerber moved to the map posted on one side of the bunker. In the dim light he could barely see it. He leaned across the wooden table for a closer view and confirmed that Bromhead was in an area full of swamps. The probable cause of the radio silence was that the radios were wet and wouldn't work. It seemed ironic. Gerber was nearly overwhelmed by the red dust in the commo bunker, and Bromhead was probably ass deep in water.

"There's nothing we can do tonight. Galvin, call Saigon and lay on a chopper for tomorrow at first light. We'll make a recon flight and check out the situation. In the meantime keep trying, but don't overdo it. We don't want the VC to know we're worried, if they happen to be monitoring our freqs."

"I seriously doubt they will be, sir. We changed all our operating frequencies just before the patrols went out."

Gerber clapped Bocker on the shoulder. "Good work. See you in a couple of hours."

SINCE THE LAST ATTACK no one had moved from the trees, and there had been no incoming fire. Bromhead didn't like it. He was afraid that it meant the VC had slipped away, and that meant Fetterman would be walking into an area where there was a lot more of the enemy than he thought.

Bromhead wasn't worried about his position, however. The tree line where the Vietcong had hidden was nearly a hundred yards away. The ground was nearly flat, and the short grass could not conceal the VC if they tried to crawl forward. Although it was night, the overcast had begun to break up so that the moon showed, giving him some additional light. A dew was beginning to coat everything and everyone, making them even more uncomfortable. His men were dug into the soft, damp earth around the perimeter he had created earlier, creating shallow foxholes with bottoms that quickly filled with swamp water. They set their machine guns behind the gravestones. The wounded had been tended, and no one was in danger of dying soon. Bromhead was sure that, in the morning, Gerber would have choppers up looking for him. He hoped that the helicopters would find him before Fetterman got into trouble.

He thought about sending out a runner, someone who could look for Fetterman to tell him that the blocking force had been ambushed and chewed up. The trouble with the plan was that he didn't have any lowland Vietnamese with him, only Tai strikers who were smaller and darker than the Vietnamese and didn't speak the same language.

The big advantage was that they were near Cambodia and some of the Cambodes looked like the Tai. The only thing to do was send a few of them out with instructions to alert Fetterman.

Bromhead crawled around until he found one of the Tai NCOs that he trusted. He told the man to pick two others, slip into the swamp and work their way to the northwest to the trail being followed by Fetterman. They were to tell the American sergeant that he would not be receiving all the support that he thought he would get and to act at his discretion.

The Tai nodded his understanding, and Bromhead watched the three men work their way back into the swamp. He heard a quiet splashing and then lost sight of the men. He hoped that they would succeed.

He sat for a moment, wiping the sweat from his forehead as he stared into the night. He hadn't done too well in the fight. He had lost most of his men, and he knew the shock of that would set in soon enough. He was hot and tired, and he didn't want to think about the next few minutes or the next couple of hours. He just wanted Gerber to bring out some choppers and get him out. He shook his head, realizing that it wouldn't happen that way and that he had things to do. He had to check the men once more to make sure that they were all alert. And he had to see if there was a radio lying around. He was sure that he would have found one of the radio operators by now if either of them had made it out of the swamp. With a deep breath he forced himself to his feet and began checking things out.

BEFORE THE SUN ROSE, Gerber heard the faint sound of a helicopter. He headed to the helipad, saw the aircraft's lights in the distance and turned on a strobe for a guide. Then he stepped back and turned his head in anticipation of the swirling dust and debris from the rotor wash.

The chopper touched down, bounced slightly as if the pilot had been a little too fast in dropping the collective and then settled to the pad. The aircraft commander leaped out. He was a tall, skinny man who had not taken off his flight helmet or his chicken plate. The helmet hid his hair, but the flowing mustache that was completely outside Army regulations and a trademark of helicopter pilots was black. He said, "Good morning, Captain."

"Ramsey, isn't it?" responded Gerber, studying the man. "Charles Ramsey?"

"Yes, sir."

"Thought after the last time you wouldn't be back."

"No, sir," said Ramsey. "You've provided the only good missions I've been on. When the operations officer asked who'd like the ash-and-trash flight with the Special Forces, I jumped at the chance."

Gerber looked at his watch. "You can shut down and grab some breakfast if you want. Be a half hour or so before it's bright enough to see."

As Gerber left the helipad, the other pilot, a very young warrant officer named Randle, said to Ramsey, "You know that guy?"

"Yeah. Worked for a couple weeks out here with him. Had five other aircraft. I thought you'd been here."

"I just flew in and out once or twice, ferrying a lieutenant to Saigon," said Randle as he followed Ramsey away from the helipad and toward the team house.

Gerber reappeared at the helicopter thirty minutes later, accompanied by two of his NCOs. He laid a map in the cargo compartment and said, pointing to a place on the map, "We've got to search this general area. We're looking for a good-sized force so it shouldn't be hard to find them." He took off his beret and wiped the sweat from his forehead. He put a hand to his eyes and looked to the east. "It's going to be a hot one today," he added.

Ramsey nodded and climbed into the left seat as Randle took the right. Ramsey leaned across the console, set the flight idle detent button, glanced through the windshield and yelled, "Clear!"

Randle looked out his side window to the right and then held up a thumb. From the rear both the crew chief and gunner shouted, "Clear!" The crew chief tapped Gerber on the shoulder, pointed to Gerber's seat belt to indicate he should fasten it and then handed him a spare flight helmet that contained a headset so he could talk to the pilots.

A moment later there was a quiet whine that built slowly until it was a hot roar. The blades began to swing faster and faster. Ramsey sat upright, his eyes focused on the instrument panel, watching the gauges. He rocked the cyclic around and then began to ease in the pitch until the helicopter trembled and jumped into the air. It hung about three feet above the pad, oscillating slightly, and Ramsey used the pedals to turn to the south. He dropped the nose and the chopper began to slide forward, gaining speed as it rushed down the runway, leaving a trail of swirling red dust and flying debris behind it.

They climbed out to the south, leaving the heat and humidity of the ground behind, and turned west over the swamp. The clouds were high and scattered. The ground was partially veiled in a whirling mist that obscured detail and then blew away to reveal it. At first they could see a trail through the light grass, but as the water became deeper, they lost sight of it. Gerber continued to consult his map, trying to guess the route Bromhead would have taken. They overflew the small clump of high-ground islands, and they could see from the crushed grass and churned-up mud that someone had been there recently.

They continued flying at about fifteen hundred feet to keep out of effective small arms range, trying to locate the column. As they veered toward a tree line, where it was possible that Bromhead had holed up for a rest, there was a short burst of AK fire. Ramsey circled, and the door gunner returned fire, his M-60 machine gun mounted on the side of the Slick pumping out rounds. Gerber could see the red tracers slam into the trees. There was a second burst from the VC, and Ramsey broke down and away.

Over the intercom, Gerber said, "We go on?"

"Not that way, Captain. Enemy soldiers there."

"What are you going to do about it?"

"Call our Operations and let them know we took fire and the location. Also tell them that it was only one weapon."

"How can you be sure that there is only one guy?" asked Gerber.

"Because," answered Randle, who looked over the seat into the back, "if there was more than one down there, they would have shot at us, too."

"Oh," said Gerber, feeling a little silly. "And we continue?" he added.

"Of course. No reason not to," Randle replied.

But just as he finished speaking, another weapon opened fire. It was followed by another and another and then the rapid chatter of a .30 caliber. The green tracers, seeming smaller in the daylight, danced skyward, disappearing into the clouds. Ramsey dropped the collective, diving toward the ground, away from the enemy weapons as both door guns began to return the fire. He felt three or four rounds smash into the side of the helicopter as they skimmed the grass in the swamp, trying to stay as low as possible until they were well away from the enemy weapons.

Randle had switched on his UHF radio and was trying to make contact with Cu Chi Arty to tell them the location of the enemy. Gerber could hear him giving the coordinates, the type of fusing and the type of terrain the artillery would be hitting.

"Can you spot?" asked the voice from Cu Chi Arty.

"Negative. We have sustained combat damage."

"Do you need assistance?" asked the man on the radio.

"Negative. Just give him hell for us."

"Roger. Hell."

Ramsey glanced at the instrument panel and saw the oil pressure begin to drop. He looked at Randle and then back at the instruments. "Let's get out of here," he said.

"We're heading back?" asked Gerber.

"Have to," responded Ramsey. "Took a couple of hits and we're losing oil pressure. It goes and we'll lose the engine. I can get another aircraft out here for you."

Gerber shook his head and thought, *I didn't like this mission in the beginning. Damn!* Over the intercom he said, "Head on back."

4

SOUTH OF THE
PARROT'S BEAK,
SOUTH VIETNAM

Fetterman wasn't overly concerned about the lack of radio contact with Bromhead. It had happened often enough before. He remembered the trouble they had had with their equipment during the river operations, and they hadn't had to move across great expanses of open water. Those radios had become waterlogged just by being close to the river. No, he wasn't concerned. Just annoyed.

The shooting that he had heard early in the morning bothered him a little more. He knew that Bromhead could take care of himself, and his force was large enough to deal with any threat that the VC could mount. At least the intelligence reports suggested that Bromhead could handle anything. The Vietcong weren't supposed to have much in the area.

At sunup Tyme, who had been sleeping under a large tree, crawled over to Fetterman. "You find out anything else?" he said.

"No. The camp hasn't heard a word."

"We going to proceed?"

Fetterman studied the younger man carefully. "Don't really see any reason to cancel," he replied. "Even if we can't coordinate with the lieutenant, we should be able to handle anything they throw at us. The lieutenant was being set up to catch anyone who might get away from us."

"I don't like this. Somebody was shooting out there last night, and now we can't make contact with one of our patrols. Our biggest one at that."

"Don't sweat it. See that the men get something to eat and then we'll move into the final positions. After that, I don't want anyone moving about until we spring the ambush."

"You talked to Kittredge?"

"Not directly. He called the camp about the shooting, too. I heard part of the message, but he was breaking up pretty badly. All I really could tell was that it was Kittredge."

"Another great mission," said Tyme. "Going out to attack the enemy and we can't even talk to the friendlies."

"You know, Boom-Boom, you're becoming a real worrywart. Didn't anyone ever tell you that nothing ever goes according to plan? Once you begin, you have to be flexible."

"It's just that I'm getting too short to be very flexible."

When they finished breakfast—canned C-rations for the Americans, rice and fish heads for the Tai—Fetterman moved them a half klick to the west. He found a well-used trail through the jungle that was lined with bushes and palm, banana and coconut trees. The trail meandered around stands of bamboo and touched the bank of a shallow stream before bending away from the water toward Cambodia. The trail itself was packed earth, three or four meters wide. The bamboo and trees rising steeply at the trail's edge provided good cover, and there were several escape routes through the jungle.

Fetterman had deployed the Tai into a modified U-shaped ambush so that his men lined both sides of the trail. No matter which way the VC broke, they would run into more shooting. He had Tyme anchoring one leg and Krung anchoring the other. He knew Krung well enough now to believe that Krung would watch the entire army of North Vietnamese walk by without shooting if he was ordered to do so. But, once given permission to fire, he would kill every enemy soldier he could see.

Fetterman had taken the base of the ambush where he could control the claymore mines set to rake the trail. Once those were detonated, the men of the ambush would begin pouring rifle bullets into the enemy. Each man had been given a specific field of fire so that he wouldn't be shooting men on the other side of the trail. Now all he had to do was wait for the recruiting platoon to walk into the death trap.

They had just gotten set when they heard distant firing. Fetterman knew that it had to be Kittredge and his men. It rolled to him like thunder diminished by distance. There were periodic explosions and the rise and fall of small arms fire. Suddenly Fetterman felt like Custer and then remembered the stories that he had heard as a little boy. His great-great-great-grandfather, William J. Fetterman, had lead a group of eighty cavalrymen and infantrymen into an ambush arranged by Sioux warriors. In less than forty minutes his entire command had been wiped out. Fetterman suddenly knew how his ancestor had felt.

Fetterman turned to his RTO. "I've got to raise the camp," he said.

AT THE CAMP Ramsey and Randle stood looking at the bullet holes in the side of the helicopter. There were two through the tail boom, peeling the light skin of the fuselage back to reveal bright silver metal. There was one on the left side that had penetrated the window of the cargo compartment door where it was locked back against the chopper. The bullet had smashed into the engine and the deck there was covered with oil. A couple of the wires to the turbine had also been severed.

"That should take care of it," said Randle. "Wouldn't be such a good idea to fly this out of here."

"Yeah," agreed Ramsey. "Maintenance is going to be pissed. Told me not to break the airplane."

Randle laughed. "Wonder if I should flunk you on your check ride. Flew into enemy fire and broke the airplane."

"Extremely funny."

Gerber broke into the conversation. "Then you're down for the day?"

"We're not going to fly this out of here, if that's what you mean. The engine oil is leaking all over the deck. We could get airborne, but I doubt we could stay that way for very long. Maintenance may fly in to try to fix it, or they may just call in a shit hook to lift it out. If we're lucky, we'll get a replacement."

Gerber did not look pleased. "Let me know what you learn. I've got to get over to the commo bunker," he said.

Gerber left the helipad, crossed the northern end of the compound and entered the commo bunker. It was a large, heavily sandbagged structure that sprouted a half-dozen antennas. The interior was dark and the air was slightly cooler than it was outside, although it was still extremely humid. Bocker was sitting behind the counter, his feet propped up, sipping a Coke and reading the latest *Stars and Stripes*.

"Any news?" Gerber asked as he walked in.

Bocker dropped his feet to the dirty plywood floor and set his Coke on the counter. "No, sir. Been real quiet except for traffic on Guard. Somebody lost a chopper up near Go Dau Ha. They're all out picking up the crew."

At that moment they heard Fetterman's voice slice through the static on the Fox Mike. "Zulu Base, this is Zulu Main."

Gerber stepped around and took the microphone from Bocker and said, "Zulu Main, this is Zulu Six."

"Roger, Six, say status of Zulu Five and Zulu Reserve."

For just a minute Gerber wasn't sure how to answer. Their codes didn't really cover the situation he now found himself in. He knew that radio operators sometimes made up the codes as they went along. Once he had been told that the grid coordinates were up five from Jack Benny's age. The thinking was that the VC would have no idea what it meant, but every American would know that the base number was thirty-nine. Gerber had never been convinced that these tactics fooled the VC.

They had just changed the frequencies so the odds were that the Vietcong could not monitor their radio transmissions. He took a chance that the VC, even if they were monitoring the Green Berets' frequency, wouldn't know the police ten codes.

"Ah, Zulu Main, we have ten seventy-seven with Zulu Five. Recon has not succeeded. We have not attempted to reach Zulu Reserve."

"Roger, Six. Understand. Please advise as soon as you can."

"Will do. Are you planning an advance to the rear?"

"Negative, Zulu Six. Have no reason to make a move now."

"Roger, Main. Will advise. Out." Gerber held on to the mike for a moment before handing it back to Bocker. "I have a very bad feeling about this," he said. "Very bad."

KITTREDGE FOUND a good location for his reserve force. He held what little high ground there was. It was grassy and fell gently away to the jungle below. Bushes were scattered around the slopes along with a couple of tall palms and a single banana tree. From his vantage point he had a limited view of the surrounding countryside. He could see a single hootch about half a klick away through a series of breaks in the jungle vegetation. A little farther to the east he could see the water of rice fields flashing and shimmering in the morning sun. The jungle nearest him was thin enough that he would be able to see anyone approaching and could bring them under fire. With the M-60 machine guns and two 60 mm mortars to support him, he didn't worry about sneak attacks.

Kittredge made a radio check to let both the camp and Fetterman know that he was in position. Then he told his men to go to half alert so that some of the men could eat and relax. The force was spread out in a circular formation with the crest of the hill in the center. Smith and one of the Tai sat there eating their breakfast. The Tai was sharing his fish heads and rice with Smith, who had given the man a can of ham and lima beans. Looking around, Kittredge didn't have the feeling that anything was going to happen.

Just after sunup one of the men reported movement in the trees to the south. Kittredge thought that it was probably a farmer heading for the rice fields a klick or so to the east. But, to be safe, he edged to the side of the perimeter to watch.

The pop of several mortars took him completely by surprise. He yelled, "Incoming!" as he rolled to the ground and tried to spot the flashes through the jungle.

The first of the rounds dropped short, exploding in the high grass on the southern slope and throwing up small clouds of dust and dirt. The next volley landed closer to the lines, and the third landed among his men. Kittredge ordered them to keep their heads down. He leaped to his feet, sprinted toward the middle of the perimeter and dived for cover. He got to his knees and saw the mortar crew huddled together, ignoring their weapon. He hesitated for a moment before running toward them to begin a counter-mortar duel and as suddenly as the mortar rounds started falling, they stopped.

On the other side of the perimeter, Sully Smith rolled into a shallow depression where he bumped into a couple of the Tai strikers who were huddled at the bottom. Smith got to his knees, looked around and dived out of the hole to land behind a rotting log. From there he could see the entire northern approach to the perimeter.

Kittredge got up and ran to the right until he found Saut, the Tai NCO who was working with them. He whispered to him, "Get ready to repeal an assault. I think we're about to be attacked."

Saut turned and began yelling quickly in Tai to the men. There was a rattling of weapons as the Tai strikers made sure that they had rounds chambered.

"Sully," yelled Kittredge, "keep your eyes open. I think they're coming at us."

Smith left his position and crawled across the perimeter. He whispered to Kittredge, "You call the camp?"

"Was about to. Let me find the number two RTO."

Together they crawled off. The RTO was lying on his back, blood running from a dozen wounds in his chest and head. His dead eyes stared at the rising sun. There was a stubble on his chin where he needed to shave.

"Shit," said Kittredge as he turned the body over. He could see the hole in the PRC-10's canvas cover. He pulled the handset out, keyed it and tried to raise the camp. When that failed, Kittredge opened the canvas, saw the hole in the radio and asked Smith, "You cross trained in commo?"

"Hell, no," said Sully. "But I do know something about radios—sometimes they come in handy to blow things up."

"Then see if you can fix this before it gets really ugly out here."

They were interrupted by a single bugle call, followed by a couple of whistles and a sudden surge of enemy small arms fire.

"Here they come!" yelled Saut.

"Fix it, Sully! Fix it quick! This wasn't supposed to happen," Kittredge shouted. He crawled off to see fifty or sixty black-clad VC running through the grass and up the slope toward them, already too close for the mortars to be effective. The VC had their bayonets out and were firing their weapons from the hip as they shouted and screamed. The enemy outnumbered them at least two to one.

As the firing increased, kicking up the dirt in the center of the perimeter and ripping apart the Tai's makeshift cover, the enemy soldiers closed with them. Smith worked feverishly to open the radio. He found that the shrapnel had not penetrated very deep, but had severed a couple of wires. Using his combat knife, he stripped the insulation from the wires, glanced at the onrushing enemy, looked at the wires and connected them. He heard the shout from the VC, shot another glance at them and twisted the broken wires together. He turned the PRC-10 on and heard the hiss of the carrier wave indicating that the radio was now operational.

But Smith had no time to make any calls. He pushed the radio out of the way, trying to protect it behind a log, and then turned to meet the coming threat. He was stunned to see that the VC were already inside the perimeter.

Off to the right Kittredge was trying to direct the fire of the machine guns, but the assistant gunner wasn't interested in feeding bullets into the machine gun. He wanted to shoot at the Vietcong so the machine gun jammed. As it did, the VC swarmed up that slope, too, overrunning the American and Tai lines. The mortar crews had abandoned their weapons, picked up their rifles and were using them.

Kittredge jumped to meet the enemy. He had one of the short bayonets attached to the front of his rifle, and as one of the enemy soldiers ran toward him, Kittredge parried and thrust. The bayonet penetrated the silk of the black pajamas and entered the man's stomach. There was a spurt of blood as the VC stopped suddenly, leaped backward and turned so that he could shoot at Kittredge. The American dropped to one knee and fired his own rifle. The bullet slammed into the VC's chest, throwing him back into the tall grass, and he died with a look of surprise.

As that happened, another enemy jumped at Kittredge from the side, knocking him to the ground. Kittredge rolled over, pain flaring in his back and side. He kicked out, cutting the VC's feet from under him. As that man fell, Kittredge squeezed the trigger twice, and he saw the body jerk as the bullets hit. Blood blossomed on the man's chest and spurted from his throat. The VC dropped his rifle, one hand clawing at his neck as if he couldn't breathe. The enemy thrashed around, pounding his heels on the soft ground, his hands raking his neck as he slowly died. When the man was dead, Kittredge got shakily to his feet, turned and saw the battle raging around him. Suddenly he was aware of the noise. Of the shooting. Screaming.

Smith was fighting two of the VC, holding them off with his rifle that lacked a bayonet. He was swinging it back and forth between the two, shouting at the top of his voice. One of the VC hesitated at the wrong moment, and Smith clubbed him with the rifle barrel, smashing into the man's skull. As the other moved in, Smith dropped his rifle and kicked upward, hitting the man in the crotch. The VC shrieked in pain and doubled over. Smith kicked again, snapping the Vietcong's head back with an audible crunch, killing him.

As Smith bent over to pick up a weapon he felt someone leap onto his back. Reaching over his shoulder, Smith grabbed the loose material of the enemy's black pajama top and slammed him to the ground. The American followed through with a punch to the neck, crushing the VC's throat.

Just as the fighting looked as if it could get no worse, the enemy vanished. It seemed that one moment there were Vietcong all over them and the next they had disappeared. Bugle calls and shouts filled the air as the enemy retreated to the trees. It meant that Kittredge would have a moment to regroup.

FAR AWAY, FETTERMAN HEARD the first sounds of the enemy as they moved toward the ambush. He'd been worried about all the shooting that he'd heard, apparently from Bromhead's group and then Kittredge's, but now he ignored that as the Vietcong began to close in. He could no longer afford to worry about anyone else.

AS SMITH PICKED UP his rifle, Kittredge crawled over to ask, "What the hell happened?"

"I don't know. It jammed somehow." He worked the bolt and saw that one of the rounds had not stripped from the magazine properly. The nose of the round was pressed into the top of the breech. Smith reached in and flipped the shell out of the way, worked the bolt and discovered that the next round was crooked.

Smith pulled the magazine from the rifle, checked it, reseated it and saw that it was now working correctly.

"You get the radio working?" Kittredge wiped the sweat from his forehead with the sleeve of his fatigues. He had lost his helmet during the fight.

"Yeah," Smith replied. "Couple of wires broken, but I didn't have time to make any calls. Got kind of busy."

"Okay," said Kittredge. "Advise the camp that we've run into trouble. Maybe they'd better pull Fetterman out. I'll check to see what kind of damage has been done."

There was a single shot, and the ground between them erupted. Kittredge rolled sharply to his right and yelled, "Sniper! Anyone see where that came from?"

One man pointed toward the trees.

"Then return fire, for Christ's sake. Don't let them get away with that shit. Kill the son of a bitch!" He glanced back at the mortar crews and yelled, "Use the fucking tubes."

But before anyone could take the sniper under fire, another enemy charge flooded across the open grounds, accompanied by a sudden eruption of shooting and yelling. There was a hesitation by the Tai and then they began firing, but the VC didn't waver.

A couple of the Tai stood to meet the charge and were cut down immediately by sniper fire. One fell back, his right arm hanging loose at his side as the blood cascaded from a shoulder wound.

And then the enemy was there among them, using bayonets and machetes to chop and slash at the Tai, hacking at them as if they were trying to clear vines from a jungle trail. The Tai fought back with their rifles, bayonets and pistols. They lobbed grenades at the VC, but the enemy kept coming, pouring out of the trees like someone had opened floodgates. Smith and Kittredge were kneeling near the center of the perimeter, shooting the VC as fast as they could pull their triggers. A dozen of the enemy fell, but then the VC swarmed past the first line of defense and spilled into the center with Smith and Kittredge. Both men stood up back-to-back, covering one another.

Using their rifles, bayonets and finally knives, they kept the enemy bodies piling up around them. Kittredge grabbed the barrel of an enemy rifle as the man tried to impale him. The American jerked the weapon forward, pulling the enemy soldier toward him and then slashed with his knife, slicing into the soft skin under the man's jaw. Blood spurted, washing down the front of the VC's uniform, staining it crimson. He collapsed to his knees and pitched forward into the grass as the rest of his life pumped out.

Another VC ran at Kittredge, his rifle hip high, bayonet extended. Kittredge turned so that his right side faced the man, jumped back and plunged his knife to the hilt into the man's chest. He twisted it and jerked it free as the man shrieked and died.

The shooting died in the mass confusion of soldiers, VC and Americans fighting hand-to-hand for their lives. There was shouting and screaming without intelligent thought. Men grunted and fell, and all the while the bugles kept blowing and the whistles kept shrilling.

Surprisingly, the VC swept past the center of the perimeter and grabbed the mortar tubes, shooting and stabbing the crews as they ran into the line on the other side and down the opposite slope. It was as if the attack had been planned that way—sweep through, kill as many of the Americans and Tai as possible, capture the mortars and then get out.

With the lull in the fighting, Kittredge checked the perimeter. Bodies were scattered up the grassy slope, and where the enemy had encountered the perimeter force, there were piles of bodies. Dead men dressed in black pajamas and khaki uniforms. Dead men dressed in the olive drab of American-made uniforms. Men with rust-colored stains on their clothes and in the grass around them. Blood that was soaking into the earth, turning the dirt to mud.

Weapons were strewn over the battlefield. Brown craters dotted the slope and the hilltop. Dead men lay near them, some of them broken, the white of bone contrasting with the red of torn flesh. Pieces of the dead littered the ground. Kittredge bent to pick up an undamaged boot and then nearly threw up when he found that there was a foot still inside it.

Still holding the boot, Kittredge slowly turned, counting the bodies, no longer caring that there were snipers. Of the fifty men he had started with, thirty-two were dead, including Sergeant Saut. More than half his men were dead. Twelve others were wounded, and of those, five were in danger of dying from their wounds. One just barely clung to life, an Army belt drawn tightly around the stump that had been his arm. His blood had dyed the side of his fatigues red.

That left him with just six men ready to fight. Seven of the wounded could hold rifles and fire into the VC when they began the next assault, but they would be useless if the enemy penetrated the perimeter. And the VC had yet to fail to do that.

Kittredge crawled to the radio, turned it on and found to his surprise, that it was still working. First he tried to call Fetterman to tell him that the reserve force no longer existed, but he couldn't reach him. Next he tried to call Gerber at the camp to let him know, hoping that he would be able to relay a message to Fetterman. Only after he failed to make contact with the camp did he realize that he could have asked them for help if he could call them. Maybe helicopters to swoop out of the bright deep-blue sky to save them. Or artillery. He could call in artillery support. Something that could be there in seconds, if he could get a radio call through.

Standard procedure, if the radio was operating and you failed to make contact, was to call in the blind, hoping that anyone who heard would answer.

Kittredge, now sitting in the center of the perimeter with his tiny command dead around him, keyed the mike and in a voice that was lifeless with shock said, "Anyone listening, this is Zulu Reserve calling in the blind. How do you hear, over?"

"Zulu Reserve, this is Black Sabbath One One. I roger your transmission."

Just as he received the response from the Army Aviation helicopter, he heard the sound of bugles and the yelling of the VC as they sensed victory. There was a rattling of rifle fire as Smith moved all the men to one side of the perimeter to deal with the threat of attack.

For a moment Kittredge stared into space. He saw the gently sloping hill with the scattered bodies of his men. Beyond them were thirty or forty dead VC lying near the trees. Kittredge knew that he and his men would not survive another assault. There were simply too many of the enemy coming. All he could do was take as many of them with him as possible.

Over the radio he said, "Black Sabbath One One, please relay to Cu Chi Arty that I have a fire mission. Over."

"Understand fire mission."

"That is correct and please hurry."

To Smith, Kittredge yelled, "Sully, we've had it! We're not going to get out of this one. I'm calling for artillery."

With bullets hitting the ground all around him, Smith wormed his way back to Kittredge and asked, "What the hell good is that going to do?"

"I'm bringing it down on us. We'll take some of the bastards with us!"

Smith looked at Kittredge's eyes and saw that he meant it. He glanced over his shoulder and saw that the VC were running up the slope and screaming, the sound of their bugles filling the air.

"You do what you have to. I think we better tell the Tai and give them a chance to bug out."

Kittredge shook his head. "Wait for the first rounds to fall. That might give them a chance to reach the trees behind us, but I doubt it."

The radio crackled to life as the Army pilot tried to contact Kittredge.

"Roger, One One," said Kittredge. "Tell Cu Chi Arty we have a reinforced VC company attacking across open ground from a tree line. Grid X-ray Sierra two five six four. Request area fire, quick fuse." He hesitated and warned, "You'll be dropping it danger close."

The pilot relayed the message and then asked, "Can you spot?"

Kittredge grinned at the radio. "I will as long as possible. The VC are about to overrun us."

Just as he made that statement, the first of the artillery rounds slammed into the trees. A plume of white from the smoke round sprouted skyward, fire spreading from it. There was agonized screaming from the VC where it had landed. A few jumped up to run, fleeing from the white phosphorus of the round.

"Drop twenty five and fire for effect." Kittredge yelled at Smith, "They'll come in groups of six. After the sixth one has hit, have everyone fall back to the north."

Firing erupted all around them as VC machine guns and grenades from the trees joined battle. When the VC were twenty yards away, the first of the artillery rounds fell. The ground all around the VC exploded into geysers of brown soil, red blood and obscured the jungle as the artillery continued. Fifteen of the VC died in the detonation of one 105 mm howitzer shell.

Then it seemed as if the entire planet was exploding as the artillerymen at the unseen fire support base got into the rhythm of loading and firing their weapons. The VC assault slowed—neither attacker nor defender wanted to stand in the midst of the artillery barrage. Everyone hugged the ground, trying to disappear into it so that the shells wouldn't kill them.

When the sixth round had hit, Smith leaped to his feet and shouted, "Scatter! Run! Let's get the fuck out!"

The Tai and the Americans got up and began to run to the north, away from the main VC assault. They were on the downslope side when the next artillery volley began to fall. They hit the dirt as the ground all around them blew up, throwing tons of deadly shrapnel through the air. Smith turned and saw Kittredge standing near the crest of the hill. He was firing at the VC as if unaware of the artillery, shooting at anything that moved as the 105 mm shells landed. Then he disappeared in a fountain of earth. Smith closed his eyes tightly, breathed deeply and counted to six again. Then he was on his feet, surrounded by the few survivors, running for the supposed safety of the jungle, away from the hilltop and the VC.

He dived to the ground as the third volley landed, and defenders and attackers alike died.

5

U.S. ARMY SPECIAL
FORCES CAMP A-555

Cat Anderson left the commo bunker and walked across the compound toward the helipad, where Gerber stood talking to the chopper pilots. When he was close, he said, "Say, Captain, we just got the strangest call. Helicopter crew asked if we had anyone in trouble."

"Don't look at me," said Ramsey. "I've been here the whole time."

"You get a call sign?" asked Gerber.

"Black Sabbath One One."

Gerber looked slightly irritated. "I mean, did they get a call sign from our group?"

"Oh, yes, sir. I think it was Kittredge's people. One One said they called in artillery. The pilot claimed it sounded like they were calling it down on themselves, but Kittredge wouldn't do that," said Anderson.

Gerber felt the blood drain from his face. "Good God!" he said. "You tried to contact them, didn't you? Really tried?"

"Of course. Couldn't raise them, but with the way the radios have been working, I'm not surprised."

"You talk to Fetterman about this?"

"Not yet, Captain. Wanted to advise you first. See what you thought about it. I thought it pretty strange that Kittredge would be calling artillery in on his own position. The pilot said he wasn't sure about that, but it sounded like it." Anderson was repeating

himself because he refused to believe that Kittredge was dead—
which was what the radio call meant if taken at face value.

"Okay," said Gerber, thinking rapidly. "Try to let Fetterman
know and suggest that he pull back. Next, get hold of Crystal Ball
and advise him and ask for immediate airlift. Ten choppers. Let
me know as soon as you learn anything else. And keep trying to
get Kittredge."

"Yes, sir."

As Anderson took off running, Gerber said to Ramsey, "How
long before your replacement is here?"

"Twenty minutes at the most."

"No way you can get this airborne?" he asked, pointing to the
helicopter.

For a moment Ramsey said nothing. Then slowly he confessed, "Given the situation, we could get it up, but I can't guarantee how long it'll stay up. We've got the leaks plugged, but we
lost a lot of the oil. Engine could quit quickly."

"But you could get airborne?"

"Yes, sir. In an extreme emergency."

"Then please consider this an extreme emergency."

Ramsey shot a glance at Randle, who nodded gravely. "Yes,
sir," Ramsey said.

Gerber stood staring at the helicopter. He felt sick. He hadn't
liked the idea when Kepler had come up with it, and now it
sounded as if his feelings were justified. Kittredge was in deep
trouble, and Bromhead was out of contact, too. It all seemed to
be too much. Not a coincidence. Bromhead and Kittredge apparently ambushed. It *had* to be a coordinated plan designed to
inflict losses on the men of his camp.

"Listen, Ramsey, get ready to take off. I mean now," Gerber
said. "I don't think we have time to fool around. I've got to get
to the commo bunker, but I'll be back in a minute."

Ramsey looked at the helicopter as Gerber took off at a dead
run. The oil still glistened on the deck, but the lines were patched
with hundred-mile-an-hour tape. He reached over to jiggle the
wires and lines and then said to Randle, "Let's crank it up and
hope for the best."

"I'm not thrilled about trying to fly this sucker out of here,"
Randle replied. "We're taking a real chance."

Ramsey looked oddly at his copilot. "We don't have a choice," he said.

FETTERMAN LISTENED to the artillery shells exploding near where Kittredge and his men were supposed to be. He'd tried to raise Kittredge on the radio with no luck. Now he had his own worries. He could see the lead elements of a VC unit and knew that he would have to spring the ambush in less than a minute.

Just at that moment there was a crackle from the radio and the beginning of a message. Fetterman shut it off. The VC had entered the killing zone. Fetterman tossed a grenade, and as it detonated, he fired the first of the claymores as the enemy's lead elements broke and ran toward him.

From the far end he heard Tyme shout and the Tai open fire, raking the trail with a devastating fusillade. Bullets smashed into the soldiers, cutting them down. Dirt was kicked up, and the trees rained splintered bark and bits of leaf. There was a momentary confusion while a dozen enemy soldiers dropped and others turned to flee.

Fetterman thought that the ambush had gone quite well. The VC had been surprised and had reacted like amateurs. They had fled in terror rather than attacking the ambushers. It was then that the mortars began to fall, first on the trail, killing the wounded VC in almost festive puffs of gray smoke and brown earth, and then among the trees, forcing the ambushers to hug the ground. Shrapnel from the enemy weapons whined through the air, ripping into everything in its path.

From somewhere came a wailing call from a bugle followed by whistles and shouts as the VC rallied and assaulted the ambush. The enemy swarmed out of the jungle, firing their weapons from their hips, screaming curses at the ambushers. The mortar barrage lifted as the enemy soldiers scattered along the trail, spreading out so that the Americans and the Tai couldn't bring them under a concentrated fire. There were at least five times more VC than Fetterman had expected.

But the American sergeant was prepared for the worst. He picked up the controls for his claymores and detonated them simultaneously. A curtain of steel balls blew along the trail, cutting men off at the knees, at the waist or at the neck. Shattered bodies bounced on the ground as blood from about fifty men spurted onto the jungle floor. There were shrieks of pain and the groans of the dying.

The claymores broke the attack, but the firing from the enemy crouching in the trees kept pouring into the ambush. Mortars began dropping again, walking along the trail and into the ambush site. They were not well aimed, but they were taking their toll as the shrapnel tore at the Tai.

Fetterman realized with a feeling of frustration and anger that the enemy strength in the AO had been badly underestimated. Suddenly he knew that both Bromhead and Kittredge had been ambushed and there would be no help. Firing from the enemy increased, the green tracers from the AKs and the SKSs pounding into the jungle around him. The mortars were joined by Chicom grenades and it seemed as if the jungle were alive with weapons firing and exploding. There were shouts from his own men, and he heard Tyme trying to rally the Tai like a cheerleader at a football game.

Suddenly Fetterman knew that to stay where he was would be disastrous. The VC would assault them again and probably overwhelm them. Fetterman ordered the first section to fall back, telling them to "Go to E and E plan two."

As the Tai, led by Sergeant Krung, began exfiltration, Fetterman moved along the northern side of the ambush. Out of the corner of his eye, he saw his men helping each other, one man leaning on the shoulder of another. It was a coordinated withdrawal, some of the men trying to cover the others, firing their weapons into the jungle. One or two threw grenades at the VC positions. The bodies of the dead lay sprawled where they had fallen.

When he found Washington, the medic's hands were covered with someone else's blood and his fatigues stained with it. He was tending a wounded Tai striker who had taken a rifle bullet in the shoulder. Then, just as Washington was tying off the bandage, he shifted the man and saw a second wound that had opened the entire stomach. The Tai's entails spilled onto the soft jungle earth.

"We've got to pull out, T.J.," Fetterman said. "Kepler got his information wrong. I think we've been set up."

Washington looked down as the Tai opened his eyes wide, as if surprised by something in the sky overhead. The wounded striker reached up, his right hand bright red with his own blood and his fingers clawing at the air. He shuddered once, kicked his foot and died without saying a word or making a sound.

The American medic shook his head, then grabbed the dead man's rifle. He and Fetterman crawled along the north side of the ambush, checking the bodies of the Tai. Three had been killed by rifle fire and the rest hit by shrapnel. They crept past the bodies, using the bushes and trees for cover as the firing continued. The sharp, flat bangs of the AKs and the crack of M-16s filled the air.

At the far end of the ambush, they found Tyme. He lay on his side, gasping for breath. His helmet had come off, and blood congealed in his sandy hair. His eyes were closed, and he'd dropped his rifle.

Enemy mortar rounds still fell to the east, where the anchor of the ambush had been. Rifle firing was sporadic, and then there was shouting from the VC and someone was blowing a whistle. It sounded as though the Vietcong were rallying for a final assault.

"Second section, pull out now!" ordered Fetterman. "Go!"

Washington had rolled Tyme to his back, had pried back an eyelid and was peering into the unfocused eyes.

Fetterman just reached down, twisted Tyme's ear and was rewarded with an angry shout.

"What in the hell are you doing?" Tyme yelled.

"Come on, Boom-Boom, I think we've overstayed our welcome. We've got to bug out."

Tyme struggled to sit up and said, "Help me to my feet." He shook his head as if to clear it and grinned at Fetterman. "We sure blew that one, didn't we?"

"I think," countered Fetterman, "that we walked into the whole North Vietnamese army. We've got to make tracks."

Tyme, Fetterman and Washington, along with six Tai, fell back from the trail. Using palm and coconut trees to shield their retreat, they moved carefully away from the scene. Running through a tree line, they emerged on the dike of a paddy field. Fetterman halted for an instant and looked around. Behind him he could hear the RPD machine guns still firing and the bursting of mortar shells. In the distance he saw the ruins of a farmer's hootch. He turned toward it, running quietly through the light trees that bordered the paddy field. "Head over there. We've got a chance to regroup," he called to Tyme.

About that time the mortars stopped falling—the VC were moving back into the ambush site. They would quickly discover that it had dissolved, and Fetterman grinned to himself, thinking that it was nice to have reversed the tables for a change. Usually it was the VC who sprung an ambush and faded into the jungle. The only problem was that Fetterman didn't have dozens of tunnels, bolt holes and spider holes to use. He only had his wits.

GERBER CURSED AS HE FAILED to raise Fetterman. He threw the mike at the sandbagged wall, watched it bounce to the floor and said, "That fucking tears it. It really does."

Both Bocker and Anderson tried to stay out of his way. He pointed at Bocker and said, "You get back to Crystal Ball and tell Bates that I need ten helicopters out here and I need them yesterday. Anderson, you get to Captain Minh and have him get two of his strike companies ready. One should stand by at the helipad, and the other has to be ready to move out on foot."

"That's going to leave us awfully thin here, Captain," said Bocker. "We've already got a bunch of people out."

"Shit! We've got to do something!"

Surprisingly, the helicopters landed less than ten minutes later in a gigantic cloud of blowing red dust and swirling debris. Nine of the ships touched down along the runway while the lead chopper broke off to land on the helipad set on the northeast side of the strip. Lieutenant Colonel Alan Bates, the B-Team commander stationed in Saigon, had found an aviation unit that had just completed one mission and had been heading to Dau Tieng. He had them diverted to the Special Forces camp, telling the flight leader that he would have to pick up the camp commander for the C and C role. They would recon the area as the rest of the flight worked on getting the strike company organized for the lift.

At the helipad Gerber, sweating heavily in the hot sun and carrying only his M-14 and a bandolier of spare ammo, found Anderson. "Cat," he said, "you're going to have to take charge down here. Get these guys organized, check the weapons and equipment.''

"I say, old boy," said Captain Minh, the Vietnamese camp commander, "aren't you forgetting about me?''

"No, Captain, I'm not. But we find ourselves in that bizarre situation again with both American officers off the camp. You have to stay here. You're the only one who can."

"Of course," agreed Minh. "Just didn't want you usurping my authority."

Gerber had to smile at Minh's British accent. It seemed so out of place—yet Minh had opted for an education in Great Britain rather than France like most of his contemporaries.

"When I've located the LZ, Cat, I'll let you know. Shouldn't take long to find it."

The big Special Forces sergeant was slightly confused. "Who are you looking for, Captain?"

"Kittredge. I know where he was supposed to be, and we have a report that he was definitely under attack. We should be able to find him quickly."

"And then?"

"We'll try to tie up with Fetterman and withdraw to here."

"What about Bromhead?" asked Minh.

"Once we get the others taken care of, we can begin looking for Bromhead again. We'll just have to trust Johnny to take care of himself for now. One more thing, we'd better get Doc McMillan, too. I'm sure his services will be needed."

With that Gerber ducked beneath the spinning roto blades of the chopper and trotted across the helipad to the lead ship. He leaped into the cargo compartment, and before he could even sit down, the aircraft lifted to a hover, turned to the north and began a rapid climb out. Gerber fell onto the red canvas troop seat and pulled his map from the side pocket of his fatigues.

Using the grid coordinates given by Black Sabbath One One, Gerber found the remains of Kittredge's patrol in less than fifteen minutes. He had the pilot of his aircraft fly over the battlefield a couple of times, looking for signs of life. He could see none. At Gerber's insistence the pilot descended and flew slowly over the hilltop.

Now Gerber could see only too well. He could see bodies in khaki, black and olive drab scattered like toy soldiers around the top of the slight hill. He could see equipment, rifles, machine guns, helmets and packs strewn everywhere. Some of the trees in the jungle surrounding the hill were still smoking from the fire caused by the artillery barrage. Others were stripped of their leaves. Everywhere he could see the fresh brown craters made by the artillery scarring the landscape like newly opened wounds. But he could see no sign below him that anyone was alive.

He had the pilots withdraw to the north, and in a voice emotionless with the shock of seeing the reserve force's remains below him, he called for the strike company. They approached from the east, landed on the hilltop among the bodies and rubble of the battle and swept downward into the trees. That done, they fell back to the hill and established security. After they had finished, they had the opportunity to examine the battlefield.

Ten minutes later Gerber landed and found Anderson standing in what must have been the center of the defense perimeter. He was turning slowly, taking it all in. As Gerber approached, Anderson said quietly, "They're all dead. Doc couldn't help any of them, but they put up one hell of a fight. There's forty or fifty enemy dead lying around here and in the trees. Quite a few weapons left behind, too."

"You found Kittredge and Smith?"

Anderson couldn't meet Gerber's gaze. "Yes, sir. That is, we found Sergeant Kittredge, or most of him." Anderson's voice trembled as he spoke. "Artillery must have got him. We can't find six or seven of his men, including Sully. Artillery must have got them, too."

"Shit! Just fucking shit." Gerber took off his helmet and ran a hand through his hair as he stared into space. "I didn't like this mission from the beginning. Not at all. You know that."

"What'll we do?"

"Get the bodies of our men lined up so that we can get them out of here. Detach a squad, maybe twenty men, and sweep around the whole area but not more than two or three hundred meters into the trees. They run into trouble, they get out. And we call in the fucking artillery."

"What about the VC?"

"Pick up the weapons and check for papers. Leave the bodies. If their own people didn't give a fuck about burying them, I sure as hell don't."

In less than an hour they were back at the camp; the bodies of the dead were stacked like so much cordwood near the helipad. Each body had been wrapped in an OD poncho liner that had been tied at both ends. Blood had soaked through some of the liners, staining them a dark red. A light breeze stirred the loose ends, providing a macabre movement among the dead.

The lead pilot wanted to be released so the helicopter unit could return to base, but Gerber didn't want them to go just yet—they might be needed to locate Bromhead and his men, or Fetterman and his patrol. There was still no word from either group. Gerber told the pilots to go and refuel and hurry back. He was afraid that the disasters for the day were just getting started.

"What now," Anderson asked as the helicopters disappeared.

"We try to identify the dead and get a list of the missing for the report in Saigon," Gerber replied. "They have to know that we stepped in some shit out here in case someone else steps in it. They'll be able to adequately evaluate the situation."

Anderson took a step backward and dropped onto a couple of sandbags. He lowered his head and put a hand over his eyes as if to shade them from the sun. He looked up, blinking rapidly and said, "This sure happened fast."

"Yeah. Too fast. I should have taken more time to study Kepler's information. It was just too good, and it gave us no time to think. Just time to react."

From behind them Gerber heard the sound of the motor-driven film advance of a 35 mm camera. He spun and saw Morrow taking pictures of the bodies and the men standing around them. "Christ!" he shouted at her. "Don't you have any fucking sense at all? Stop that."

Morrow let the camera fall from her eye and stared at Gerber. "What are you talking about?"

"Robin, we've just come back from the field with the bodies of our friends. We don't know exactly what happened, except that they were all killed. Then you stand around taking fucking pictures."

"The people have a right to know."

"Shit! I don't want to get into that now. Just don't take any more pictures, okay?"

She was going to argue and then saw the hard look in his eyes. "Okay, Mack, I understand. I'm sorry. I wasn't thinking."

"Forget it."

Then from near the commo bunker came a shout. "Captain Gerber! Quick!"

Gerber broke into a run, coming to an abrupt halt in front of Bocker. "What? What is it?"

"South gate, sir. They say there is a group of men moving toward it. They think it might be Lieutenant Bromhead."

Without a word Gerber spun and took off toward the south gate. Before he got there, he could see the green smoke from the trees in the distance before the men revealed themselves. He stood by impatiently as the men worked their way through the elephant grass and began to wind their way along the concealed and irregular path that had led through the rolls of concertina wire protecting the wall.

Gerber could see Bromhead leading them. He looked dirty and tired. One sleeve of his uniform was badly ripped, but he didn't seem to be injured. He was followed by some of the Tai and then a couple of men being helped along by their friends. Four men carried two stretchers with bodies on them. Several of the men had large blood-stained field dressings wrapped around their heads or shoulders or chests. But there weren't nearly enough of them. They had been badly shot up.

As soon as Bromhead was within talking distance, Gerber said, "What happened?"

Bromhead stepped beside Gerber, but before he answered his commanding officer's questions, he waved his men past and told the senior BCO, "Get a weapons check made and a muster. I want a roster in ten minutes of the men who came in with us. I also want to know who's missing and who's wounded and how badly they're hurt. You understand?"

"Yes, sir," the man said with a nod.

"You get together with Lieutenant Bao and have him help you," he said as the man ran off.

"Johnny, what happened to you?" Gerber repeated.

"They were waiting for us, Captain. They seemed to know exactly where we were going and how many men we had. The ambush was set perfectly. I think they underestimated our resolve to get out of the swamp. Otherwise, I think we would have all been killed. But they had everyone placed perfectly. I don't think we could have set it any better."

"Okay, Johnny," said Gerber, studying the younger officer. He could see the strain on his face and in his eyes. "Let's head to my hootch and get a drink. Then you can tell me what happened."

"How are the others? How's Fetterman?"

Gerber stopped walking and stared at his executive officer. "I think it's bad all over. Kittredge is dead. Sully's missing, but I think he's probably dead, too. We haven't been able to talk to Fetterman. It's getting fairly grim."

"God, Captain. It seems that we've been had."

IN THE SMALL HOOTCH hidden deep in the Cambodian jungle, Major Vo, Commissar Dau, Major Ngoi and a Chinese officer sat around a rough wooden table hammered together by a long forgotten rice farmer. The hootch had a dirt floor, a single window with no glass and a doorway with no door. The thatch of the roof was in poor shape. The mud walls were crumbling and did nothing to keep out the heat, or the humidity and the insects.

Standing at one end of the old table was a young Vietnamese covered with sweat and breathing hard. He had just run a long distance to bring news of one of the counterambushes. He looked longingly at the cigarettes that burned in the ashtray made from half a coconut shell but did not ask for one. He was frightened by the North Vietnamese officers and he directed his comments at Major Vo because Vo was the one man that he knew and was his commanding officer.

Slowly he told of the fight between the Green Berets and their puppet soldiers and the Vietcong and NVA. He told how they had made a final charge toward the perimeter and how they had penetrated the defense of the Americans and the Tai when the artillery barrage began.

"The Americans must have made a mistake," the young soldier reported as the sweat dripped from his face and stained the collar of his already wet shirt. "The shells began exploding all over the hillside, killing them as well as us."

The Chinese officer, who had been partially hidden in the shadows of the hootch, leaned forward and put out his cigarette. "I think not," he said. "I believe it was a deliberate act by the Americans. An act to prevent their capture."

"It gained them nothing," said Dau.

"It denied us the prisoners we sought," said Vo bitterly. He turned his attention to the Chinese. "You have promised me prisoners. You didn't expect the Americans to die rather than be captured."

"You forget, Major, that there are other teams in the field, each in contact with the Americans. You will have your prisoners yet."

A lizard scurried across the dirt floor, scrambled up the mud wall and disappeared into the rotting thatch. Vo watched the creature until it disappeared. He said to the Chinese, "And what if each group does the same? What if each group denies prisoners to us by sacrificing themselves?"

"It was a fluke," said the Chinese. "We shall have our prisoners." He pointed to the runner and said, "You searched the field after the battle, of course." It was a statement rather than a question.

"When the shells stopped exploding, we began to search, stripping the dead, but enemy helicopters appeared, and we were forced to abandon the search."

"Abandon the search," repeated Dau. "You abandoned the search?"

The young Vietnamese looked at Vo for support and then turned his attention back to the commissar. "Yes, comrade," he said. "We were told that it was very important that we not be engaged by other Americans and to abandon the field if the helicopters came."

"Why was that?" asked Dau.

"Because," snapped the Chinese officer, "to let the Americans engage our troops takes the initiative away from us. We do not let them catch us in the field. We catch them."

"How many were killed?" asked Ngoi.

"We found the body of one American and nearly forty of their puppet soldiers."

"Only one American?" asked the Chinese officer.

"Yes, comrade."

The Chinese smiled shyly. "Major Vo, it is my experience that the American soldiers do not work alone. There should have been a second American body. Possibly more, but certainly more than one. I believe that one American escaped. You must capture him."

Vo got to his feet and stepped to the door to order his men to prepare for another patrol. Outside, he could see three of his NCOs crouched near a small fire barely visible in the bright sunlight. Behind him he heard the Chinese officer say, "It is only a matter of time before we have the prisoners we need for the next phase."

6

SPECIAL FORCES CAMP
A-555

It was only early afternoon, but the day had already been a disaster. Gerber sat in a hard wooden chair and stared at his executive officer. Bromhead's uniform was sweat-stained and torn in a dozen places. There was mud caked on it, some of it obscuring the left breast pocket and the patch that read U.S. ARMY.

Gerber waited for Bromhead to speak, and when that didn't happen, he reached into a drawer for his bottle of Beam's. Wordlessly he handed it to Bromhead and watched as the young lieutenant drained nearly half the remaining liquor.

As Bromhead handed the bottle back, he asked again, almost as if seeking confirmation, "How are the others?"

"Kittredge and Smith were ambushed and wiped out. Kittredge is dead and Smith is missing," Gerber replied.

Bromhead nodded, dazed. "What about Fetterman?"

"No word from him for a couple of hours. Just as soon as the helicopters return from refueling, we're going out in force to look for him." Gerber paused, letting the weight of what had happened sink in. Then he said, "Sounds like you did everything you could."

"You mean I didn't get wiped out," Bromhead said in a deadpan voice.

"There is that. But I was thinking more of the way you handled the ambush. You did the only thing you could think of and it worked. You got as many of your people out of the swamp as you could."

Bromhead stared at the Beam's. "What are you going to do about Fetterman?" he asked.

"Like I said, go get him. Troops are standing by." As Gerber finished his sentence, he heard the sound of helicopters in the distance. "In fact," he said, standing up, "I'm going to get him now."

"Mind if I come along?"

Gerber stopped at the door and thought. "No, Johnny, you've got plenty to do here. Check on your men, see who needs to get evaced. I'll leave McMillan here with you. Washington is out with Fetterman."

"Yes, sir," Bromhead said forcefully.

As he walked away, Gerber wondered how much Bromhead held him responsible for what had happened.

FOR THE MOMENT THEY WERE SAFE, or as safe as they could be. The farmer's hootch had no roof and one wall had collapsed. There were the remains of a bunker in one corner of the hootch and a disintegrating bamboo mat on the dirt floor. Tin and thatch from the roof littered the inside.

The hootch was nestled inside a small grove of coconut and banana trees. It might be dilapidated, but it offered some protection, maybe even sanctuary. For now it provided Fetterman and the few men with him a chance to figure out what to do.

As soon as they were inside the hootch, Washington made Tyme sit down. He examined him closely and found a lump on the side of his head where a bullet had grazed it but had not broken the skin. He also had a gigantic bruise on his chest as if he had been hit with a large rock, probably thrown up by a mortar shell exploding.

Washington moved off to look at the Tai. Only one of them seemed to be badly hurt, and he was not in danger of dying. The wound in the man's thigh, although deep, had formed a scab and the bleeding had stopped. Washington dusted the wound with sulfa powder to combat infection and covered it with a large, clean field dressing. There was little more he could do. He didn't have the equipment or the time.

Fetterman posted his security and then sat back. He took one drink from his canteen. Like the others, he was tempted to drink it all, and normally he would have finished off the water to prevent it from sloshing in the canteen as he tried to sneak through the jungle. But he knew that as the day progressed, he would need the water. He saw a couple of the Tai drink their canteens dry. Maybe they figured there wouldn't be too much of the day left for them.

When he saw Tyme staring at him, Fetterman smiled and said, "How you doing, Boom-Boom?"

"I'm fine." Tyme gingerly touched the side of his head and asked, "What do we do now?"

"Hang loose. The captain will be looking for us before long, and if he doesn't, we'll just have to make our way home."

"You sure this is a good place to hole up?" Tyme asked, gesturing at the hootch.

"It's lousy, but it's better than anything else I saw. We have a good field of fire, some protection in the packed mud walls, and if we have to bug out of here, there are a couple of ditches and that mud wall over there to use for cover. Lots of ways out."

Suddenly there was a snap from the jungle, and a single bullet struck one of the inside walls, showering dirt everywhere. Fetterman grabbed one of the Tai and threw him down before he could return fire. He stopped two others and whispered, "Hold it. They may not know we're here and are trying a recon by fire. Just hold it."

A moment later a single mortar round exploded in a puff of gray-white smoke and was followed by four VC rushing from the trees. Fetterman could see no point in letting them advance. He raised and fired his M-14 as fast as he could pull the trigger. The first two VC went down in a burst of blood and bone. The third was staggered by the heavy 7.62 mm round and dropped his weapon, but he kept running. The fourth turned to flee, threw himself behind the mud wall, hesitated and then leaped to his feet. Fetterman cut him down as the staggering man collapsed in front of the hootch. There was a wail of pain and then silence.

From the jungle came a sustained burst of RPD machine gun fire that was quickly joined by a dozen AKs. Fetterman ducked quickly as the walls of the hootch began to disintegrate from the machine gun bullets ripping into it. When the enemy firing started to taper off, Fetterman and a couple of Tai popped up and returned it. They had no visible targets so they just hosed down the trees in front of them, hoping to keep the VC pinned down.

Tyme kept an eye on the jungle behind the shelter and watched a dozen or more VC rush from the cover. He shouted a warning, but the others didn't seem to hear him over the staccato of their own weapons.

Tyme fired his M-16 on full automatic and several of the enemy soldiers fell, bullets in their chests or heads or stomachs, spreading stains of red dying their khaki uniforms. But the others kept coming, and Tyme quickly emptied his weapon. He fumbled for a new magazine, pulling at the pouches on his pistol belt, but somehow he seemed to have lost them all.

Tyme threw the now worthless weapon to one side and pulled his Very pistol. As three of the VC jumped over the short wall, Tyme pulled the trigger. The noise from the weapon was tremendous, as was the recoil, but all three of the Vietcong fell as the number four buckshot pellets spread and drove into them. Two VC were screaming in pain.

Two more VC leaped the wall, and Tyme was ready for them with his combat knife. He had dropped his pistol to the floor of the hootch, when there was a burst of rapid firing beside him as one of the Tai soldiers turned and fired. One of the enemy went down, a bullet blowing away half his face. The other dived for cover, popped up to shoot and ducked again. When he jumped up to flee into the jungle, the Tai striker was ready. He pumped four rounds into the man's back.

Quiet descended around them. For the moment the VC assault was over and Fetterman used the time to check his men. Two more had been wounded. One of the Tai had been shot in the stomach, and he was holding himself, moaning quietly and asking for water. The other had been clipped by shrapnel or flying rock that had torn through his right hand. Washington was wrapping a bandage around the man's hand. Tyme sat with his back against the wall and wiped sweat from his face. He was breathing hard, as if he had just sprinted a mile. He drained one of his canteens.

As he reloaded, Fetterman said, ''They'll try a little finesse during the next round. I don't think they'll mount any kind of frontal assault. Time is on our side.''

Washington was trying to help the Tai with the stomach wound. There wasn't much he could do, given the medical supplies that he had brought with him. He used sulfa powder, trying to limit the infection, and knew that they would have to evacuate the wounded man quickly, or there would be no way to save him.

As Washington glanced up, he saw nearly a dozen VC. ''Here they come again,'' he yelled as he dropped his medical bag and picked up his rifle. He fired single shots, carefully picking out his targets until the whole open area in front of him seemed to be crawling with VC. Then he switched to full auto.

Tyme set his rifle down, leaning it against the mud wall of the hootch and got out his last four grenades, lining them up in front of him. Then deliberately he pulled the pin of the first, threw it, got the second ready and threw it. After the first two explosions, he popped up and threw the third and the fourth.

The attackers seemed to waver, then regroup, and the VC surged forward, screaming and shouting. Tyme picked up his rifle and began killing the VC. More of the enemy fell while others scrambled for cover.

Fetterman was directing the fire of the Tai who could still hold a weapon. Two of the others were now unconscious because of blood loss from wounds. Another one had been so badly shot up that, although he was conscious, he couldn't sit up.

They were all firing on full automatic, but the attack didn't seem to be slowing. It reached the mud wall and a couple of the VC hurtled it, but they were quickly cut down, tumbling into bloody heaps. The remainder of them seemed content to hide behind the wall, afraid to either attack or retreat. The two sides were now separated by only about thirty yards. It seemed that each side had found some momentary protection.

As the last of the firing died away, Tyme looked over his shoulder at Fetterman and asked, ''And now what?''

''Doesn't seem like we're going to get a reprieve until dark,'' said Fetterman. He looked at the men with him as they crouched behind the flimsy protection of the crumbling mud walls and rotting thatch. Shell casings littered the floor. In some places they were a couple of inches deep. To his right the man with the stomach wound moaned quietly, semiconscious. "I suppose we'd better see if we can't get out of here."

"We can't move the wounded," countered Washington.

"Yeah, I know," said Fetterman. "But I sure as hell don't want to be captured, either."

"That's okay, Tony," responded Washington. "I'll stay behind, hold off the VC as long as I can and then surrender to them. We might be able to get some medical help for the men."

"That idea stinks. I don't want any martyrs or medal winners here," Fetterman replied.

"You have an alternative? We can't hold this place much longer. It makes no sense for all of us to be captured," argued Washington.

Fetterman peeked over the wall and saw that the VC hadn't moved. He shifted his attention to Tyme and said, "What's it look like back there, Boom-Boom?"

"Clear right now. I haven't seen anyone moving in the trees. We might be able to sneak off."

"If we can get to the trees, we should be able to get clear," Fetterman said. He turned his attention back to Washington. "Look, T.J., I'm sure the captain is trying to get in here, but there's no way we can hold out. I'm not leaving anyone here who can travel. You've got one wounded man who won't survive until nightfall and two more who might live to be evaced if we had a way of doing it."

"And I'm not going to leave the wounded," said Washington. "There is no way that I can leave the wounded."

Fetterman shot a glance over the top of the wall again. He could see a couple of the VC running through the trees in the distance. He ducked again and said, "T.J., I want you to make the wounded as comfortable as possible. Give them everything you have in your medical bag of tricks. Leave the bag. The next time the VC rush the front of this place, we throw up a cloud of steel for a couple of minutes and then E and E out the back. Everyone understand?"

There were nods all around except for Washington. "I said that I can't leave the wounded."

"You have two choices, Sergeant Washington," said Fetterman with a hard edge to his voice. "You can either treat the wounded as best you can and prepare to leave them, hoping that the VC will have a doctor, or you can watch me shoot them right now."

Washington held Fetterman's gaze for a few moments and then dropped his eyes, "You won't shoot the wounded," he said.

"No, maybe not," agreed Fetterman. "But I'll fucking drag you out of here."

Washington didn't say anything. He merely nodded.

"Okay," said Fetterman, "I don't know how well this is going to work, but it's the only plan we have."

WHEN THE HELICOPTERS LANDED, Gerber issued his instructions. Minh would be in command of the assault troops, and Bromhead would be responsible for the camp's defenses in the event of an enemy counterattack. Gerber told them that, as soon as he had learned something, he would call.

The helicopter lifted off, coming to a hover and then racing along the ground to gain airspeed. The pilot hauled back on the cyclic, turned to the nonthrust and began a low-level flight along the path that Fetterman was supposed to have followed. All the time Bocker sat in the commo bunker trying to raise Fetterman on the radio.

On the ground around them, Gerber could see nothing. He trusted the pilots to follow the route he had shown them on the map, and looking out, he could see many of the landmarks, canals, roads and abandoned hamlets. But the ground was rushing by too fast for him to spot anything of significance. If Fetterman had come this way, he had been very careful not to leave any sign.

As they neared the operational area, there was a burst of firing from the ground and the green tracers of the enemy flashed far to the left of the aircraft. The pilot broke in the opposite direction and was immediately taken under fire by a .51-caliber Soviet-made antiaircraft machine gun. The door gunner opened fire, but the rapid chatter of the M-60 made no impression on the enemy, who kept hammering away and trying to walk the tracers into the helicopter.

They dived away from the antiaircraft fire, trying to put a tree lie between the helicopter and the enemy. They raced to the north and then turned back to the west, low-leveling toward the camp. Over the intercom Gerber shouted, "We can't go back to the camp!"

"Captain," said the pilot, "I understand what you need, but if I get shot down, what good will that do you? If I go down and they come out to rescue us and the rescue ship goes down, how does that help? We need to get an air strike to suppress the anti-aircraft fire. The bad guys have some big shit in here."

Gerber didn't like what he was hearing in the least. Time was wasting, and everything he did seemed to take more time, but none of it moved him any closer to the answers he needed. He wanted to get in there and learn the fate of Fetterman and his patrol, but he could see the point being made by the pilot. It would do no good to get shot down.

"Can we spot for the air strike?"

"Yes, sir. Sure can. I've got the request in, and we can direct the artillery in there now if you want."

"Okay, put the artillery in. Can you put me through to my camp?"

"You bet. Hill, you want to set the captain up to make his call?"

The crew chief turned the selector switch on the radio control head to the number two position so that Gerber could talk on the radio. The pilot had already dialed the proper frequency into the radio. A moment later the crew chief yelled to Gerber, "Press the button when you're ready to transmit."

"Zulu Base, Zulu Base, this is Zulu Six."

"Roger, Six. Go."

"We have taken heavy fire. Will be directing LZ prep. Get the flight off the ground. I say again. Get the flight off the ground."

"Roger, Six. Will do."

The aircraft commander came on the intercom. "What are you planning on doing?"

"Insert my people as close to Fetterman's position as possible and walk in. We're not that far from him."

"Captain, I might remind you that we'll have an air strike coming. It might be quicker to wait for that and insert closer to their location."

Gerber looked at his watch. It was now after two. Fetterman had been out of touch for nearly five hours. In that time Gerber had learned that Bromhead had been ambushed and Kittredge killed. He felt that he had to act quickly but couldn't see the point in getting more people killed through unnecessary haste. He had been running almost since sunup. He sat in the back of the helicopter, shaking because he was forced to sit in one place. He wanted to be on the ground doing something. Again he thought about the information that Kepler had provided that had started the mission. Too much, too fast, and it was getting worse.

"How long until the jets arrive?"

"Maybe ten minutes."

Gerber nodded but didn't speak. He had to make himself relax. He took a deep breath and closed his eyes. He forced himself to concentrate on what he was going to do when he got on the ground. He would have a company of strikers. About the size of the force that Bromhead had had the night before. Bromhead hadn't been able to do much with them, but then Bromhead hadn't really been expecting trouble. Gerber had the advantage there. Not to mention air mobility. If he walked into trouble, he could get out of it quickly, or he could get reinforcements quickly. And he had all kinds of radios that were working.

The one thing that he had to guard against was making a mistake by hurrying. The adrenaline was pumping through him, making him nervous. He needed to think everything through carefully. He had to remember that he had the time to make intelligent decisions. It would do no good to fly off half-cocked and get another company ambushed. He would have to be patient.

At the moment, there wasn't much for Gerber to do. The whole flight was airborne but still fifteen minutes away. Artillery was falling on the antiaircraft positions they had identified, and the Air Force was coming. He tried to get the pilots flying in an ever-expanding search, looking for Fetterman. Unfortunately they couldn't fly too far to the north for fear of fouling the gun-target lines of the fire-support bases. And they couldn't fly too far west because they kept encountering enemy antiaircraft. All they could do was fly east and south, and there was nothing that Gerber wanted to see in either direction.

THE SHOOTING STARTED AGAIN after a fifteen-minute break. It started slowly with one VC firing a single shot. He was quickly joined by several others using a full auto until the RPD opened up. Fetterman emptied a whole magazine at the VC, then tossed a grenade over the mud wall to stir them up. Three or four tried to jump up, but Washington gunned them down. The others escaped into the jungle. Fetterman picked off the stragglers, but he wanted the others to make it to the trees. He didn't want to waste ammo keeping them pinned down behind the mud wall.

When the VC had escaped and the enemy shooting was coming from the jungle, Fetterman whispered, "That's it. Let's get out."

Washington checked the three badly wounded Tai. The man with the stomach wound looked at him and grabbed the front of his uniform. Slowly, carefully, Washington peeled the Tai's fingers free and laid the man's hand beside him.

Tyme crawled to the rear, pushed two of the unwounded Tai forward and pointed toward the jungle. He turned and glanced at Fetterman, who waved him forward. Tyme pushed another of the Tai out as Fetterman joined him.

Together Fetterman and Tyme began crawling along the ditch, keeping their heads down. Behind them they heard the firing increase and then heard a bugle call. There seemed to be a shout from the jungle. Fetterman looked in time to see a dozen more of the enemy rush the hootch.

Ahead of them came more firing as the Tai ran into a couple of VC. As Tyme rose out of the ditch, he was shot once in the shoulder. He cried out in surprise and pain, fell back and rolled to the bottom of the ditch out of sight.

Fetterman crawled to him, shook out a field dressing and pressed it to Tyme's shoulder. He reached down, took one of Tyme's hands and pressed it to the dressing. He saw the young sergeant try to smile. Then Fetterman crept past him to the end of the ditch where he got to his feet. He rushed to the jungle's edge and leaped into the trees. He spotted a VC who was drawing a bead on one of the Tai. Fetterman clubbed him with the butt of his rifle, and as the enemy fell, Fetterman shot him, the round penetrating the VC's back.

The fighting on that side of the clearing degenerated into hand-to-hand combat. Fetterman pulled the short bayonet from its scabbard and fixed it. He whirled in time to see a VC running among the trees. Fetterman fired from the hip and turned the man's head into an explosion of red mist as the high-velocity bullets connected.

Spinning to his right, he saw another VC. Fetterman lunged and was surprised when the Vietcong parried and thrust. Fetterman jumped back, faked a thrust and came around with a vertical butt stroke, smashing the side of the enemy's head. The man fell to one knee but tried to ram his bayonet into Fetterman's stomach as he fell forward. Fetterman knocked the rifle from his hand and then jabbed the bayonet into the man's neck. He ripped the bloodstained blade free and spotted still another enemy soldier. He fired once and the VC was thrown forward, his rifle flying from his hands. Then Fetterman ran forward, halted and waited. He saw two Tai attack one VC, killing him. Both of them then fell to the ground and fired into the jungle as if they had suddenly seen more enemy soldiers.

Fetterman ran to them, saw that they were shooting at shadows and ordered them to stop. He found two others and told them to establish a tiny perimeter so that they could guard one another.

"I have to go back to see about Boom-Boom," he said. "He went down wounded. You wait here."

There was still some shooting near the hootch as Fetterman cleared the jungle and entered the ditch. He could see Tyme lying on his back, staring into the sky. He had dropped the field dressing and now clutched his rifle in both hands so that it was across his chest. He looked as if he held it at port arms.

"Boom-Boom," he whispered, "you okay?"

"I'm hurt, Tony. I'm hurt."

"Can you move?" Fetterman asked.

"Yeah. I think I can move. Just help me get out of here."

He reached Tyme and looked at the bullet hole in the fatigue shirt. He took the first-aid kit off Tyme's pistol belt and used Tyme's knife to cut the shirt away. He pressed the bandage to the bleeding wound. He held it there for a moment, released the pressure and saw that the bleeding hadn't slowed.

"I've got to get you out of here so that I can work on you."

Tyme didn't respond. He stared upward.

11

VC P.O.W. CAMP
NEAR HONG NGU

The rooms were okay, Fetterman decided. He'd stayed in worse accommodations in France and Korea, but the service and the attitude of the staff left a lot to be desired.

Fetterman had mentally christened the camp the Jungle Hilton because of Major Vo's continual references to them as his guests. That, he figured, made Vo the manager, with Lieutenant Trang the concierge or keeper of the keys and Sergeant Bat the bell captain. He hadn't figured out who the head waiter was yet, and he had a hunch that he wouldn't either, because so far the VC had shown no inclination to feed their prisoners or give them any water.

The camp was situated among the trees and was virtually invisible from the trail. Fetterman had been able to glimpse only the one hootch from the clearing, apparently a guard shack of some kind, and had almost missed it because of the camouflage. A well-trained soldier looking for something might or might not notice it. Fetterman had little doubt that a passing peasant would have small likelihood of spotting it and even less interest in investigating it. Besides, it was undoubtedly well inside a defensive perimeter of some kind. At the very least they had to have a few pickets or patrols out beyond the clearing.

There wasn't much chance of being spotted by an aircraft passing overhead, either. The thick, leafy tree branches formed an almost impenetrable canopy overhead that effectively screened the camp from air observation and cast the compound into a kind of twilight world. The reduction in light had the curious effect of making things warmer, not cooler, since the closeness of the trees also effectively blocked any breeze. In addition it brought the mosquitoes out in hordes, the bugs' biological clocks oblivious to the fact that it was midmorning.

It was hard to get a really accurate idea of the camp. The ground had been cleared only where absolutely necessary, and the remaining trees and ground cover made it impossible to see more than one or two dozen yards in any direction. It made for effective camouflage both outside and inside the camp.

In addition to the guard shack at the edge of the clearing, they had passed two longhouses on the way in that were apparently used as barracks for the camp's garrison, a small hootch without windows and with the door wired shut, which Fetterman thought to be a storage hut of some kind and a third longhouse with a packed mud fireplace at one end, apparently the mess hall for the guards. All of the structures were set on stilts or earthen mounds, which suggested seasonal flooding of the area, and that, in turn, indicated the nearby presence of a river or major canal.

All the structures in the camp had a new but solid look to them, suggesting that, although the camp had only recently been constructed, it had been built with long-term occupancy in mind. There was even the beginnings of a system of elevated bamboo walkways paralleling the pathways within the camp, a further indication of seasonal flooding and that the Vietcong intended to occupy the camp for some time to come. Fetterman noted that most of the cut bamboo used in construction was still green.

Major Vo and his Chinese friend had obviously planned to have several guests in residence at their little jungle hotel. Fetterman counted eight "bungalows," with three more under construction. There could have been more, but his view was blocked by the trees.

Each of the "guest cottages" consisted of a bamboo cage measuring about five feet wide by ten feet long, with a thatched roof around five-and-a-half feet high at the center ridge that sloped to about four feet above ground level. The roof overhung one end of each cage by about a meter, making a sort of floorless porch over the doorway. The door itself was a cross work of bamboo with

"Give me your rifle and then hold the bandage in place. You've got to apply pressure, or you'll bleed to death."

"Okay," he replied absently.

"I'm going to have to drag you out. I'm afraid that it's going to be painful."

"Okay."

Fetterman took the rifle and used the sling. He grabbed Tyme by the collar of his jungle fatigues and pulled. Tyme used his feet to push and lifted his wounded shoulder off the ground, sliding on his other. They had almost reached the safety of the jungle when the shooting suddenly stopped. Fetterman glanced toward the farmer's hootch but saw nothing. Then he heard the unmistakable sound of a bolt slamming home.

At that moment Fetterman looked up into the barrel of an AK-47 and the grinning face of an NVA lieutenant. Fetterman held the lieutenant's eyes, thinking that he could kick the man's feet out from under him. Then he saw three VC and knew that there was nothing he could do. He smiled at the lieutenant and let go of his rifle that he held in one hand. Then he shrugged his shoulder so that Tyme's rifle slipped to the ground.

THE ARTILLERY LIFTED, but the Air Force still hadn't arrived. Gerber tapped the helicopter pilot on the shoulder and said, "We don't have any more time to waste. Let's try again."

The AC nodded. "Okay. I think they might have silenced that big gun."

They turned back to the west and descended so that they were only a couple of feet above the trees, dropping close to the ground whenever there was a large clearing. They circled one area, saw nothing and took no fire.

Then, as they were drawing close to the place where Fetterman should have been, they were taken under fire again. This time it wasn't just a couple of weapons, it seemed like a hundred. The AC broke away, fleeing the heavy fire.

Over the intercom, he said, "There's no way to get a flight in there, Captain. They'll all be shot down before they can land."

"Head back to the camp," he said. Gerber shook his head. This was deep shit. "We'll rendezvous with the flight and find an LZ somewhere else. We'll have to walk in."

"I may be talking out of turn, Captain, but it seems to be a very large enemy force in there."

"I appreciate your concern. We'll work something out."

Far in front of them, Gerber spotted the other helicopters. His own chopper joined the flight and turned back to the west. Gerber told the lead pilot where he wanted to go, that the arty prep had been completed and that there was still a possibility that an air strike would be going in if they encountered resistance of any kind.

But as they approached the area, firing erupted around them again. The door gunners returned it, but that didn't seem to slow it down. The VC were swarming all over the area, and since Cambodia was less than ten klicks away, they could reinforce their troops quickly or pull them out.

With the amount of antiaircraft fire increasing, Gerber realized that he was badly outnumbered and outgunned. To land anywhere near Fetterman would spell disaster.

He gave the order to return to cover.

At the camp he was met by Bocker, Anderson and Kepler. As Gerber got out of the helicopter, they all began shouting at him.

"What the fuck are we going to do?" Kepler asked.

"We got people out there. We've got to do something," Anderson chimed in.

"I know all that," Gerber shouted right back at them. "Now, if you people will join me in my hootch, we'll try to work something out."

Bocker looked at Anderson, who shrugged. "Yes, sir," said Bocker. "I'll see that Lieutenant Bromhead is there, too."

"That's fine."

"What's the plan, Captain?" the lead pilot asked as he got out of the helicopter.

"You guys need to hang loose for a while. Shut down and I'll get with you in a moment."

"We have orders to get out of here as soon as you've finished with us. We do have other commitments."

"I understand that. But I still have fifty people in the field that I can't find. And a hell of a lot of Vietcong who may have already found them."

"Yes, sir."

In his hootch Gerber found Anderson, Bocker, Bromhead and Kepler. They were waiting patiently for him, none of them speaking, each man staring at the floor.

"First things first," said Gerber by way of preamble. "We couldn't land because I could tell by the amount of antiaircraft fire we were encountering that we wouldn't survive very long on the ground. The size of the enemy force is a lot larger than estimated." He turned significantly to Kepler.

"All I had, Captain," Kepler replied, "was the one report from that old woman. A recruiting platoon would be moving through. But without being allowed to move into Cambodia to gather data, the VC could move an entire division in there and we wouldn't know it."

"What about reports from Nha Trang?" asked Bromhead.

"I know what you're thinking," Kepler continued. "The recon flights over the area showed nothing significant, but the short distances the enemy have to travel would allow them to move into position in just a couple of hours. The overflights showed no significant movement or buildups. The first indications we have are the ones we're running into."

"Okay," said Gerber. "We've got to think of something. Fetterman and his people are still missing out there, and until we find out what happened, we've got to keep moving."

"We could put out two strike companies from here," said Bromhead slowly, as if he were working out the details of the mission as he spoke. "Maybe get a couple of others moving into the area from other bases."

"No good, Johnny. Not enough time to coordinate it. I just don't want things to break down any further than they have. We've already taken more casualties today than we have since the VC tried to overrun the camp six months ago."

"What are we going to do?"

"I'm not sure yet," answered Gerber. "But I know that I'm not going to send a bunch of people out to get killed for no good reason. We're going out but not until we have a definite plan that will allow quick reinforcements and air and artillery support. I'll speak to Colonel Bates."

7

SOUTH OF THE
PARROT'S BEAK, RVN

Fetterman climbed slowly to his feet, still smiling and holding his hands open, palms down, away from his body. He glanced over his shoulder and saw Washington, his hands in the air, walking toward them.

"You my prisoner now," said the NVA officer. Fetterman's captor stood about five-and-a-half feet tall. He had straight jet-black hair. His oval face was shiny with sweat, and his uniform was stained with it. One knee of the trousers was torn, and there was mud caked on the front. He was grinning as he said, "You do as I say, or I shoot you."

"I understand, sir," said Fetterman, nodding gravely. "We will give you no trouble."

"See that you don't, Yankee dog."

Washington, who now stood with them, asked, "What about the wounded? Some of the men have been badly hurt."

"We will take care of your wounded as soon as we finish treating our injured," said the officer with a contemptuous smile.

"You speak remarkably good English," commented Washington.

"Yes. I was forced to take training in the United States at your Fort Benning. I found it necessary to learn your harsh and uncomfortable language."

"Christ," muttered Washington, "we trained the son of a bitch."

Fetterman shot him an angry glance but said only, "You learned your lessons quite well, sir."

"Shut up!" He pointed at Fetterman. "You help your friend now, or we will have to shoot him."

Fetterman crouched and checked Tyme's bandage. He saw that the bleeding had slowed considerably. Fetterman tied the bandage and said to Tyme, "Can you sit up?"

"I think so," Tyme replied, looking at the NVA officer and the VC who surrounded him.

"Okay. We'll take it easy now. If you feel woozy, you speak up. I don't know what these guys have in mind, but I think you'll probably have to walk ten, twelve klicks to get out of this area and into Cambodia, where they think they'll be safe."

"You stop that talking," commanded the NVA officer.

"Yes, sir," responded Fetterman. "I was trying to determine the state of mind of Sergeant Tyme."

Tyme was horrified by Fetterman's use of his name, but Fetterman said, "Don't sweat it. We'll have to give them names anyway." He lowered his voice. "If we make it look like we aren't real sharp, things might go a little easier."

"I would like to check on the wounded," said Washington.

"You are a doctor?" asked the NVA, studying the big, black American soldier. "You have medical supplies?"

"No, ah . . ." He hesitated.

Fetterman spoke up. "He's a medic. Probably could assist your doctors or your medics."

Now it was Washington's turn to be amazed. He tried to catch Fetterman's eye, but Fetterman was busy working on Tyme. Washington crouched, examined Fetterman's work and nodded his approval.

"I have some medicine in my bag," said Washington, pointing back toward the dilapidated farmer's hootch. "I left my stuff there."

"My men will find it," said the officer. "I will give it to my men."

"What about our wounded?" asked Fetterman.

There was a burst of machine gun fire followed by three quick pistol shots. The officer turned toward the sound, smiling, and then said, "Your injured have succumbed to their wounds. I'm afraid nothing more can be done for them."

GERBER WAS UP AND PACING. Inside his tiny office were all the Special Forces men still on the camp—Bromhead, Bocker, McMillan, Kepler and Anderson—and Captain Minh. They were sitting on Gerber's cot, on the floor or in the lawn chairs that he had gotten in Saigon. Minh was leaning against the wall, his arms folded across his chest. They were all trying to work out a plan.

"We've only got four, maybe five hours of light left," said Gerber, checking his watch. "What's the status of the choppers?"

"They're here until we release them," said Bocker. "Oh, and Ramsey said to let you know that he was off. Chinook airlifted that broken helicopter. Ramsey and Randle went with it."

"I suppose that we've heard nothing from Fetterman on the radio."

"No, sir. He hasn't checked in."

"Christ!" said Gerber. "We're really working in the dark on this one. No idea of the size of enemy forces or where they are."

Kepler felt that he had to say something. "We had no indication of enemy movements or buildups. But we do know where some of them have been operating, based on our troubles." He bent over the map spread out on Gerber's flimsy desk.

"Don't sweat it, Derek," said Gerber. "Right now we've got other things to do."

"What are we going to do, old boy?" asked Minh.

"I think we need to put a strike company into the field near the place Fetterman was supposed to set up the ambush and let them sweep through the area. We'll have a second company on standby here in case they need reinforcements and coordinate with Henderson's people in case we need more people than we have. He's running the Mike Force now.

"Galvin," Gerber continued, "I'm going to want you to head over to the commo bunker and start the coordination efforts. Alert the various fire-support bases about the possibility of some fire missions. Call Bates and have him start working on the air support. Also, call Henderson and see what kind of shape he's in."

"Yes, sir."

"I understand that two of your strike companies are ready," Gerber said, turning to Minh.

"And waiting," Minh replied.

"Good. Strip the defenses as best you can and see if you can scrape together a third. Some of the stragglers from Bao's strike company can augment if necessary. Is your new exec very good?"

"I'm afraid that I don't trust him very much, considering he was recommended by a general in Saigon. I just don't know him that well, old boy. I suppose that he's probably as good as anyone," said Minh with a shrug.

"Leave him in charge from your end. I'll leave Johnny here, too."

"Wait a minute, Captain," Bromhead protested.

"No, Johnny. You wait. You were out all night. You'll be of more help here."

"Yes, sir," said Bromhead bitterly. He understood Gerber's statement, but he didn't have to like it.

"Cat, I'll want you on the first shift. Derek, you and the doc should be on the second. Captain Minh, I think you should be with them, too, if you approve."

"Sounds fine to me."

Gerber turned and walked over to one of the maps. He studied it carefully and then pointed to an area south of the Parrot's Beak. "There are a couple of good LZs right in here. We'll go into one of them and sweep northwest into Fetterman's ambush location. If we run into trouble, we'll call for the backup. We'll make a radio check every fifteen minutes, and if we don't, it means that we need help."

"And then I come to the rescue?" asked Minh.

"Yes, if you think it wise. Any questions?"

When there were none, Gerber said, "All right. I'll want to see Minh and Bromhead in the commo bunker before we take off. We'll mark the LZs on the maps there. As soon as that's done, we're going in."

The flight lifted off twelve minutes later with the pilots staring into an orange sun that was dropping toward the horizon. Gerber sat on the right side of the helicopter, his eyes moving back and forth over the terrain shooting under him. He could see nothing that told him what to expect—just the rice fields, the swamps, the groves of coconut or banana trees and the scattered hootches of the farmers. He saw abandoned hamlets, some of them smashed by American artillery or VC rockets and mortars. There were only a few people visible. Old farmers in their black pajamas or khaki shorts and coolie hats, working their fields and refusing to look up at the American helicopters that flashed by.

Gerber, using a set of headphones and boom mike given to him by the crew chief, finally asked the pilot, "Are we getting close?"

"Yes, sir," said the AC. "Took some fire in this area last time we passed by."

But they flew on without being shot at by anyone. Now they had gunship cover, provided by the armed helicopters assigned to the helicopter company—C-Model Hueys loaded down with 2.75-inch rockets and machine gun bullets. One of them had the new mini guns that could crank out six thousand rounds a minute and put a slug into every square inch of an area the size of a football field with a single ten-second burst. High overhead was a C and C containing the air mission commander. He had wanted Gerber to stay up with him, but Gerber preferred to be on the ground with his men. Air and artillery support could be coordinated through the C and C, as could reinforcements.

Using his map, Gerber had told the C and C where he planned to land. In turn, the air mission commander called the gun team leader and told him. Together, from altitude, they flew by the LZ and took no fire. They relayed the information to the flight.

Gerber acknowledged the information with a grunt. He was thinking how complex the mission had become and yet how quickly he had gotten all the assets he needed. The men in the helicopters were highly trained professionals, and if he let them do their jobs they would give him an edge. He didn't have to understand the operations of an assault helicopter company. All he had to do was tell them he wanted to make a combat assault into a certain area, and they would take care of their end of it.

All at once he saw a Charlie-model Huey appear in front of him. Over the radio he heard the pilot of the oncoming aircraft contact the AC of the flight lead. As the contact was established, the gunship turned, diving back toward the ground as if leading the Slick.

"We're making our approach, Captain," said the aircraft commander. "Please get your people ready."

From the open cargo-compartment door Gerber saw another gunship dive beyond them, firing rockets two at a time into the trees. He saw bursts of smoke at the sides of the chopper and two bright lights that were the flames of the rockets. Seconds later there were bursts of black smoke and orange fire below. On the other side of the flight, another gunship used its mini guns to rake the trees. The sound from the Gatling-type machine gun sounded like a buzz saw, and the tracers reached down like a red ray. The gun team leader led the flight to the LZ, flew through it, and two small objects tumbled from the cargo compartment. The smoke grenades fell to the center of the LZ.

Over the radio Gerber heard the AC say, "ID yellow."

"Roger, yellow. Negative fire."

Gerber stripped his headset, tossing it on the console between the two pilots. As he donned his steel pot, he heard both door guns open fire as the men behind the M-60s began a routine suppression. He checked the magazine of his M-14 and then worked the bolt.

As the helicopter touched the ground, its nose hidden in the billowing cloud of yellow smoke, Gerber leaped into the grass being flattened by the rotor wash of the chopper and fell to his knees. Around him, the men of his company jumped from the other ships, which took off as soon as they were unloaded. It was a classic air assault into a cold LZ.

Immediately Gerber signaled his men forward toward the trees, forming them into squads. Anderson and a couple of Tai hurried forward as a point and slack. As they entered the trees, the last of the men fell into a rear guard.

They held their interval well and had a couple of flankers out on both sides because they were using a trail. Gerber didn't like walking on a trail, where he could easily be ambushed or trip any number of booby traps, but he felt that speed was important.

Thirty minutes later they stopped. Gerber crawled forward to see what was wrong. Anderson held his map out and whispered, "I think we're getting close."

Gerber checked his compass and consulted his map. He nodded to Anderson and said, "You're right. I don't hear anything, do you?"

"No, sir. I sure don't."

Gerber waved at the RTO, who carried the heavy PRC-10. He called the C and C. The gunships had been crisscrossing the area, looking for a target or trying to draw enemy fire, but not a shot had been fired at them. It was as if all the VC had pulled out.

Having confirmed that nothing had been seen by the helicopters, Gerber waved his men forward. They spread out carefully now, watching the ground near them for signs of booby traps. The advance was slow and it was another twenty minutes before they discovered the first evidence of what had happened to Fetterman's ambush. They found the body of one of the Tai strikers. The VC had taken his weapon, his clothes and anything else the man might have carried. Then they had mutilated the body. Some of the mutilation was obviously trophy taking. There were no fingers or ears. And some of it was obviously designed to terrorize the other strikers. There was a gaping, bloody hole in the man's chest where his heart should have been. Gerber turned and looked at his strikers. What he saw wasn't terror or fear; it was anger.

Now they began a leapfrog advance, half the men covering the rest as they moved forward. Once they had deployed, the remainder of the strike company moved up and took positions. It slowed the advance but made if safer.

A few minutes later they found a second body. The Tai had been shot fifteen or twenty times, but only a couple of wounds would have been fatal. It looked as if the man had been captured alive and then shot to pieces as a form of torture. Once he was dead, he had been stripped and mutilated. He was missing one hand, three fingers from the other and his head.

They found several more bodies near a trail. From the evidence—trees riddled with bullets and shrapnel, craters in the ground from exploding grenades and mortars and the remains of claymore mines—Gerber knew that they had found the ambush site.

They swept through it, looking for signs of the enemy. They saw more bodies, all stripped and mutilated. But there were no weapons or booby traps. Nor did they find the bodies of Fetterman, Tyme or Washington. Once they knew that the area was clear, they began a detailed inspection to determine what had happened.

Gerber could tell from the evidence of the mortar craters that Fetterman had run into something a lot larger than he had expected. Fetterman had apparently been able to hold his position for quite a while. Again it was the evidence left behind—the damage to the trees where the bullets had slammed into them, the number of mortar craters, the blood trails and the large pools of blood—that suggested that many of the NVA or VC soldiers who had been killed had been dragged away. They also found the body of the RTO, the remains of his radio shot full of holes. Anything that was of value had been stripped from the carcass of the radio.

"Now what?" asked Anderson quietly. It was the second time in less than twelve hours that he had stood looking at a battlefield.

"We sweep through again to see if we can find a trail to follow," growled Gerber. "Fetterman and the rest of the strikers have to be somewhere."

"It will be getting dark soon, Captain," said Anderson.

"Yeah, Cat, I know. But according to the map, there's a good LZ about half a klick from here. We can use it. That means," said Gerber, consulting his watch, "that we can stay here another twenty or thirty minutes."

The search failed to turn up anything useful. They found a couple of dead strikers a hundred meters behind the ambush. Once again the bodies were stripped and mutilated. Each had had the heart cut out. The heart of one of them had been set on a nearby log as if it were some kind of warning. Behind the dead Tai they found still another body, also mutilated, but this one wasn't a striker. From the remains of the khaki uniform, they could tell that it was an NVA NCO.

"Looks like they didn't find all their dead," commented Anderson.

"And from the mutilation," said Gerber, "it appears that our Sergeant Krung survived the ambush and managed to escape in this direction."

"You think he's still out there?" Anderson asked, looking into the dense vegetation.

Gerber smiled. "Knowing Krung, he's still out there carrying on his private war. We could probably find him by following a trail of dead NVA and VC who were mutilated. I think all we have to do us wait for him. He'll show up at camp carrying a bagful of trophies."

"What about Fetterman?"

"That, Cat, is the question. I can't see Tony getting himself captured. I suspect that he's faded into the jungle."

"Do we continue to look?"

Gerber shook his head. "Not now. We've got to get out of here. Tomorrow we organize a battalion-sized sweep through the area and see what we can find. Right now we've got to get back to camp."

Gerber turned to his RTO, grabbing the handset of the PRC-10. He radioed the flight and asked that they use the small LZ to the west of the ambush site. The VC or NVA had probably escaped to Cambodia.

The flight back to the camp was somber. Although the whine of the Huey turbines and the roar of the engines made conversation difficult, the men usually joked with one another at the completion of a mission. But not this time. Too many friends were dead and too many were missing. He would have Bocker try to arrange aviation support for the next day. Gerber knew that he had to divert some of his assets the next day to collect the bodies. The Tai expected it and the Vietnamese demanded it. If the dead weren't picked up and buried properly, Gerber knew that he would no longer be able to count on the Tai or the Vietnamese in a fight. He made a mental note to coordinate with Bates and have Bao command the detail, with Bocker or Anderson to advise.

The mood in the camp was not happy. Bao and his strikers were mourning their dead in their own way. Gerber and most of the Americans that were left were in the team house. Bocker had added to the gloom by telling them General Crinshaw had denied airlift, explaining that the LZs were within walking distance and the aviation assets were needed elsewhere. No one spoke too much. A bottle of Beam's sat on one of the tables and periodically someone would take a swig from it.

Morrow came in about an hour later and saw them all sitting around. She went directly to the refrigerator, took a barely cool beer out of it and held it up. "Anyone else?"

"I'll have one," growled Anderson.

"Me, too," said Gerber.

As she handed the beer to Gerber, she asked, "Shouldn't you be doing something?"

"Such as?"

"Planning your operation?"

"Right now the operation is off. We have orders from Saigon. Crinshaw to be exact. We don't have an airlift."

Morrow sat down next to Gerber and popped her beer using the church key she wore around her neck. "And you're going to let that stop you?"

"Of course not!" said Gerber. "It's just that there isn't a whole lot to do right now. Bocker is still trying to get us one helicopter for recon. Bromhead is out organizing the men. I thought it would be good training for him. He's getting to be fairly senior and will get promoted to Captain soon. And I don't know why I feel compelled to explain all this to you."

"Maybe you're feeling guilty," she said and then wished she could bite her tongue off.

But Gerber just smiled. "No. Not guilty. We received some information and acted on it. By the time we hit the field, the information was outdated. Now we're trying to recover from that. But right now there's nothing we can do but wait."

8

MACV HEADQUARTERS, SAIGON

"Thank you for seeing me at this late hour, General Hull," said Lieutenant Colonel Alan Bates, saluting the tall, thin, balding man behind the heavy steel desk. As he did so, Bates couldn't help comparing Hull's office to that of Brigadier General Billy Joe Crinshaw's.

Crinshaw's office was opulent, the floor newly carpeted, the mahogany-paneled walls lined with bookcases or decorated with weapons captured in battle from the Vietcong, none of which, Bates knew, had been captured by General Crinshaw. Crinshaw had used his influence as a general officer to make himself a very comfortable inner sanctum, where he held court from behind his massive oak desk, resplendent in his Class A blouse bedecked with several rows of ribbons, the most important being a Bronze Star without V device. That is, he was resplendent in his Class As when he wasn't huddled in a field jacket to protect himself from the icy blast of his new air conditioner, which would have been sufficient to handle the walk-in freezer at the Tan Son Nhut Officers' Club.

Major General Garrison Hull's office was spartan by comparison, the walls painted a light shade of restful green, the desk the regulation military issue in battleship gray, topped with a small green blotter and two OD metal in and out trays that seemed always to be full. There were stacks of papers and file folders neatly arranged along one edge of the desk and a single black telephone and photograph of General Hull's wife and daughter along the other edge. On one painted wall hung a picture of Eisenhower before he had become President, talking to some troops in the field. Hull, then a captain, stood second from the left in the line of soldiers. A second photograph, this one autographed, showed Hull as a major, receiving the Army DSC from General Patton. The other wall held a large map and a Renoir print of a young girl who bore a striking resemblance to the general's daughter. Bates noted that the map, unlike the one in Crinshaw's office, was covered according to regulations. Behind Hull was the officer's one concession to the privileges of rank—a large set of double windows stood open to the night air, which an ancient ceiling fan stirred languidly, the faint, warm air currents providing the illusion of a breeze.

"No problem, Al. I was catching up on some back paperwork anyway," said Hull, returning the salute. "Besides, I usually figure when you want to see me it's about something important. Have a seat and tell me how I can help." He motioned to a battered armchair set near the window and turned his own chair so that he could face Bates without the desk being between them. Then he leaned back in the chair and dug into the pocket of his OD jungle jacket for his pipe and tobacco pouch. It was a bit early for the single bowl of Whitehall he allowed himself in the evenings, but the paperwork was getting monotonous, and he welcomed the break created by Bates's visit.

"Thank you, General," said Bates, taking the offered chair and then leaning quickly forward, sitting on the edge to avoid sinking into the overstuffed cushion as the worn springs creaked loudly. He considered how different this meeting was from the one he'd had earlier in the day with Brigadier General Crinshaw. Both Crinshaw and Hull were USMA graduates, both career soldiers, yet there the resemblance ended. Major General Hull was a man that Bates admired, respected and liked, someone he trusted and as much of a friend as a lieutenant colonel could be friends with a major general. Crinshaw, on the other hand, was the perfect example of the kind of officer that Bates despised—a loudmouthed garret trooper leg, who still thought wars could be fought and won using the kind of tactics employed at the Battle of Hastings.

"Well, General," began Bates, "as you probably know by now, Mack Gerber's A-Detachment stepped into it in a big way out by An Minh early this morning."

Hull nodded. "I was just reading the initial report before you came in. Gerber's a good man. Has he located all his people yet?"

Bates suddenly felt very tired. "He's located some remains he believes to be those of Sergeant First Class Steven Kittredge. He was the team's heavy weapons specialist. It appears that he called artillery fire in on his own position as he was being overrun by the Vietcong."

Hull stopped sucking on his pipe in middraw and slowly lowered it. "The poor bastard. Did he have any family?"

Bates nodded. "He left a wife and a four-year-old daughter."

Hull turned his head toward the desk and stared at the photograph of his own wife and daughter. The silence stretched out for several seconds before he asked, "What about the men with him?"

"The strikers were slaughtered to a man, stripped and mutilated. Staff Sergeant Sully Smith was with Kittredge as second advisor. He's listed as missing at this time. He was—is—the team's demolitions specialist."

"And the rest of the operation?" asked Hull, still staring at the picture. He sensed that the worst was yet to come.

"Well, you'll know from the preliminary report that Lieutenant Bromhead made it back to camp with what was left of the blocking force. Sergeant First Class Tyme, the team's light weapons specialist, and Staff Sergeant Thomas Jefferson Washington, the junior medical specialist, were with the ambush party under Anthony Fetterman, the team sergeant. All three are missing. Same story as before with their strikers—no survivors. Except possibly one. Captain Gerber indicated that he had reason to believe one of the senior Tai NCOs may have escaped. He didn't say what the reason was."

Hull seemed not to have heard the last part. "Tony Fetterman? Wiry little guy, mild mannered, claims to be descended from the Indian fighter, or sometimes Aztecs?"

"That's the one. I didn't realize you knew the master sergeant," said Bates with some surprise.

"And I didn't know he was even still in the Army. Take another look at that picture of Eisenhower before you leave, Al. The skinny little short kid to the far right with the corporal's stripes. That's Tony Fetterman. He carried me five miles through German lines one night in France. I don't remember too much of the trip because I had a sucking chest wound and kept passing out. I found out later that Fetterman had been shot through the left shoulder and thigh, and he carried *me* out. I owe Tony Fetterman, and now you tell me he's missing in action."

"I'm sorry, General, I didn't know. I knew you knew Captain Gerber from Korea, but I didn't know about Master Sergeant Fetterman. Which doesn't make the next part of what I have to tell you any easier. Captain Gerber suspects, and given the absence of bodies—" Bates broke off, immediately regretting the turn of phrase. "What I mean to say, General, is, given the absence of evidence to the contrary and the massacre of the strikers, Captain Gerber suspects, and I'm forced to agree with him, that all four men may have been captured by the Vietcong."

It was an obvious statement but one that had to be made.

Hull nodded slightly. "What's being done to get them back?"

"Captain Gerber took two companies into the field late this afternoon to search for survivors. They were forced to abandon the search at dusk because of a lack of adequate supporting fire and a suitable night defensive position. There was also a high probability of a large VC force in the area."

"And in the morning?" asked Hull.

"And in the morning, nothing," said Bates quietly.

"What the hell do you mean, nothing, Al?" snapped Hull.

"Captain Gerber had planned to strip the camp and conduct a battalion-sized sweep of the area. I was going to loan him Dave Henderson's Mike Force as well, but the plan has been scotched."

Hull was incredulous. "Why on earth would Nha Trang do that?"

"SFHQ would never do that, General. Special Forces takes care of its people. Colonel Andekker's even offered a couple of companies from the Moc Hoa area." Bates had bristled at the implication, then shrugged it off before continuing. "The problem isn't in Nha Trang. It's here in Saigon. General Crinshaw—"

Hull practically exploded. "God damn the man! I should have suspected Billy Joe was making an ass of himself again the minute you walked in. What's the mental midget done this time?"

Bates couldn't have agreed more with Hull's assessment of Crinshaw, but he also couldn't express his agreement. Lieutenant colonels didn't speak that way about general officers, especially not in the presence of another general officer. Not even if that other general officer said so first.

"We need airlift support to mount an operation of this size," Bates began carefully, "and I'm afraid that General Crinshaw..."

"Who has a certain amount of say-so over the allocation of aircraft in such matters, has denied the airlift," Hull finished for him. "Am I correct?"

"Yes, General."

"And did Brigadier General Crinshaw give you a reason for his decision?" asked Hull, his voice dangerously calm.

"Yes, General. He said that other requirements of the military assistance effort prevented the allocation of the numbers of aircraft necessary for an operation of this size at this time, that the very nature of such an undertaking constituted an inefficient waste of manpower and that, in any event, an operation of this magnitude would take at least three weeks to coordinate with the ARVN staff."

"By which time our boys will be in northern Cambodia, enroute for Hanoi, or dead. Well, by God, I'll not let the silly bastard get away with it. If those men are going to have any chance at all, we've got to find them, and I mean quickly."

"Yes, sir. That's pretty much the way Captain Gerber and I have it figured."

As the conversation had developed, Bates had watched Hull grow increasingly angry. Now the major general was almost trembling with barely controlled rage.

"Alan, you call your Captain Gerber and you tell him to have his people ready to move at first light. Where can I reach you later this evening?"

Bates was exhausted. He had been planning to go to his quarters to try to get some sleep, but this put things in a different light.

"I'll be in my office, General. No, on second thought, I'll be at the B-50 TOC. You can reach me at B-Detachment Tactical Operations Center anytime after, say, thirty minutes from now."

"All right, Alan, I'll call you as soon as I can. Just make sure Gerber and the Mike Force are ready. I'll find you some god-damned helicopters if I have to go all the way to Westmorland to do it."

SPECIAL FORCES STAFF SERGEANT Sully Smith lay shivering in the darkness beneath the low, drooping limbs of a thicket of broad-leaved giant ferns and fought hard to slow the pounding of his heart and quiet the wheezing of his breathing. The night air had turned cool, chilling him as the almost undetectable breeze evaporated the perspiration from his skin and sweat-soaked fatigues. But he knew the trembling was more the result of the adrenaline coursing through his bloodstream than anything else.

Smith wasn't afraid. Indeed, he'd felt a curious sense of calm detachment ever since he'd seen Kittredge die. The image was still clear. He'd glanced back to see where Steve was when he'd realized he wasn't running beside him, and he'd seen the heavy weapons specialist standing calmly upright, as if he were trying to get a better view of the onrushing enemy, the handset of the PRC-10 radio still held to the side of his head. Then the next salvo of artillery had landed on the slope of the tiny knoll, and Kittredge had disappeared in a big geyser of mud, water and bodies. After that, it had seemed as though that entire region of swamp had started blowing up, and it had become a highly unhealthy neighborhood. There had been no point in going back. Steve Kittredge was dead. Smith hadn't seen any point in compounding the situation with his own death.

There had been a brief, fierce firefight when he'd reached the tree line with four or five strikers and run smack into a VC squad. He remembered shooting a couple of VC. Then it had gone hand-to-hand and somebody had smacked him on the side of the head with a rifle butt. He thought that he'd killed the man with his knife, but he couldn't remember for sure. Things had gotten pretty confusing after that. When his head had cleared, he'd been a few hundred meters away from the fight. He'd lost his rifle somewhere but had picked up one of the old heavy Garand M-1s

and most of a bandolier of eight-round clips. Presumably he'd taken them from a dead striker. The strap of the bandolier had been cut, and he had the loose ends and his knife clenched in one hand, the semiautomatic rifle in the other. Two large demo bags were strapped over his shoulders. He'd also had a splitting headache, with occasional blinding flashes of white light before his eyes, and blood streaming down the right side of his face and neck.

Smith had spent most of the afternoon running as fast as he could. Several times he'd risked the few trails he'd come across, hoping that the better footing would allow him to put more distance between himself and the short-legged Vietcong. Smith knew that at least some of the trails would be mined or booby-trapped, *dap loi* toe poppers if nothing else. But he'd taken to the trails when the sixth sense a soldier develops in combat told him that the enemy was closing in on him, then broken off into the jungle again when that same sixth sense told him that he'd stayed on the trails too long.

At one point he'd realized with horror that he was leaving tracks along a section of trail where the packed earth had turned soft from the recent rains, his Panama-tread jungle boots leaving painfully obvious footprints that even the greenest VC recruit couldn't fail to spot. Smith had turned the situation to his own advantage, stepping off the trail and doubling back to string the trip wire of a pair of claymore mines that he dug out of one of the demo bags he carried. He set the mines to rake the trail in both directions. It had cost him seven minutes to rig the trap and another fifteen minutes of struggling through the dense growth flanking the trail before he'd dared come back to it, but it had been worth it. He'd still been within earshot when he'd heard the mines blow.

"That ought to slow the bastards down a bit," he'd muttered through clenched teeth and then he'd run on.

Sometime during the afternoon the bleeding had stopped. A bad contusion from the feel of it. He probably had a mild concussion, too, but he couldn't be bothered with trivialities. He was still alive, and as long as the Vietcong didn't get hold of him, he had a chance of staying that way. If the VC caught up with him, chance wouldn't enter into it. Not with all the plastic explosives and other goodies he was carrying in his shoulder bags. There had

been some instances down in the Camau Peninsula, near the Rung U Minh—the Forest of Darkness—where Special Forces men or MACV advisors had been captured by the Vietcong. What had been left of them when the bodies had been found wasn't nearly as pleasant to think about as the prospect of blowing yourself to bits and maybe taking a few VC along with you.

He wasn't, however, in any hurry to rush the situation. When the time came, he'd pull the pin on a detonator or pop the spoon off a grenade, but until then old Victor Charlie was going to have to work like hell if he was going to get the best of Francisco Giovanni Salvatore Smith, and he wasn't going to get one damned bit of help from Franchesca Smith's little boy, Sully, in doing it.

Sully Smith had not come to Vietnam to fight and die for his country. He had come to fight and live, and let some other poor dumb bastard die for *his* country. That was why they all had come. Only Kittredge had forgotten.

Smith jerked his head upright, causing another of the blinding flashes as his temple began pounding once more. His mind had been wandering, and he'd nearly dozed off. He couldn't afford to do that. It wasn't just because the Vietcong might find him. He didn't know how serious the concussion might be. If he let himself fall asleep, he might never wake up.

He would have to rest, but he couldn't sleep. He was too tired to go on, despite the adrenaline telling his body it should be running. But it was too damned dark to tell where he was going. He would have to find some way to occupy his mind. That was the trick. Let the body relax, but keep the mind alert. If only he could concentrate . . . But he was so tired.

Think, you stupid bastard, Smith swore at himself. You want to stay alive, you've got to think so use your mind. He could feel the leeches crawling across his hands and face, but he was too exhausted to brush them away. Wouldn't do any good anyway. The underside of the ferns must be thick with the bloodsuckers. Some had already fastened themselves into place, but he didn't dare light a cigarette to burn them off. Someone might see the light. Tomorrow he might risk it, after he was another klick or two closer to the camp, if any of his cigarettes were still dry enough to light. His head nodded, and he snapped it back up. The pain helped.

Now he needed something to occupy the old gray matter, and his mind turned to what he knew best. . . .

The individual tetrytol M-1 chain demolition block is two inches square by eleven inches long and weighs two-and-one-half pounds. . . .

He heard a sudden sound, and his senses were jerked into alertness. Was somebody moving out there? he wondered. He listened hard, swearing he could hear something, then telling himself he was imagining things. He was getting tired, but he had to stay awake. Had to keep alert.

Composition C-4 is a white plastic explosive, more powerful than TNT, but with no offensive odor. It is plastic over a wide range of temperatures, and has about the same sensitivity as . . .

He stopped. There was that damned noise again! He couldn't be imagining it. But what the hell could it be? he asked himself. Leeches falling off the ferns? Some kind of jungle cat? VC looking for him? VC! Definitely VC!

Smith moved his sweaty hand forward along the stock of the Garand M-1 with agonizing slowness. His entire left arm felt as if it were made of lead. When his fingers finally reached the trigger guard, he had to push a leech out of the way before he could ease the push-through safety off. It seemed as if he barely had the strength to do what was needed. But the adrenaline was pumping again. Not much, but enough. He'd manage. Somehow. They weren't going to take him without a fight. His other hand found the fore end of the rifle, steadying the heavy weapon against his shoulder.

All right. I'm ready for you sons of bitches now, Smith thought. Come on, you bastards, it's time for fun and games. Then he heard it. So quiet that at first he was not sure that he'd heard it at all, but after a few seconds it came again. This time there could be no mistaking it. A soft, whispering voice. He shifted the rifle slightly so that it was pointing in the direction of the voice and strained his ears, trying to catch the words.

"Sergeant Sully," the voice said in heavily accented, broken English. "Sergeant Sully, you there?"

9

THE JUNGLE NEAR HONG NGU

Fetterman had a pretty good idea where he was, despite the blindfold and all the marching back and forth that the VC security team had put him, Tyme and Washington through in an effort to confuse the Americans. It had started as soon as the Green Berets had been blindfolded and turned around several times, but Fetterman had judged that he was still facing more or less the same direction when they'd finished as he had been before they'd started. He'd simply paid attention to the number of times a hand had touched his left shoulder to turn him and had ignored the other touches. The touch of the hand had felt the same each time—first the heel of the palm striking his biceps, then the fingers curling behind the arm to jerk him around to the right. Since the hand grabbed him in the same fashion and at the same location each time he felt its touch, Fetterman reasoned that it belonged to the guard in front of him and was therefore a useful indicator of the general direction in which he was facing. He'd had a pretty good idea of his directions before they were caught, and after that it was just a matter of noting turns and counting paces as the VC hustled them along a series of trails.

Fetterman was concerned about the other two prisoners, particularly Tyme. Washington had only been allowed to glance quickly at Tyme's pressure dressing before the VC lieutenant had slapped his hand away.

Fetterman was also concerned about Washington's mental state. When they'd heard the gunfire indicating that the VC had killed the wounded strikers, Washington had thrown himself at the VC officer, intent on wringing the man's neck. The big medical specialist would likely have succeeded had not Fetterman pulled him off. The master sergeant had seen a second VC soldier raise his rifle to shoot. Washington had not. Afterward they'd each received a vertical butt stroke from the lieutenant for their trouble and had had their wrists and elbows bound tightly behind their backs. The VC lieutenant had then taken the time to kick Washington in the groin and had admonished Fetterman with, "Master Sergeant, you keep your men in line, or I shoot them. Then maybe I shoot you, too."

The VC had, of course, immediately taken their weapons and equipment belts; their floppy jungle hats, helmets, wallets and wristwatches had disappeared at the same time. They had been allowed to keep their boots until they stopped at a tiny hamlet of not more than half a dozen hootches. Fetterman estimated the time to have been around 2200 hours, based on the 40,259 steps he had taken since they'd been blindfolded following their capture.

The VC marched them into the village, made them kneel in front of one of the huts and then removed their blindfolds. Fetterman was relieved to see that the others were still with him, and although he couldn't tell if the bleeding from Tyme's wound had stopped entirely, the young sergeant seemed to be doing fairly well considering the situation. Tyme nodded in Fetterman's direction and flashed him a tight grin but was kicked between the shoulder blades when he'd tried to speak.

Fetterman then took in his surroundings and was a bit surprised to find the huts. He didn't recognize the ville, and hadn't realized there were any settlements quite that small in the area. What really surprised him, though, was the lights. Each of the huts had a kerosene lantern burning, either inside or hung outside the door. A light like that in the jungle at night was an invitation to either get shelled or bombed, now that the American pilots had begun flying some of the combat missions. Unlike the VNAF, the Americans weren't hesitant to fly at night and frequently had an O-1 Bird Dog out looking for likely targets for Puff or the fast movers out of Saigon. Fetterman couldn't decide if it meant that the VC felt the tiny village was secure, or if it was all an arranged show, designed to impress the Americans with how safe the VC felt here.

The villagers were all paraded by, were given a chance to look at the despicable Yankee dogs and were encouraged to shout insults and spit at them. Then the VC lieutenant came forward and ordered the prisoners to stand. After they had struggled to their feet, the VC officer nodded to one of the other Vietcong, who untied their arms and gave each of them a cigarette. Fetterman noted with amused interest that the cigarettes were American, Chesterfield Kings, Tyme's brand, and undoubtedly had been taken from him earlier.

"You see," said the VC lieutenant, "you think the Front is your enemy. But we are not your enemy. It is the people who hate you, not the Front. The Front gives you your lives rather than kill you in the battle. But the people hate you because they do not want you in their country. Your presence here helps to prop up the puppets of the corrupt Saigon regime, and the people rightly hate you for this and would kill you. You must learn the error of your behavior and correct it if the Front is to continue to protect you from the people and keep you safe until you have learned the wrongness of your ways and can be returned home to your families again."

It was the biggest speech he'd heard so far, and Fetterman replied humbly, "Thank you, sir, for your lenient treatment of us and for the cigarettes. And please accept our thanks to the Front for sparing our lives."

It was difficult to say who wore the most stunned expression, Washington, Tyme or the VC lieutenant. It was obvious that, whatever they had expected the master sergeant's reaction to be to the VC lieutenant's canned propaganda speech, this wasn't it. But Fetterman knew the rules, and rule number one was do not antagonize your captor.

The VC officer was quick to recover. He smiled and stepped forward to light Fetterman's cigarette. Fetterman recognized the lighter but said nothing. It was his.

"You see, we are not so bad," the VC said easily. "We all want to be reasonable. But you must learn to understand the wrongness of your position here. Soon you will be taken to a camp where you will begin school to teach you the truth of our revolutionary struggle. How soon you can be returned to your families will depend upon how soon you learn the lessons of your mistakes. I urge you to study hard when your classes begin and learn your lessons quickly so that the generosity of the Front may return you to your families in the shortest possible time.''

The lieutenant knew his stuff. He kept referring to the men's families. If you make a man sentimental, you make him weak. If he's weak, he's already yours. Fetterman wondered how many other Americans the lieutenant had used to perfect his routine.

"Thank you for your advice, sir," said Fetterman. "I'm sure we all want to go home as quickly as possible. I know that I'm very anxious to get back to my family. Do you suppose the Front would mind if we used these cigarettes to get rid of a few leeches, sir?"

Tyme was so disgusted that he felt nauseated. He just couldn't believe the way Fetterman was caving in to this guy. The team sergeant was absolutely the last person he'd ever expected to knuckle under to the VC, no matter what the situation. Yet the sergeant was practically kowtowing to a slimy VC bastard. Tyme wanted to kick the VC in the nuts the way the VC had kicked Washington. He wanted to spit in the man's face. Goddamn it, they were professional soldiers, and the Code of Conduct was very clear. They were to resist the enemy by whatever means possible. If captured they were to continue to resist, by passive noncooperation if nothing else.

The VC lieutenant checked his new watch—Fetterman's watch—and seemed to consider for a moment. Then he nodded his assent. "The Front grants its generous permission for you to remove the leeches. You may help each other."

"Thank you, sir," Fetterman replied. He moved toward the other two Americans, feeling the tingling burn of blood pumping through his arteries and veins as the circulation returned to his forearms and hands. The VC soldier who had tied him up, using a split bamboo thong at both wrists and elbows, had been a little too enthusiastic about his work, and Fetterman fumbled the cigarette as he held it between clumsy fingers.

"What's the big idea, Fetterman?" whispered Tyme. "I thought for a minute there you were going to kiss that son of a bitch's hand."

"I'd kiss his ass if I thought it would keep us alive, Boom-Boom," answered Fetterman. He used his cigarette to burn off some of the leeches clinging to Tyme's arms and legs, while Washington checked the bandaged shoulder. Tyme's face was ashen, and he was highly diaphoretic.

"Damn it, Tony, what about the Code of Conduct? Do you have to be quite so helpful to them?" Tyme spoke with his words strung out, breaths interspaced between them, as if each word were costing him considerable effort.

"Come on, Boom-Boom. I haven't told them anything they don't already know or won't figure out pretty quickly. Besides, you know what these guys think of the Code and the Geneva convention. I can't see where it's going to hurt us to be polite to them. It might buy us some time, and it isn't going to help our situation any if we piss them off."

"Time for what?" Washington asked.

"Who knows? We've been out of contact with the camp for a long time and missed three routine radio checks. Captain Gerber will have people out looking for us by now. Best thing we can do is try to stay alive and see what happens." Fetterman glanced at Washington, who shook his head.

"I think part of the bullet is still lodged in there. I need a chance to dig it out and get some antibiotics in him. If it stays in, it's going to get infected."

"I'll see what I can do," Fetterman said. "Just don't either of you guys get that VC lieutenant pissed off again."

"No whispering!" snapped the VC officer. "You talk, you speak so I can hear you."

"Yes, sir," said Fetterman. "I was just asking Sergeant Washington about the condition of Sergeant Tyme's wound. He believes the bullet is still lodged in Sergeant Tyme's shoulder and needs to come out. We were wondering if the Front would be generous enough to return Sergeant Washington's medical bag long enough for him to remove the bullet and give Sergeant Tyme some medicine."

"No!" the Vietcong said adamantly. "Your man is responsible for his condition. Besides, I need all the medicine for my own wounded. We must go on in a short time to camp. The doctor there will treat your man if he needs medical attention."

Fetterman tried another approach. "Sergeant Tyme has been greatly weakened by his wound. Sergeant Washington is concerned that he will not be able to continue to walk to your camp if it isn't treated soon."

"No medicine until we reach camp. If your man cannot walk, we must leave him behind." The lieutenant's voice had the ring of finality.

Fetterman didn't like the sound of that. He had no doubt that if they had to leave Tyme behind, the VC would care for him in the same manner as they had the wounded Tai strikers.

"We understand your concern for your own men must come first," Fetterman told him. "I'm sure that Sergeant Tyme will not mind waiting until we reach your camp to have his wound looked at by your doctor."

"He must be able to walk when we are ready to move. If he slows us down, we will have to leave him behind."

Fetterman shot a doubtful glance at Tyme, who returned it with a tight grin that twisted his face into a grimace.

"It's okay, Tony. Tell the representative of the Front I'll be fine until we get there," said Tyme, gasping and swaying uncertainly on his feet.

At that point another VC came up and said something to the Vietcong officer, who checked his new watch again and nodded to the VC who had given each of the Americans one of Tyme's cigarettes. He came forward, passing out fresh ones and taking away the half-smoked ones. A group of civilians was arranged around the Green Berets, all smiles this time, and the VC officer stepped up and struck the flint of Fetterman's lighter, holding it out toward the cigarette that Washington, who was at the end of the line, held. Another VC appeared, equipped with a 35 mm camera and flash, and started snapping pictures. When he had taken a dozen photographs, the VC soldier that had passed out the smokes collected the still unlighted Chesterfields and tucked them back into the pack. The man with the camera disappeared, and the three Americans had their wrists and elbows tied together once more and their blindfolds replaced. Shortly after that someone came and took their boots and socks away.

They marched steadily throughout the remainder of the night, pausing only twice to rest briefly before continuing. The narrow jungle trails would have been bad enough without the blindfolds. With them it was a nightmare. Vines and fallen branches crisscrossed the trails, and Fetterman stumbled over logs so many times that he lost count, pitching facedown onto the jungle floor, unable to break his falls because his arms were bound behind his back. Each time it was a bigger struggle than the last to get back to his feet, and the only help offered by the VC was an occasional kick or a gun butt. His feet were past aching and full of thorns. Snakes and venomous insects were things he tried not to think about. There was an old joke about Vietnam having one hundred varieties of snakes—ninety-nine were poisonous, and the last one could swallow you whole. Fetterman hoped he wouldn't get the chance to put the theory to the test.

As bad as it was for him, Fetterman knew that it must be worse for Tyme. The young sergeant hadn't looked good at all back in the village, but Fetterman was encouraged by the fact that there had been no gunshot.

After it began to get light, the going wasn't quite so bad. The blindfold, which seemed to be made of an old strip of burlap, hadn't been tied all that well, and Fetterman discovered that he could see just a bit of ground if he pitched his eyes steeply and peered out from under the bottom of it. By tilting his head, he could see a short distance in front of his feet, only a foot or so but enough to prevent him from stumbling over any more vines or branches. Once, his new sight saved him from stepping squarely on a scorpion that was apparently late getting home and a bit slow scurrying out of the way.

In spite of the very difficult terrain, Fetterman stubbornly continued to keep track of the number of steps he took and a general sense of direction. He estimated that they had come only about four-and-a-half klicks from the village when the VC lieutenant called a halt.

For about twenty minutes nothing happened. Fetterman stood waiting, swaying slightly on tired legs, feeling the oppressive heat that always signaled the start of a new day in the land of eternal

summer. He could barely see his feet beneath the blindfold and
wished he couldn't. They were filthy and covered with scratches
and cuts from the brambles and thorns, a real invitation to infection. And that was only the tops of his feet. The soles, he knew,
would be even worse. He wondered how many thorns and pebbles he would find embedded there if he got the chance to examine them. What parasites could you pick up from the soil? His
feet were beyond pain now. There was only a dull, tired throb-
bing, much the same as followed any long march, suggesting to
him that the nerve endings in the outer layers of skin might possibly have abraded.

As he waited for whatever was going to happen, he flared his
nostrils and strained his ears, trying to catch some scent or sound
that would give him a clue to their surroundings. Curiously he
thought he could detect the faint odor of a cooking fire, but the
only sound he heard was a dull thud, like someone dropping a sack
of potatoes. He stood there, part of his mind searching the en-
vironment, while another part continued to assess the organism.

Feet bad, need boots. Legs weak, but probably okay. Something crawling up the left thigh toward the groin, probably one
of the ubiquitous leeches. Try not to think about it; nothing can
be done right now. Hands numb again—try to work fingers and
keep blood flowing past bamboo thong. Shoulders ache but don't
seem dislocated.

The assessment was interrupted by the sudden removal of the
blindfold, leaving him blinking in the bright sunlight filtering
through an open space in the jungle canopy overhead. He was
facing east and thought that Camp A-555 would be about fifteen
klicks east by southeast. He judged the time to be about 0900 before glancing quickly to either side. To the left he could barely see
the dim outline of a camouflaged hootch across a small clearing,
maybe twenty meters away. To the right was a packed mud wall
with punji stakes pointing inward, distance perhaps fifteen meters, with a punji moat in front, width about four meters. Beyond
the moat and wall was the jungle. About halfway to the moat
Washington was sprawled facedown. His body was in a small mud
puddle, but his head was out of the water. His upper body was
rising and falling, indicating that he was breathing heavily. Closer
to Fetterman, only five or six feet away, Tyme lay on his side, his

face turned toward the master sergeant, looking like death. His breath came in short, jerking gasps. His eyes were closed, and his skin was the color of a corpse left too long in the water.

"Gentlemen. Welcome to your new home."

The words startled Fetterman. They had been spoken in English, and although they had a rusty, creaking tone about them as if the speaker had not used English in a long time, the grammar was more precise than that which had been spoken by the VC lieutenant. The voice brought Fetterman's attention back to the front. He had to squint to see in the strong sunlight, but there were two groups of men in front of him.

A little to one side stood the VC lieutenant and a couple of the guards. The other group was made up of four men, two wearing the dark green uniforms of the NVA and the other two wearing the khaki and green uniforms sometimes worn by Main Force Vietcong units.

"My name is Major Vo," said one of the men in khaki and green. "And you men are my prisoners. No doubt Lieutenant Trang has filled your head with a lot of nonsense about your being prisoners of the Front. Permit me to dispel any notions that may have arisen from his zealousness. You are not prisoners of the Front. You are my prisoners. I am the commander here, and you men belong to me.

"Later we will have much to talk about. I will ask you questions, and you will give me answers. There is much that I want to know about your camp and your Captain Gerber, and I know that you will want to answer all my questions because I am very good at asking."

Another man, one that Fetterman had missed in the glare of the sunlight, emerged from behind the two NVA soldiers, casually lighting a cigarette. Fetterman felt himself stiffen. The man was dressed in the full khaki uniform and Sam Browne belt of a Communist Chinese officer.

Hello, thought Fetterman as he stared at the man's face. I've seen you before, old friend. Over the sights of my rifle. You just keep making a nuisance of yourself, don't you? Like a toothache.

"Major Vo, if you would permit me to interrupt," the Chinese officer suggested mildly. "Perhaps before you begin questioning your prisoners, you should have your doctor take a look at this man.'' He pointed toward Tyme. ''Otherwise, I believe he may well bleed to death before he can even tell you his name, rank and serial number.''

Major Vo glared at the Chinese, then gave a deprecating gesture with his hand. ''Trang! See to it! We must not allow one of our guests to leave us before we are ready for him to do so.''

The VC lieutenant spoke briefly to his men, and the two guards grabbed Tyme under each arm and dragged him roughly toward the camouflaged hootch. Lieutenant Trang brought up the rear.

''Now, then, as I was saying,'' continued Vo, addressing Fetterman directly, ''I want to welcome you to your new home. We have spent a great deal of time preparing it especially for you. I think that you will find that our preparations have been more than thorough. Actually, I must admit that we had expected to entertain a few more of you. But do not despair, gentlemen, I am sure that the rest of your team will be joining us shortly. I especially look forward to many long conversations with your Captain Gerber.

''I trust you will find the accommodations adequate. I do not think that it would be quite fair to call them comfortable. Still, for the moment at least, you will have plenty of rooms to choose from. I do hope you will enjoy your stay, gentlemen. Because you will never leave.''

Vo made a quick motion of his hand, and Fetterman crumpled under a blow to the right kidney, delivered by an unseen guard behind him.

''Sergeant Bat! Take our guests to their rooms, please. And do be more careful with the older one. After all, we must show appropriate respect for our seniors.''

Then Vo threw back his head and laughed. He laughed at the new day and the spectacle before him. He laughed at his own little joke. He laughed because it was good.

10

THE JUNGLE NEAR
AN MINH

"Sergeant Sully, you better now? You maybe want another drink from canteen? Want another C-rat?"

Sully Smith smiled happily at the diminutive Tai striker and had his smile returned with Krung showing two rows of teeth filed to even points, which was an improvement over the four rows he'd been seeing earlier.

"No, thanks, Krung. I'm just fine now. I've have plenty to eat and drink, and I've had five-and-a-half hours of sleep. But, best of all, you don't have a twin brother anymore."

Krung looked puzzled. "What you mean? I never have a twin brother. I had brothers once, but VC kill them all. You know that."

Smith was instantly sorry for his choice of metaphor. "I'm sorry, Krung. I know. What I meant was, when I looked at you earlier, I saw two of you because of the bump on my head. But now I can see that there is only one Sergeant Krung, and it makes me very happy. It means the injury wasn't as bad as I thought it was."

Krung squatted next to the stocky Green Beret demolitions man and digested this information for a few minutes. Then he shook his head.

"Sergeant Sully, what you say make no sense to Krung. I think maybe knock on head shake something loose inside. Make you say funny things. Maybe you rest some more, okay?"

Smith chuckled. "I'm okay, Krung. Really." He gingerly felt the bandage on the side of his head. "You're partly right. It did knock something loose, but I'm fine now. Let me have my rifle, will you?"

Krung reached behind himself and passed the heavy Garand to Smith, who unloaded the weapon, checked to make sure that the bore was clear and that the rifle was functioning properly, and then inserted a fresh clip.

"Well, I guess we'd better be going. Captain Gerber will want to know about what happened to Sergeant Kittredge and the others, and we've still got a long walk back to camp."

Krung wasn't totally convinced of Smith's condition yet. "How about you rest here another thirty minutes before we go? Krung go make recon, scope out area, make sure no VC follow Sergeant Sully and Krung's tracks. Then when come back here, we go on to camp. Okay fine?"

Smith chuckled again. "Okay, fine. Only let's make it twenty minutes. We don't want to keep the captain waiting."

Krung glanced at his wristwatch, a U.S. Army-issue OD plastic model that Smith had given him some months before. "Twenty minutes, okay." With that he picked up his carbine and moved off, disappearing into the jungle as quietly as he'd arrived.

While he waited, Smith checked his resources. There were five full clips for the Garand in the bandolier, plus the full one in the rifle and the five rounds from the partial that had been in the M-1, fifty-three rounds in all. Not the sort of load a man wanted for a serious firefight. He still had his .45 pistol and three mags, plus one up the spout, making twenty-two rounds. But the .45 was essentially a close-in defense weapon, and he didn't want the situation to get down to that.

There was still his knife. But if they got into it again before they made it back to camp, they were going to have to break contact damned fast and run like hell. Of course, there might be a way of slowing their pursuers down a little.

Smith rummaged in his haversacks, looking for anything that might prove useful. Ten pounds of plastic explosives, always handy to have around but not very useful in this situation. A fifty-foot roll of det cord; might be able to do something with that, he thought. A small roll of safety fuse and a couple of fuse lighters. An assortment of electric and nonelectric blasting caps. A pressure release device, two pull release devices and a fifteen-second delay detonator. Crimpers. Two more claymores and two WP grenades.

With all that and the three frags he still had on his webbing, he thought he should be able to do something, certainly with the grenades and claymores—if there was time to set it up right. The rest of his gear wasn't particularly useful for killing people. He still had his LBE, a few more rations, a compass, map and his nickel-plated whistle, which he sometimes used to spring an ambush or for signaling. That and two smoke grenades, one green, the other yellow.

Smith considered ditching the yellow smoke. He couldn't see it as anything but extra weight, and it might be smart to leave it and part of the C-rations behind to lighten his load. He'd already donated his poncho and liner to the jungle landscape during yesterday's marathon run. He'd need the green smoke to signal the perimeter guard when they got back to camp.

It seemed to be taking Krung a long time to get back. Smith glanced at his watch and saw that Krung's twenty minutes were not yet quite up. Worrying over nothing again, he told himself. The man would be on time. They'd evaded the VC this long, and another three or four hours would put them back at the camp.

That was something that Smith wasn't really looking forward to. While making it back to the camp represented safety from the Vietcong, at least of a sort, it also meant that he'd have to explain to Gerber about Kittredge and the others, and he wasn't looking forward to that.

He also wasn't happy about all the questions that would go unasked by the rest of the men, both the strikers and the team. He could see their silent, questioning glances already, the looks from eyes that would be quickly averted when he returned their stares.

"Sully, old boy," the looks would be asking, "tell us, please, just how is it that you're the only one who made it back while Steve and all the rest of them died?"

It wouldn't be as though any of them really believed that he'd turned tail and run away to avoid a fight. They all knew him too well for that, and the head injury would confirm that he was no coward. But there would still be that little niggling doubt.

"Sully, wasn't there *something* you could have done to help Steve? Anything, Sully? *Anything at all?*"

How could he tell them that there was nothing any of them could have done but run away? That they'd underestimated the cleverness of the enemy and got caught with their butts hanging out in the breeze? That the VC had been better equipped and better led than ever before and had been waiting for them with a vastly numerically superior force. And that they'd all just walked into it, fat, dumb and happy, and found themselves up to their necks in deep shit?

The enemy had been waiting for them. Kepler wasn't going to like that. He wasn't going to like that at all. The mission had been his idea, and it hadn't just gone sour. It wasn't just a chance encounter with a big VC unit that had happened to be in the wrong place at the right time. The VC had been waiting for them. Kepler had been had. They'd all been had. And Kittredge and all the strikers had died because someone had guessed wrong. It wasn't a question of someone being stupid or making a mistake. Military disasters were seldom that simple. It was a question of guilt by association, and no one involved would escape the blame. Not in a fiasco this size.

The brass hats back in Saigon would try to hang the captain out to dry because he'd authorized the mission instead of just passing the information on to Nha Trang, where it could work its way up through the chain of command and be useless by the time anyone decided whether to act on it. Then they'd try to hang Kepler because he was the one who'd gotten the information in the first place and conceived the mission. Then they'd probably hang Smith and Krung for having been unfortunate enough to survive the massacre. After all, they must have done something wrong, or they'd have died like everyone else, right?

Well, at least we're alive to be hung, thought Smith. And Christ only knows what happened to Fetterman's bunch and Bromhead's group. I hope to good God that they didn't get clobbered the same way we did. Goddamn it! Those bastards *knew*. They knew we were coming, and they waited for us to do it and then closed the trap. How did they know? How could they have known? Security had been tight on this one. Real tight. There was no way they could have known.

Unless they had known all along. Unless they had always known, known from the very first. *Unless they'd planned it.*

GERBER WAS PUSHING HIMSELF too hard. They all were, but he was being especially hard on himself. He'd had six hours' sleep in the last forty-eight, and the last of that had been over thirty-five hours ago. The Benzedrine tablets that McMillan had reluctantly prescribed for him when he had refused to rest were still in the left pocket of his jungle fatigues. He knew that he'd have to take them soon if he was to keep going, but he also knew they'd only prop him up for so long, and when he crashed off the bennies, he'd be out of it for a long time. McMillan had warned him that he might sleep for two or three days straight once the pills ran out and he came down. And Gerber had a hunch that McMillan wouldn't be willing to prescribe a second batch for him, no matter what the situation. So Gerber continued to hoard the bennies until he absolutely needed them, functioning now on sheer willpower and helped by strong GI coffee. He didn't know how many cups he'd had. He'd lost count somewhere around forty.

Bates's call had come in around 0100. Bocker had found Gerber working at his makeshift desk, trying to rough out plans for the ground search that he intended to mount in the morning. Bocker had noted that Robin Morrow, the young photojournalist who seemed to be trying her best to attach herself permanently to the captain, had curled up under a poncho liner and gone to sleep on Gerber's bunk. Bocker hadn't quite figured out yet if she was interested in Gerber in a boyfriend-girlfriend fashion or just thought the captain made good copy for her readers back in the World. He also figured it wasn't really any of his business, but he couldn't help wondering. It was common knowledge among the team members that Gerber and Morrow's sister, Karen, an Air Force flight nurse, had once been lovers. There were no secrets in so close-knit an organization as the Special Forces A-Detachment. Bocker was concerned that the captain had enough on his mind right now without the complication of a romantic involvement with a former lover's sister. Still, if it was an affair, it was the captain's affair and not his place to bring it up. Besides, maybe I'm just a little bit envious, Bocker thought.

"What is it, Galvin?" Gerber had asked, looking up from his work and rubbing his eyes.

"Crystal Ball is on the horn, sir," Bocker had answered him. "He asked to speak to the Actual."

"Bates wants to talk to me? At this hour? The colonel's keeping some pretty late hours," Gerber had replied.

"Yes, sir," Bocker had told him. Then had come the carefully not expressed implication that Bates wasn't the only one keeping long hours. "I told him you might be asleep, sir, but he said to wake you."

"You told him I was asleep?" Gerber had seemed puzzled.

"Yes, sir," Bocker had finished, not quite so subtly the second time. "I'd hoped you might be, sir."

"Uh-huh," Gerber'd grunted, finally picking up the hint. "Any idea what it's about?"

"No, sir. Just that the colonel said it was important."

It had been. Bates had informed Gerber to have the two Tai strike companies and one of the PF companies ready to move at first light. General Crinshaw, it seemed, had been induced to modify his position on the denial of airlift support.

The helicopters had come in shortly after dawn, two flights of CH-47 Chinooks, each accompanied by a two-ship Huey gun team. Dave Henderson's Mike Force had come with them.

Gerber had been so busy pumping his old friend's hand and thanking him for the added help that he failed to notice the other passenger until Henderson hitchhiked a thumb over his shoulder.

"Good morning, Captain Gerber. Hope you won't mind my tagging along. After all, I did convince Billy Joe to give you the helicopters." Standing there in his old but still highly shined paratrooper boots and chin-cup helmet and armed with an M-1 carbine with a folding stock was Major General Garrison Hull.

Gerber was stunned.

"Had to bring him along." Henderson grinned. "You ever try to say no to a general when he wants you to take him somewhere?"

"No," admitted Gerber, "I don't believe I've ever tried. To what do we owe the honor of this visit, General?"

"You know how stuffy it can get in Saigon—conferences one minute, briefings the next, paperwork sandwiched in between. Just thought I'd get out in the country and get myself a bit of air," said Hull flippantly. "Truth of the matter is, Mack, that Al Bates told me you were having trouble locating Tony Fetterman and a couple of the boys, and I really was getting bored around the old office so I thought I'd come out here for a day or two and give you a hand. I scrounged myself a couple of air assets and rounded up Henderson's bunch for a security team—we generals aren't supposed to go out in the field without a security team, you know— and here I am."

Gerber's expression said he didn't believe a word of it, but he couldn't very well call a general a liar. Especially one he'd known and been friends with since Korea.

"It's good to see you again, sir, but I can't really say that I'm happy to see you," Gerber said truthfully. "We've apparently got a large, well-directed Vietcong Main Force unit operating in our area. I'd hate for anything to happen to you while we were out looking for the others."

"Mack," said Hull, raising one eyebrow and lifting his carbine slightly. "I used to be pretty good at looking out for myself with this little popgun, and I haven't forgotten how to use it. I'm not here to take over and try to run things. This is your show. Just think of me as a useful adjunct if you have any trouble getting support, say from Cu Chi Arty or Stinger Ops. In the meantime just put me anywhere you can use an extra pair of eyeballs and a weapon, and I'll keep my mouth shut until you ask me to open it. Tony Fetterman is an old friend of mine from the Deuce. I'd like to help, that's all."

Gerber looked at Henderson, who gave him a shrug and a grin. "See what I mean? You say no to the guy if you want to. I can't."

"Well, General, I must say I applaud your judgment in selecting a rather large security detachment. Have you completely emptied Saigon of Special Forces personnel, or is somebody still minding the shop back at B-Detachment?"

"Colonel Bates is still coordinating things back at B-Team TOC," said Hull. "He'll be mad as hell when he finds out I came out here without him."

They all laughed at that, and somehow the laughter seemed to drain the tension that had permeated the entire camp since yesterday's disaster. For a moment Gerber even felt less tired. Then he saw Morrow walking across the camp toward them.

"All right, sir. I guess I don't know how to say no to a general, either. I've got my executive officer supervising the loading. He'll be coming out with the second lift. I'd have had to put him in the stockade to keep him from coming along. It's not SOP, but Captain Minh is a very competent officer and he'll be in charge here while we're out. If I could impose on Dave to introduce you to him and my XO, I think I'd better go deal with our representative from the press. She's going to be real happy with me when I tell her she can't come with us."

Hull raised a quizzical eyebrow again, and Henderson gave him a blank look. "She? As in female-type reporter?"

Gerber moved his head slightly in Morrow's direction. "Morrow, Robin E., shade tan and blond, eyes green. Seriously she's a damned good journalist, and she isn't going to like being left in camp one bit."

"Morrow? I don't think I like the sound of this. Any relation to your lady friend the nurse?" asked Henderson.

"Ex-lady friend," said Gerber sourly. "This one is her sister."

"I definitely don't like the sound of this. General Hull, maybe we'd better make ourselves scarce for a bit."

"Somebody want to tell me what all this is about?" asked Hull.

"No," said Gerber.

"How about that! He can say no to a general," said Henderson. "This way, please, General. I think we ought to let Mack wing this one on his own."

Hull shot Gerber another questioning glance, noted the correspondent's approach and acquiesced. "Lead on McDuff. I'm not looking for any literary entanglements."

They turned and walked off down the flight line, moving quickly but casually.

Morrow's walk was purposeful, determined. She was close enough now for Gerber to see the fine line of her jaw, which was set. He knew this wasn't going to be easy.

It wasn't. Morrow started in when she was still fifteen feet away.

"All right, you male chauvinist bastard, what's all this bullshit about not letting me go out with the search party? I spent half the night sitting up with you, then I dragged my ass, my camera and my notebook down to the far end of the runway to find out from Lieutenant Bromhead where I'm supposed to ride, and Bromhead told me you say I can't go. And after all I've done in the past for you and Fetterman and all the rest of the guys. This is a good story, and I'm not going to miss out on it. I'm going so you'd just better think again."

"Sorry, Robin. Not this time. That's the way I want it."

"The hell with that noise. I'm going."

"No, you're not. And that's final."

"You can't stop me. I'm a member of the press."

"I can stop you," said Gerber, "and I have. You're not going on this one. Not even if I have to put you in the stockade to keep you here."

"You wouldn't dare!" she muttered.

"I will if you make me."

"Why, for Christ's sake?"

"Because it's safer here."

"Oh, that's just great. I'm supposed to tell my editors that you made me stay in camp because it's safer here? Since I've been here, I've been sniped at, mortared, gone on a secret mission into Cambodia and had the wonderful experience of finding a cobra in my sleeping bag. And now you tell me I can't go out and help look for Fetterman, Smith, Washington and Tyme because it's safer if I stay in camp? How in the hell am I supposed to do my job if you won't let me?"

"That's exactly the point. How am I supposed to do my job if I'm spending all my time worrying about what might happen to you? We don't know how big a force we're up against. I've already got one of my team killed and four missing, and I will not allow you to be put in a position where you might be joining them."

"You won't allow . . . Just who in the hell gave you the right to be my keeper, Mr. Supersoldier? Wait a minute. Oh, you rotten SOB. You're doing this because I'm Karen's sister, aren't you?" She was almost shouting in his face now. "When will you get it through your thick head that I'm not her, I'm me?"

She swung an open hand at him, but Gerber saw the slap coming and caught her wrist before the blow could land. He pulled her in close to him, snaked his right arm around her shoulders and grabbed the back of her head. He kissed her hard.

She tried to pull away and pounded on his back with her other fist, but slowly her resistance subsided. Gerber could feel the anger ebbing out of her body as he held her until finally she returned the kiss. He broke the embrace and held her at arm's length. The expression on her face was a mixture of surprise and confusion. Gerber wondered briefly what his own expression must look like.

"Yeah," he said quietly. "I'm doing it in part because you are Karen's sister. But not for the reason you think. Robin, I'm confused about us right now, and I need time to think things through. But I can't do it right now. My first responsibility is to my men. If you go out in the field with us, I'm afraid I won't be able to do my job right. That will put you in danger, me in danger and my men in danger. I'm not talking about the kind of day-to-day dangers we all face out here. I'm talking about the kind of avoidable, preventable, unnecessary danger that results when the commanding officer hasn't got his mind on the job. I don't want anything to happen to anybody else because I was thinking about you instead of doing my job. Is that what you want?"

"No, Mack. Of course not," she said softly. Her eyes searched his face, trying to see into his mind to understand what had just happened.

"Then just this once do this one thing for me. Stay here, where I know you'll be relatively safe, and I can concentrate on finding my men. We'll talk about it when I get back."

Morrow was in a state of confusion. Something had happened between them, something more than had taken place on that last night in Saigon over a month ago. It was something that she'd been trying hard to bring about during the last two months that she had known Mack Gerber, but it had somehow remained one-

wrapped wire hinges, secured by the simple expedient of being wired shut after the prisoner had been placed inside. The precaution was hardly necessary, however, because of the clever arrangement of leg irons.

The leg irons illustrated the VC penchant for making do without benefit of the more sophisticated devices and techniques used by Westerners. They consisted of a long iron rod bent into a large loop at one end and a small hole drilled through the rod at the other end. A pair of U-shaped iron pieces with loops bent into each leg of the open end of the U were fastened at the bottom. The U-shaped pieces could be placed about a prisoner's ankles and the rod inserted through the small loops in them. The large loop kept the prisoner from slipping them off that end, and the smaller end could be inserted through a hole drilled through a large wooden stake that had been driven into the ground outside the cage and then wired to it. The result was even more effective at limiting motion than a set of Peerless leg irons, didn't require a padlock or key, which could be lost, and assuming that it had been made from scrap materials, cost zero to build. A series of stakes, driven at intervals along one side of the cage, made it possible to lock up more than one prisoner in the same cage, limit the prisoner's movement as punishment, or, with a second set of irons, stretch the prisoner out spread-eagled on the floor of his cage. Fetterman appreciated the ingenuity of the leg irons's inventor, but under the circumstances he really couldn't say that he found the man's inventiveness admirable.

The VC didn't start to work on them right away, and Fetterman was thankful for that. It gave him a chance to assess their situation and plan a course of action. The basic situation did not look good. He had no doubt that Vo had meant it when he'd said that he would ask the questions and they would be glad to give him the answers. They were prisoners not just of the VC but of a man who had made it clear that he did not consider them to be prisoners of the National Liberation Front, but rather his own personal property. Vo had also made no pretense of concealing a clearly sadistic bent of mind.

Fetterman knew the assumption among Special Forces personnel had always been that, if they were captured and were not killed outright, then they would be taken to one of the VC sanctuaries in Cambodia. And that, he knew, was what Gerber would expect, too. If the captain had been able to mount any kind of rescue operation at all, he'd be looking for them along the border itself, not here, well inside Vietnam and, at the most, a day or two's forced march from Camp A-555. That would give the VC plenty of time to work on their prisoners, and he had no doubt that Major Vo would have a number of highly original persuasion techniques in mind. The permanent-looking nature of the camp suggested that Vo had anticipated having plenty of time to employ his methods as well. Sooner or later, Fetterman knew, those methods would produce results, though just what Vo hoped to learn from them, he didn't know. The man already seemed unusually well informed about them. He had known they were from Camp A-555 and that Gerber was their commanding officer. Deducing they were from the camp wouldn't have been any real trick, but how had the man known Gerber's name?

"I will ask you questions, and you will give me answers," Vo had told them. When ya got 'em by the balls, their hearts and minds will follow.

The Vietcong had placed the prisoners in separate cages but left them within sight of each other. Fetterman recognized the tactic. It was a way of isolating the Americans so that they couldn't help each other. But at the same time it provided a visual reminder that, if you weren't cooperative, the same sort of thing that had just been done to the other guy could happen to you. From a psychological standpoint, Fetterman wasn't sure that it wouldn't have been better, from the VC's point of view, to have completely isolated the prisoners. That would have left considerable doubt in each of the American's minds as to what had happened to the others, giving each a feeling of total dependency on the Front for their continued existence. It might also have been a better softening-up technique. But then, he reminded himself, they weren't prisoners of the Front. They were Vo's prisoners, and somehow he didn't seem to be the type to go in for subtle psychological interrogation techniques.

Washington's cage was about fifteen meters away and partially screened by trees and brush. Tyme was somewhere out of sight, presumably still being seen to by the camp's doctor. While he waited for some sign from the others, Fetterman amused himself by taking stock of his own condition.

His feet were an absolute mess. They were cut, bleeding, full of thorns and the wounds were filled with dirt and pebbles. For the first time in his long military career, Fetterman was thankful that he'd kept his immunization record up to date. He might die of infection, but at least he wasn't going to have to worry about tetanus. The raw flesh and oozing blisters were things that he tried not to think about.

He did, at least, have the use of his hands again. One of the guards had seen fit to cut through the split bamboo thongs at Fetterman's wrists and elbows after they'd got him safely locked up in the leg irons, and sensation was beginning to return to his fingers.

The wrist thong had bit deeply into the flesh over the radius and ulna, and the ragged edge of the bamboo had caused some cuts. Fetterman noted that the blood flow was a slow oozing of bright red, indicating capillary bleeding. It would be sore as hell tomorrow and was another outstanding opportunity for infection. He wasn't in any danger of bleeding to death, and although his fingers tingled and were clumsy, it didn't seem as though any permanent damage had been done.

Fetterman's back ached all the way into his groin from the blow that Sergeant Bat had delivered to his kidney, and he didn't know if he was hemorrhaging internally or not. His pulse seemed normal. And although he knew it was the poorest of tests, considering that he had to judge for himself rather than being evaluated by an unbiased observer, he hadn't noticed any decrease in his own level of consciousness or mental ability, which was one of the early symptoms of hypovolemic shock. As far as he could tell, if he was bleeding inside, it was a slow bleed.

Fetterman worked his trouser leg up until he found the leech. It was happily sucking away. The VC had pretty well gone through his pockets, including the thirty-odd ones sewn all over the outside of the camouflaged jungle jacket that he'd had custom made in Cholon, and he didn't have any insect repellent, salt or matches to encourage the nasty little slug to let go. Pulling on it wouldn't work. That would only leave the head firmly embedded in his thigh, enhancing yet another risk of infection. All he could do was try to encourage the little bloodsucker to let go, and he could only think of one way of doing that.

Bending painfully forward, Fetterman picked up the leech's tail and bit the slug in two, spitting out the rear part and tossing it clear of the cage. The leech didn't care for that. It thrashed madly about on his leg for a bit, finally loosening its grip enough for Fetterman to pull it free without leaving the head behind. He tossed it out after its tail.

Fetterman checked himself over as best he could without finding any other injuries or leeches. The mosquitoes, which seemed to number in the thousands, had discovered his raw feet and were having a picnic. Fetterman plucked out what rocks and thorns he could reach and squashed a few hundred mosquitoes in the process, getting a few flies as a bonus. Clearly, though, the jungle had more mosquitoes to offer than he could hope to deal with in so direct a fashion, and he finally struggled out of his jungle jacket and used it to cover his bloody feet, figuring that his upper body could stand the bites better. In the unlikely event that an escape opportunity presented itself, his most valuable equipment, outside of a well-trained and inventive mind, was going to be those feet. Bad as they were already, he couldn't afford to let them get any worse.

After that, there was nothing to do but wait and see what happened next. That and periodically smash a few of the mosquitoes that were finding his face interesting, now that the more attractive meal of his feet had been covered up.

About half an hour later Fetterman saw Washington slowly sit up in his cage. When he finally spotted Fetterman, the big medical specialist flashed him a weak smile and gave a brief nod of his head between ineffectual swipes at mosquitoes. Fetterman returned the grin and winked. It was his way of telling the staff sergeant that he was okay. Washington responded by giving him a quizzical look and scratching his head. The seemingly innocent gesture was plain enough to Fetterman. He shrugged his shoulders in the universal gesture and silently mouthed, "I don't know where Tyme is."

Neither man attempted to speak. Although they could see no guards, it was likely that some were nearby and might overhear the conversation. Fetterman knew that at least Vo and Trang

Tyme's voice was coming in ragged gasps now; the effort of speaking was costing him a great deal.

"Tony? You still there?"

"I'm here, Boom-Boom."

"Tony, I'm sorry I screamed like that. I couldn't help it."

"I know, Boom-Boom. It's all right. Don't worry about it."

"I tried not to, but I couldn't help it when he stuck that poker in my shoulder."

"I said it's all right. Forget about it. It couldn't be helped."

"Tony... There's something I've got to tell you... I want you to understand...."

"Forget it, Boom-Boom. I understand. I said it's all right."

"No. You don't understand.... I've got to... tell you we're... not alone...."

Tyme wasn't making any sense.

"Listen to me, Boom-Boom. You're weak. You've lost a lot of blood. I want you to be quiet now and rest."

"No! You don't understand! We're not alone... not alone here.... There are others."

"Other what, Boom-Boom? Other guards? Other prisoners?"

"Americans... other Americans here."

Fetterman sat up straighter.

"Americans? You mean there are other American prisoners here?"

"Got to understand... Yes. Other American prisoners... here."

"How many, Boom-Boom? How many other prisoners are there?"

Tyme was silent.

"How many, Boom-Boom? Tell me how many there are."

Still no response.

"Sergeant First Class Tyme," said Fetterman a bit louder, trying to break through the other man's increasingly befuddled state, "I order you to tell me how many other prisoners there are here!"

"Two... Washington and..."

Christ! thought Fetterman. The kid's delirious. He means Washington and me.

spoke English, and it was possible that some of the ot...
well. He didn't know if Washington had been consciou... s
to have heard Vo's little welcoming speech or not, but \...
ton knew about Trang and was playing it safe as well.

A long scream answered the question of whether Tyme \...
alive. There was really no way to be certain that the screa...
longed to the weapons specialist, but it was a pain-filled...
malistic protest that reminded Fetterman more of a puma'...
than a human being's. It was followed a few moments later \...
second much longer scream and then finally a third, very we...
this time.

About ten minutes later a couple of guards dragged Tyme's lim...
body down the trail and dumped him unceremoniously inside a...
cage about five meters from Fetterman's cell. They didn't even
bother with the leg irons, just wired the door shut, then disappeared back up the trail, laughing and sharing a cigarette between them. When the sound of their voices faded, Fetterman
cupped his hands to his mouth and risked a low whisper.

"Boom-Boom! Can you hear me?"

There was no answer, and he tried again, slightly louder.
"Boom-Boom! It's me, Fetterman. Can you hear me?"

This time there was a faint response.

"Tony? I'm okay, I think."

"What did they do to you? Did they hurt you?"

"Stupid question. Of course it hurt. Oh, you mean… No. That
was just the doctor performing a little minor surgery. He got the
bullet out but couldn't control the bleeding so he had to cauter-
ize the wound. He wanted to give me some morphine from
Washington's kit, but there was some officer there that wouldn't
let him. Bastard seemed to find the whole business very funny.
Kept laughing every time it hurt too much and I had to scream."

"That would be Major Vo, our host. The camp commander,"
Fetterman told him.

"Nice guy, I'm sure. You'd better hope you don't get sick 'cause
the doctor here is just some kid who was in his first year of medical school in the North when the Front drafted him."

"How'd you find that out?"

"He told me. Didn't seem like a bad kid for a VC. I think he
was sweating more than I was."

"Washington's okay, Boom-Boom. I've seen him. Is that what you meant about there being other prisoners here? Is it?"

"Washington fine? Yes. No. Not you and Wash... Others, Tony. There are two others."

"What two others? Did you see them? Where are they?"

"Didn't see... didn't see them, Tony. Heard... Vo and that lieutenant nabbed us... heard them talk... talking. Two Americans brought here last night."

"Boom-Boom, this is very important. Think. Did you hear who they were? Were they part of our team?"

"No. Not our... guys. No. Rock... Rockford... Rock somebody. Can't remember... Rock something and Corbett. I think the other guy's name was... Corbett. I... Sorry, can't remem..."

"Okay, Boom-Boom, that's fine. You just rest easy now. We'll talk more about the other guys later."

"No time... no time for that. Fetterman... you don't unders... Damn it! Shoot them. The VC..."

Fetterman felt a chill run up his spine despite the heat.

"Shoot who, Boom-Boom? Shoot the VC? Are the VC going to shoot us? Are they going to shoot the other prisoners? Who's going to shoot whom?"

"The other guys. Vo's going to shoot... the other guys."

"When? Can you still hear me? When is he going to shoot them?"

"Tomorrow... maybe day after tomorrow. He's... waiting."

"What's he waiting for, Boom-Boom? Why is he waiting to shoot them?"

"Waiting for word from... from..."

"From where, Boom-Boom? He's waiting for word from where?"

"Hanoi."

Fetterman tried for several minutes more to get Tyme to talk to him, but there was no further response. He didn't know if the young soldier had passed out or died. There was no way he could check and no way he could reliably communicate Tyme's information about the other two Americans to Washington without running considerable risk of being overheard by one of the guards, who might or might not understand English but who would certainly understand that the prisoners were not allowed to talk to one another. Right now there didn't seem to be anything that he could do but wait. He didn't have to wait for very long.

Three VC soldiers, two carrying carbines and one carrying an M-14 that might have been Fetterman's own rifle, came down the trail and unwired the door to Fetterman's cage, as well as unwiring his leg irons from their attachment to the wooden post.

"Di!" one of them shouted at Fetterman. *"Di di mau lien!"*

Evidently Fetterman didn't move fast enough to suit them. One of the guards stepped into the cage and rapped Fetterman on his head with a carbine while one of the others yanked viciously on the rod of the leg iron arrangement, drawing the narrow end through the bars into the cage, scraping the skin from the backs of Fetterman's ankles in the process. They shoved Fetterman out the door, and he pitched face first onto the path. One of the guards clubbed him again, on the back this time, then two of them grabbed him by the arms and dragged him along the trail until they came to a small bamboo hootch with an overhanging porch roof, similar to those on the cages but bigger.

Fetterman wasn't a large man. He was short and thin but surprisingly strong for his size. This was not the time to exhibit that strength, however, so he simply let himself go totally limp, making things as difficult as possible for the guards. Even so, the VC, who were nearly as big as Fetterman, had little difficulty half holding him up between them. One of them got a hand under Fetterman's chin, after trying unsuccessfully to find any hair long enough to grab on to, and tilted the master sergeant's head back so that he was forced to look up the two small steps to the entrance to the hootch. A smiling Major Vo looked down at him. Behind Vo, Fetterman could see the Chinese officer seated on a folding canvas chair inside the hootch. He was smoking and appeared to be reading something, showing a total lack of concern for what was going on outside the hootch.

"Good morning again," said Major Vo. "Or perhaps I should say afternoon. It is a few minutes past the twelve o'clock I see by my new watch."

Fetterman noted the watch on Vo's wrist. It was Fetterman's. Evidently Vo had relieved Lieutenant Trang of the responsibility of looking after it for the Front.

"The time has come for us to have a little talk," Vo continued.

"Of course," said Fetterman mildly. "I'll be happy to tell you whatever you want to know."

Vo looked genuinely surprised, and Fetterman noticed that the Chinese officer straightened and turned partway toward the door before catching himself. It confirmed that the Chinese advisor also spoke English.

Vo was quick to recover, however, and wasn't about to be deprived of his entertainment by a cooperative prisoner.

"Yes, of course. I am sure you will be happy to tell me whatever I want to know. There has really never been any doubt of that." Vo smiled. "But first, I think, we shall have a little lesson, shall we say. In order to ensure the honesty of your cooperation."

He gave a quick nod, and the two guards dropped Fetterman on his face and bound his hands behind him.

"You will be interested to know, I am sure," continued Vo, "that I have devised a number of means that are very effective in ensuring the honesty of cooperation of my prisoners."

Vo addressed his remarks to the guards but kept them in English to make sure that Fetterman understood. Evidently one of the guards spoke English, or they knew the drill.

"Take the prisoner to the hanging tree," said Vo, still smiling. "And string him up." Then he turned and walked back into the hootch, laughing loudly, as though someone had just told him a very funny joke.

Christ! thought Fetterman. I am in a world of shit.

12

THE JUNGLE NEAR
AN MINH

"Sergeant Sully, we are in a world of shit," said Krung, pushing breathlessly through the vegetation to Smith's side.

"What is it, Krung? What's the matter?"

"Krung make bad mistake, Sergeant Sully. Me see three VC come along trail look for us. Kill two, but one get away. Shit!" He spat. "Krung must be getting old."

"What happened?" asked Smith.

"Krung go take look, like we say. Check back trail, hear someone come, so hide quick to watch. Only one of VC see me when stop to take piss. Me move quick, but not quick enough. Shit!" He spat again. "Krung getting slow in old age."

"I didn't hear any shots," said Smith, struggling into his gear.

Krung looked at him aghast. "Krung no rookie trooper. Know better than to draw big crowd of VC with shot. Use knife, but not quick enough to get all three."

"You tried to kill three armed VC with your knife?" said Smith, then wondered why that really didn't amaze him somehow. After all, he was talking to Sergeant Krung.

"No biggie," said Krung. "Besides, one have dick in hands. Not hard for Tai to kill three Vietnamese when one have dick in hands. Only Krung fuck up, let one get away. Krung getting too old for this shit." He spat. "Krung very sorry."

Smith picked up the heavy Garand rifle and pushed himself to his feet. "Why didn't the VC shoot?"

"Two VC no have time to shoot," said Krung matter-of-factly. "Third VC drop rifle and run away. Fucking garret trooper. Krung chase, but not catch. Think maybe better stop chase before chase right into beaucoup VC. Think maybe best come back tell you what happen. Krung sorry let one get away, Sergeant Sully. You no think Krung dumb leg for make this FUBAR?"

Smith clapped the little tribesman on the shoulder. "No, Krung, I don't think you're a dumb leg. You did as well as could be expected under the circumstances. Are you sure these guys were looking for us? Maybe it was just a couple of local guerrillas out wandering around with their guns to get away from a nagging mama-san."

"They look for us," said Krung definitely. "One who stop to piss have this under arm." He reached behind him and pulled a bundle from beneath the H-straps of his web gear. It was a poncho and blanket liner with Smith's name and serial number neatly stenciled in one corner.

"In that case," said Smith, tucking the poncho and liner into his own web gear, "they've got to have a bunch of friends around here somewhere, and I don't think we ought to hang around waiting to be introduced. I think we'd better di di most rickey-tick. You want to take point? I'll try to hang back about a hundred meters and see if I can't figure out some way to slow them down a bit."

Krung nodded and moved toward the trail.

"Try not to get too far ahead," Smith called after him. "I may need a little time to set up a surprise. We'll follow the trail about a klick and see what happens, then decide whether to stay with the trails or make our way through the jungle to the camp."

Krung nodded vigorously and waved to show that he had heard, then disappeared quickly down the trail.

Smith considered the possibilities of the trail, but it really wasn't conducive to booby-trapping. Not in this particular area, anyway. He could rig a simple trip wire to one of the grenades. The enemy would be excited and in a hurry to catch them, and the trip wire might be overlooked until it was too late. If they hit it, it was sure to make them cautious and slow them down a bit, which was the general idea, but it wasn't enough. Smith wanted something that would bring the VC to a screeching halt and hurt them. He wanted something massive.

He ran for almost a full klick and had nearly caught up to Krung when he found the perfect spot.

The trail had widened a bit, becoming almost as wide as a single lane road, which made it possible for soldiers to bunch up three or four abreast. Based on Smith's experience, he knew that that was exactly what the average soldier tended to do when he was in a hurry. And the VC would be in a hurry. Further, there were two deep ditches on either side of the trail, providing exactly the sort of cover a soldier would instinctively seek when fired upon, and there was a small side trail leading off to the south that would look like a good escape route to anyone wanting to run away. The whole setup was, Smith decided, perfect for a Sully Smith demolitions extravaganza.

Smith moved rapidly ahead to find Krung, knowing that he'd need someone to cover him while he set up the fireworks. Krung also had the one piece of equipment that would add the finishing touch to the plan. He'd seen it thrown over the Tai tribesman's back when he'd moved out—a PPS-43 submachine gun, which the Tai had taken from one of the VC in his earlier encounter.

Krung didn't like the idea of doubling back on their trail, wasting time when they could be putting more distance between themselves and the pursuing Vietcong, but when Smith explained his idea for killing many VC, Krung happily agreed. If there was one thing in life near and dear to Sergeant Krung's heart, it was killing many VC.

As he worked feverishly to set the trap, Smith explained to Krung how he hoped the firing chain would operate once the VC activated it. For Krung, it was a detailed lesson in the complimentary arts of mayhem and death. For Sully Smith, it was all just part of a day's work, doing what he liked to do best—making things go bang.

"I figure it this way, Krung," said Smith, pausing to wipe the sweat from his brow with the back of his hand before crimping a length of time fuse into a blasting cap. "Those three VC you ran into were either an independent search element of a larger unit, say fifteen or twenty men to a platoon, or they were a point element for a really big unit, maybe company size.

"If they were a search team from a platoon, the one who got away will hotfoot it back to the RP, and they'll collect all their buddies before coming after us. If they were point for a company, their CO will send the lead platoon after us while he tries to get the rest of his troops in front of us. He'll then use the lead platoon to locate and fix our position while he maneuvers the rest in for the kill, like drawing the string shut on a bag.

"Either way, we can reasonably expect about a platoon of Vietcong to come charging down this trail in short order. If those guys are even half-assed trackers, they've got to know that they're only chasing a couple of guys. They'll put speed ahead of caution, figuring two guys won't be dumb enough to try to ambush a whole platoon of Vietcong. That's where they're wrong, and that's how we're going to kill them. You set this claymore up at the end of this ditch," Smith said as he pointed to his left. "Then take this spool of wire and run me about three sets of trip wires lengthwise down the ditch for about fifteen meters or so. Just stake them out at the far end. Make the wires about a meter apart. I'll show you how we'll tie them all together when you've finished."

Smith finished his work and moved across the trail to the other ditch to deploy the second claymore.

"The trick is to get all of them, or at least as many as we can, into the killing zone. Since we can't guarantee the VC will cooperate with us, what we have to do is set up a killing zone big enough to sucker them all into it, then make sure none of them can get out.

"The first step is to bait the trap properly. I wrapped my extra smoke grenade up in my poncho and liner after removing the pin. If they pick it up the wrong way, or unroll it, the yellow smoke will drop out, and the grenade will pop about a second and a half after the spoon flies off. The idea is the VC won't know it's only a smoke grenade and will dive for cover. The only good cover is the ditches, and when they hit them, they'll hit the trip wires, triggering the claymores. With luck, we might get five or ten of them right there."

Smith made sure the claymore was properly sighted, then began stringing the second set of trip wires.

"We can't be sure they'll do that, however, so we'll improve the trap. Farther up the trail we'll string a trip wire across the trail itself and attach it to a pull release detonator inserted in a block of C-4. We'll put another blasting cap in the other end of the C-4, tape it to a twelve-meter piece of det cord with another blasting cap on the far end and insert that into a second block of C-4. We'll open up all our C-ration cans and fill them with pebbles from that little stream over there, then pack them around the C-4 blocks to create a shrapnel effect. Well, almost all of the cans. I'll need a couple for the grenades, but I'll explain that later. The first block of C-4 goes up—'Boom!'—throwing the rocks out in a circular fan-shaped pattern about knee-high, the det cord tears up the middle of the trail in a fast ripple, mangling anybody still on the trail, then sets off the second C-4 and shrapnel bomb, smack in the middle of the VC. Surviving VC once again seek shelter in the ditches, and our claymores, if they haven't already claimed a few, get put to good use.''

Krung had finished staking out his trip wires, and Smith showed him how to attach them to the claymore so that a pull on any of the three wires would trip the mine, filling the ditch and raking the edge of the trail with a hail of seven hundred and fifty steel balls.

''Got the idea?''

Krung nodded a vigorous affirmative.

''Okay. You finish the other one while I work on the rest of our little surprise.''

Smith cut a piece of safety fuse with his knife, lighted the fuse and timed its burning with his watch.

''Thirteen seconds . . . that's a little long.'' He cut a slightly shorter piece and crimped it into a pull fuse igniter.

''The pull on the trip wire attached to the pull release device will also activate this fuse igniter and light this piece of fuse. When it burns through, it will release a wire attached to a fifteen-second delay detonator attached to another piece of det cord, which is in turn attached to a third shrapnel-surrounded block of C-4 placed just about five meters short of the point where the back trail narrows, creating a natural bottleneck.

''If all goes well, the first two explosions, three counting the det cord between the C-4 blocks, clear the trail of the advance element of VC. The survivors in the middle jump into the ditches where the claymores take care of a few more of them. Whoever is left runs back the way they came, right into the third block of C-4, or the tail of the VC unit coming forward to reinforce the point takes the third charge in the face.''

Krung reported that he had finished with the second claymore, and Smith set him to work preparing the C-ration cans.

''When you've finished with the cans, gather four or five helmetfuls of rocks. Try to get mostly small ones, about the diameter of your thumb, but don't waste time looking. If you can't find real small ones, take whatever's there. The more rocks we have, the more VC we'll kill.

''I'm going to go a little way down the side trail and string another trap—trip wire designed to drop a Willy Pete grenade out of a tree onto the trail. I'll string it so the grenade drops in front of the man who triggers the wire, and also tie it into a second piece of fuse and igniter so that it will drop a couple of frags onto the path at the mouth of the trail about seven seconds later. That ought to catch anybody that the Willy Pete misses and stampede them back toward the main trail. I'll splice a twelve-second piece of fuse into the end of the seven-second fuse, cap it and connect it to the rest of the det cord, tying it into the third C-4 and shrapnel bomb. That way, even if they check the side trail first, it'll trigger the whole firing chain in reverse.

''When you've got the rocks, fill all the C-ration cans but one. Save me one of the long cans. Then pack the cans and the rest of the loose rocks around the C-4 and cover them with dirt. I've scooped out a shallow hole around each of the C-4 blocks so they won't be quite so obvious. Try not to mound the dirt up too high or the VC may spot them. If the Vietcong show up before I get back, fire a warning shot and take off. Can you find your way back to camp from here without me if you have to?''

Krung gave Smith an insulted look in reply.

Smith nodded. ''Sorry.'' Then he moved about three dozen meters down the side trail, found a good spot and began rigging the secondary mechanical ambush. When he returned, Krung was putting the finishing touches on concealing the C-4 and rock bombs.

Smith inspected the Tai's handiwork briefly, nodded his approval and asked him for the submachine gun, noting as Krung handed it over that it bore Chinese markings. The weapon was, in fact, a Type 43, a Red Chinese copy of the M1954 variant of the PPS-43, which had been developed during the Second World War by the Soviet military engineer Alexei Sudarev, rather than the original Russian weapon that Smith had at first assumed it to be. Smith would have preferred a PPSh-41 with its larger, 71-round drum magazine over the 35-round box of the Type 43, but beggars could not be choosers. Besides, he had a hunch that it would be enough.

"Sergeant Sully, why you want burp gun?" asked Krung.

"It's the icing on the cake," Smith explained. "We'll put it up the trail, near the point where the pathway bends to the left, and tie it to a tree. Then we'll wrap a wire around the C-ration can you saved for me. We'll wrap the wire in two different directions and tie a rock to one end. The rock is held up by a forked stick attached to the trip wire and pull-release arrangement. When the wire is tripped, it pulls out the stick, allowing the rock to descend. As the rock lowers, the turning of the can lets wire out in the other direction, releasing pressure on a bent branch so that it will pull a wire loop with a slipknot in it down tight against the trigger and the grip, causing the weapon to fire. The submachine gun will continue to fire until the magazine is empty and will spray the trail with bullets. Most of the rounds should impact just about where we're standing now. With luck, one or two of them might even kill somebody. But that's not important. What is important is that the sound of the firing will convince the VC that this is an ambush, not just a few booby traps. And that will make them very nervous. Perhaps nervous enough to panic. If they do that, we might kill a whole lot of them with our booby traps before they figure out that they're the ones setting off the explosions."

Krung grinned, showing his sharply filed teeth. "Good."

13

VC P.O.W. CAMP
NEAR HONG NGU

Fetterman tried hard to find something good about the situation that they were in. It wasn't an easy thing to do.

At least I'm still alive, he told himself, then whispered it softly, as if the sound of his own voice would reassure him that it were true. "At least I'm still alive."

Fetterman had fully expected that not to be the case. He'd expected to be cold and dead by now, the rigor mortis stiffening his limbs as the ants made an early supper of his eyeballs and the flies crawled in and out of his dead mouth.

Vo had told his men to take Fetterman to the hanging tree and string him up. That cheerful news, coupled with Tyme's information that there were two other Americans in the camp that the VC were preparing to execute, had led Fetterman to believe that he could expect to be hung by the neck until dead. Instead, the VC tied his elbows together behind his back and hauled him up by his wrists, hanging him by his hands a few feet above the ground until he was thoroughly miserable.

The experience was unique, to say the least. Fetterman could not recall a time when he had felt such pain, including the times during the Second World War and Korea when he had been wounded. The pain was so exquisite that he hardly noticed the severe beating that two of the guards administered to him with split bamboo poles as he hung helpless from a tree branch. He couldn't remember if he had screamed or not but decided that he probably had. It was not the sort of punishment that even a man in good physical shape could stand up to for long, and Fetterman could hardly have described his physical condition as good following the long bootless march through the jungle to the camp. Sometime during the process his left shoulder was dislocated, although Fetterman couldn't say if the dislocation had been caused by the beating or by being hung up.

Every few minutes Major Vo stepped out on the porch of his hut to inspect the proceedings, making sure that the beating was progressing at a satisfactory rate and intensity. On one such occasion the Chinese advisor put in a brief appearance, gazing at Fetterman, cigarette in hand, with a look somewhere between mild curiosity and recognition, before turning wordlessly and reentering the hut.

Fetterman fainted sometime after that. He didn't know how long he remained unconscious. He'd been awakened by having a bucket of liquid thrown in his face. It wouldn't have been fair to have called it a bucket of water. Fetterman strongly suspected that the bucket had been used as somebody's chamber pot. It was sufficient, however, to bring him back far enough to something like consciousness to see Vo's laughing face swimming nauseatingly before him. After that he'd passed out again.

Sometime later he'd regained consciousness a second time, and one of the guards had gone to summon Vo. The Vietcong major stood before him, positively beaming with delight.

"Ah, Master Sergeant Fetterman, I see that you have rejoined us. How good of you to do so," said Vo. "I trust that my staff have now properly welcomed you and that you did not find the accommodations too uncomfortable."

Fetterman wondered how Vo could know his name and rank. As a matter of course, the Special Forces advisors wore neither rank insignia nor name tags on their uniforms when in the field, and practically no one in Vietnam bothered with dog tags except Saigon commandos. They were a nuisance, no one used them for anything and they had an annoying habit of clinking together at the wrong time while on patrol unless they were taped together. It was simpler just to leave them in camp.

"Unnecessary," Fetterman managed to whisper between cracked, dry lips.

"I'm sorry. I could not hear you," said Vo mildly. "What did you say?"

Fetterman worked hard, trying to form enough spit to frame an answer. "Unnecessary," he finally got out. "I'll answer your questions."

Fetterman had already carefully constructed what he hoped was a highly creative tale that still contained enough elements of the truth to be believable. He figured that Vo wanted information on Camp A-555's defenses, and Fetterman hoped to give him the kind of information that would cost Vo a few dozen of his men when the time came for the VC to check out that information. He also hoped that, by appearing to cooperate with the Vietcong, he might be able to keep Washington, Tyme and himself alive long enough to be able to figure a way out of this mess—or for Gerber to find them. He knew that it was a long shot, but it was the only game in town at the moment.

Vo flashed him a warm, almost friendly smile. "Of course, Sergeant. You see . . ."

He was interrupted by the hasty approach of a Vietcong messenger, clamoring for his attention. Vo wheeled on the man and fixed him with an icy stare.

"How dare you interrupt me when I am interrogating a prisoner! You will show proper respect for your superior officers in the future, or I will have you reduced in rank, Corporal. I could have you shot for such an insubordinate display of ill manners."

The messenger blanched, and Fetterman noticed from beneath half-closed eyelids that the man's lower lip trembled slightly.

"Yes, Comrade Major," the messenger said. "I confess that my behavior has been inexcusably rude, and I am truly sorry for the dishonor I have brought upon the Front and our just Revolution by it, but I bring you important news. Good news."

"Well? What is it, then?"

"Comrade Lap's patrol reports that they have made contact with the missing American Smith and one of the hired mercenary dog Tai. They are following their trail and should apprehend them soon."

Vo's countenance softened. "Excellent. Excellent indeed. You may go now. I order you to spend one hour in self-criticism for your unprofessional behavior."

"Yes, Comrade Major. Is there any reply for Lieutenant Lap?"

"Only that the American is to be brought straight here to me immediately upon his capture. Lieutenant Lap may dispose of the Tai as he sees fit. Now go."

"Yes, Comrade Major." The man went.

Vo turned back to Fetterman. "As I was saying, Sergeant, of course you will answer my questions. But you see, I haven't asked you any questions yet. It is a question of propriety. You cannot answer my questions until I have asked them, and I am not ready to ask them yet. I think, perhaps, that it will be some time before I am ready to ask you anything at all. A very long time perhaps. But take heart, Sergeant, take heart. Soon you will have yet another of your men here with you to share your misery. Won't that be nice?"

Then he turned to one of the guards. "You may let him down now and take him back to his cage. I think, perhaps, that we shall entertain the black soldier this afternoon. After all, we don't wish to tire any of our guests too early. And prepare another guest cottage. I think we can expect a new visitor soon."

As he walked back into the hut, Vo threw back his head and laughed. Today it had been very good indeed.

LIEUTENANT LAP TUNG LUONG considered the evidence in the middle of the trail before him. While it would, in truth, not be entirely fair to say that they had found the enemy, they had certainly made contact with him. The flies swarming over the blood-encrusted bodies of the two Vietcong soldiers lying lifeless before him were solemn, mute testimony to that fact.

"Private Lim, tell me once again how it is that your two comrades, Privates Chi and Rho died."

"As I said, Comrade Lieutenant, we were surprised and ambushed by the enemy. We put up a heroic fight, but there were too many of the devils. I was lucky to escape with my life and be able to inform you that we had found them."

"I see. You put up a heroic fight, but there were too many of the devils." He knelt and picked up the two Mosin-Nagant rifles that had been left lying near the bodies, opened the bolt of each in turn and checked the rounds in the magazines. "If there were so many of them, why do you suppose they did not take these rifles with them?"

"I have no idea, Comrade Lieutenant. Perhaps they were afraid I would bring back help and defeat them. Besides, the Americans and their Tai have better weapons. Perhaps they did not want the rifles," Lim finished lamely.

"And perhaps you are exaggerating the truth?" Lap asked calmly.

"No, Comrade Lieutenant. We tried to fight, but there were too many of them. And see, they took the submachine gun that Rho carried," Lim finished hopefully.

"You tried to fight. Liar! Then why have neither of these weapons been fired? Why are there no spent brass casings on the ground? Do you expect me to believe that the enemy took the time to pick up all the spent casings, both theirs and yours, and left behind two rifles? Do you think that I am a fool? There is not even a single bullet wound in either of the bodies! Your comrades were killed with a knife, not a gun!" He grabbed Lim roughly by the cloth of his black pajama top and shoved him toward the bodies. "Look! Look at them! Look at their wounds! You allowed the enemy to take you by surprise and kill your two comrades, and you did not even so much as fire a single shot while they were being knifed to death! You are both a coward and a liar!"

Lim said nothing.

"You fought heroically, but there were too many of them, were there?" Lap continued angrily. "Then why is there only one set of footprints made by the crosshatched pattern that the Americans and Tai wear? One rather small set of boot prints at that? Oh, fine, brave soldier of the Front! You and your comrades allowed yourselves to be surprised by a single enemy soldier, a small, filthy animal Tai at that, and you let them be killed because you ran away. And then you compound your cowardice by lying about it. I should have you shot. I should shoot you myself."

Lap's hand drifted downward toward the pistol holstered at his belt, and for a moment Lim was afraid that his lieutenant might do exactly that.

"You let your two comrades be killed, and then you come to me with a wild story claiming to have found the American we seek. There is not even any sign that the American was ever here."

"But the poncho!" Lim tried desperately. "We found the American's poncho. It had his name on it."

"Are you telling me that you can read American now? I was not even aware that you could read Vietnamese."

Lim shrugged. "Rho could read Vietnamese. He said it was not a Vietnamese name."

Lap looked dubious.

"I see no poncho, Private Lim. Where is this poncho with this American name?"

"Perhaps the enemy took it with him," said Lim quickly. "After all, they took Rho's submachine gun."

Lap still looked skeptical. "What was this American name that was on the poncho?"

Lim shrugged again. "I do not know, Comrade Lieutenant. I cannot read American."

"Bah! You are lying again."

Lim noticed the hand straying toward the holster again.

"No, Comrade Lieutenant! No! It is true, I swear. I can remember what it looked like. I can sketch it for you." He knelt and began drawing in the dirt of the trail with a stick.

When he had finished, he stood up and Lap examined his handiwork. It said: THE IRVING AIR CHUTE COMPANY, INC.

Lap stared at the strange symbols and scratched his head. One thing was certain. It was not a Vietnamese name.

"Sergeant Nguyen," said Lap abruptly to his senior NCO, "take your best tracker along the trail for two hundred meters and see if you can find any evidence that the American came this way. It is just possible for once that this excremental excuse for a soldier is telling the truth. I will await your report here."

The two men returned within ten minutes.

"Comrade Lieutenant," said Sergeant Nguyen, "approximately one hundred and fifty meters from this spot we found a partial boot print and evidence that the trail had been swept with a branch to hide other boot prints. The size of the partial print we found was much wider than the prints here. A short distance beyond we found other prints, the same size as the ones here."

"Very good, Sergeant. Thank you."

Lap turned toward Lim, tossing one of the rifles at him. The VC private failed to catch it but hurriedly picked it up.

"Private Lim, your story is still in doubt. I have decided, however, to give you a chance to redeem your unworthiness in the eyes of your comrades. You will take the point."

Lap glanced at the two emasculated bodies lying in the trail. They were not the first such bodies he had seen since their ambush of the American and Tai unit the day before.

"You should have no difficulty locating these enemies of the Front. This Tai particularly is not a hard man to follow. He leaves dead bodies wherever he goes."

FETTERMAN LAY ON THE FLOOR of his cell feeling the sweat bead on his forehead and run down the side of his face and neck. He was amazed that there was enough moisture left in his body to sweat. His lips felt cracked and dry and his mouth felt like someone had stuffed it full of cotton balls.

Fetterman had lain on the floor of the cage for an indeterminable time after the guards had thrown him unceremoniously back inside and wired the door shut. They hadn't bothered with the leg irons, and the leg irons hadn't been necessary. Fetterman drifted in and out of consciousness repeatedly before his mind finally cleared enough for something like coherent thought. He didn't know how long he'd been out of touch. It might have been only minutes. It might have been days.

When he tried to move, there was a sudden, blinding pain in his shoulder, and a wave of nausea washed over him. He turned his head quickly to one side in order to keep from aspirating his own vomit. There wasn't much despite the racking spasms, and he realized how truly dehydrated he must be. If the VC didn't water their prisoners pretty soon, they might not have to worry about beating them to death.

Still nauseous, Fetterman used his right hand to explore his injuries. Tilting his neck only slightly, he moved his head as little as possible to minimize the urge to vomit again. His right side hurt when he breathed, but his fingers found no obvious deformities so he suspected that he only had a couple of cracked ribs, information he regarded as good news. Well, at least better news than broken ribs.

His upper body was covered with yellowish-purple bruises and crisscrossed with long but fairly superficial lacerations from the beating that the guards had given him with the split bamboo poles. The trousers of his jungle fatigues hung in tatters, revealing cut and bruised legs. His entire body ached and his testicles felt swollen, although he couldn't remember being struck there. Aside from the possible rib damage and the dislocated shoulder, however, most of his injuries seemed to be more discomforting than disabling.

Fetterman knew that, if he was going to have any chance at all of making a success of what he now hoped to do, he was going to have to do something about the dislocated shoulder. He knew that reducing a dislocated shoulder was a job for a doctor, but as it seemed unlikely that Vo would allow Washington to take a look at it for him, Fetterman didn't see that he had any choice. Moving carefully and with infinite patience, Fetterman inched his way across the floor of the cage until he could reach his jungle jacket. He wadded up one of the sleeves and stuck it in his mouth to give himself something to bite down on and help muffle the scream of pain that he knew would come with what he must do, then worked his way to the side of the cage and grasped one of the bamboo bars with his left hand.

He was perspiring heavily now and felt faint, but he did his best to ignore both the faintness and the persistent nausea as he bent his legs and drew them up, placing his battered feet against the bamboo bars of the cage wall. He felt the shoulder with his right hand, making sure of the position of the dislocated joint, and took in several deep breaths through his nose. Then, when he was ready, he set his feet and pulled until the head of the humerus popped back into the socket of the acromial-clavicular joint. He was hardly aware of the scream when it came.

When it was over, Fetterman lay quietly on the floor of the cage, his chest heaving from the effort, the injured ribs causing him pain with each breath. But the pain was not so bad now. Not at all like the pain of the dislocation. Carefully he checked to make sure that the procedure had not impaired his circulation by pinching the nail beds of his left hand with the thumb and forefinger of his right. The capillary refill might have been just a bit slow, but that was to be expected under the circumstances. There was no numbness or tingling to indicate that he had pinched a nerve in the process of reducing the dislocation. He moved the arm slightly to check the range of movement. It still hurt, but it worked okay. Finally Fetterman turned himself onto his injured right side. It seemed to make breathing a little easier and would allow for fluid drainage from his mouth should he vomit again. Only after that did he permit himself the luxury of fainting.

14

THE JUNGLE NEAR
AN MINH

"You know, Krung," said Sully Smith as he put the finishing touches on the triple-triggered, booby-trap firing chain, "the one thing I'm kinda sorry about is that we won't be around to see this baby when she blows. If it works right, we ought to take out a whole bunch of Cong."

"Yes," agreed Krung, sharpening his M-3 combat knife. "That would be good."

The Tai sheathed the knife and unslung his M-1 carbine, slipping out the long, curved banana magazine to check the loads. He tested the spring tension of the magazine follower against his finger, hefted the magazine in his hand and decided it was about half empty. He tucked the partial magazine into a pocket of his tiger-striped jungle fatigues, removed a full magazine from one of the canteen covers on his belt that served as an ammo pouch and snapped the new magazine into place. Then he rechecked the safety.

"But me think, Sergeant Sully, that this one time even Krung believe it's best we don't hang around to wait see what happen. Think maybe best we *di di mau* back to camp. Only *dien cai dau* soldier hang around when odds twenty to one and low on ammo. We make beaucoup too much time here already now."

"I couldn't agree with you more, old friend. But first I've got just one more thing to do. The pièce de résistance. Hand me that last C-ration, will you?"

Krung did as he was asked, and Smith took the can, noting that the meal consisted of ham and lima beans, a military gastronomic delicacy best described as tasting like bits of truck tire mixed with pieces of greasy cardboard—unless you had the opportunity to heat it up. Then it tasted like warm bits of truck tire mixed with pieces of greasy cardboard.

"Beans and motherfuckers," muttered Smith, almost happily. "Offhand, I can't think of a better use to put this to." He pulled out the P-38, which was tied to the bootlace fastened to his belt, and began opening the can.

Krung stared at him aghast. "Sergeant Sully, what you do? This no time to eat. We go now."

"I know, Krung. I know," Smith answered. "I'm just making it a little easier for the VC to be sure to come the way we want them to."

Smith cut the lid most of the way around and bent it back. Then he peeled the plastic spoon out of its cellophane wrapper and stuck the spoon with some difficulty into the unpalatable mass. He set the can down just to the right of the middle of the trail and carefully poured the remaining contents of the combat meal onto the ground next to it, adding a handful of dirt to the empty cardboard carton so that it wouldn't blow away. Then he took the shiny, nickel-plated whistle on the lanyard from around his neck and hung it on a low branch overhanging the trail just above the pile of cans, envelopes and box that made up the combat meal. The main trip wire was about six feet away, with the poncho and smoke grenade bait another ten feet or so beyond that. Smith wanted to be sure that the VC saw what appeared to be the hastily abandoned remains of a meal soon after they saw the poncho. It would add urgency to their pursuit and give them plenty to think about other than trip wires. The poncho and smoke grenade might well initiate the firing chain that Smith had laid out, but he was betting on one of the trip wires to actually do the job. A pull on any of them would initiate the entire firing sequence in a timed order dependent upon which wire was tripped first. Even if the VC had somehow gotten ahead of them and came down the trail from the wrong direction, the initial couple of explosions would probably claim a few and the burp gun rig would hit them from behind.

Smith made his final check and was about to speak when Krung suddenly held up a hand and motioned for him to be quiet, cupping a hand to his ear to indicate that Smith should listen.

Smith strained his ears, at first hearing nothing, then faintly, in the distance to the southwest toward the Cambodian border, he could hear them. Helicopters. Big ones, and a lot of them from the sound of it. It sounded as if a large operation of some kind were underway, but Smith couldn't figure out what it could be. He nodded at Krung.

"Sounds like we're not the only members of the VC Hunting Club out this morning," said Smith. "I hope those guys have better luck than we did yesterday. Too bad they aren't coming our way. I wouldn't have minded a ride back to the camp or a little help. Come on. Let's get out of here."

They moved down the trail past the burp gun trap. A few yards farther they turned off the trail into the jungle. The dense foliage made the going slower, but it was safer than the trail. It would be harder for the VC to track them. Smith had decided that, if they encountered any other trails, they would follow them only as long as they were headed in the right direction. When he reasoned that they were within a klick of the camp, they would leave the trail system entirely and proceed carefully on an indirect course through the jungle. He didn't want to risk being ambushed at the last moment. As he stepped off the trail into the brush, Smith checked his watch. It had taken nearly twenty-five minutes to booby-trap the trail. The Vietcong could not be far away.

HAD SMITH ONLY KNOWN IT, the help he had wished for was not far away, either.

Acting on a hunch, Sergeant First Class Derek Kepler had persuaded Captain Gerber to let Sergeant Anderson and himself take a small reconnaissance patrol to the vicinity of An Minh while the main search effort was being conducted farther west along the Cambodian border. The nine-man patrol had spent most of the night and a good part of the morning walking to the area from the camp. Airlift support hadn't been available at the time, but Kepler had considered stealth more important than a comfortable ride.

Corporal Phung, one of the better Tai NCOs, and Specialist Shoong, a Tai medic trained by Doc McMillan, walked with them while a Tai with an M-79 grenade launcher brought up the rear. The command group was preceded by a BAR team, and a hundred meters in front of them was Private Krak, one of the best trackers in the Third Independent Tai Strike Company. Between Krak and the BAR team a seventh striker picked up the slack, checking the compass and pace.

Kepler wasn't sure what he hoped to find. The battle areas to the southwest and east of the village had been well searched the day before without finding any sign of the missing men, and the village itself had been checked and found temporarily deserted. It was a common enough occurrence in Vietnam whenever there had been a sizable fight near a small hamlet before the operation had even started.

Still, Kepler couldn't shake the feeling that this time the villagers were hiding from the Americans and the Tai and Vietnamese PF strikers from Camp A-555. The old woman had indicated that they were hiding from the Vietcong when he and Washington had been there only a few days ago for the MEDCAP visit, but Kepler was no longer sure that he believed the old woman. The men sent out to ambush the VC recruiting patrol had themselves been ambushed by a large, well-organized VC force. That couldn't have been the work of local guerrillas. It had to be the result of a Main Force VC unit, and it would have been the most improbable of coincidences for the strikers to have simultaneously blundered into the VC unit in three different widely separated places. That left only one highly unpleasant alternative to think about. They had been set up.

Kepler didn't know if the old woman had been a VC agent or had been duped by the VC. It was hard to imagine her allowing herself to be subjected to the kind of burn that the old woman had exhibited. Still, some of the Vietcong could be most fanatical in their dedication to the Front. In the final analysis it didn't matter. The Americans had been suckered and had paid a heavy price for it. Kepler felt that he'd been suckered most of all, and he didn't like the feeling.

The whole setup had seemed so perfect, such an easy way to strike a sharp blow at the VC's prestige in the region, for the A-Detachment to finish its tour with a final parting victory. It had been too perfect, too easy. Maybe that was what Gerber had sensed and why he had been opposed to the operation. But Kepler had argued in favor of it, finally persuading the captain to his point of view. Steve Kittredge and a lot of strikers had died because of him. Fetterman, Washington, Tyme and Smith were missing. The only person they'd found any evidence to suggest might have survived was Sergeant Krung, and if the VC found him, he wouldn't survive for long.

Kepler couldn't shake the feeling that it was all his fault. He'd made his recommendation to Gerber based on what appeared to be good information, but he'd underestimated the cunning of the enemy. It was a bitter pill to swallow.

A lot of the strikers had wanted to put An Minh to the torch yesterday afternoon, especially after they'd found the bodies of the men that the Vietcong had so obviously executed after they were wounded. For the Tai, the philosophy of the war was a simple one. Let me win your hearts and minds, or I'll burn your damned huts down. And why not? The Vietnamese had been doing it to them and all the other ethnic minorities for years. As little as a year ago, VNAF pilots had had standing orders to drop any unexpended ordnance on Montagnard villages.

Kepler had sympathized with the Tai. But there was no proof that the villagers had betrayed them. Even if some of them had, what good would burning down the villagers' homes do? Prove that the Americans and Tai who worked with the ARVN were no better than the Vietcong? It would have been playing right into Charlie's hands. The VC would have pointed a finger at the warmongering Americans and their hired Tai killers, and the leftist liberal press would have had a field day hyping it up back in the World.

Yet Kepler had felt that there still might be something to learn at the deserted village, some evidence or clue as to what had gone wrong and what had happened to the other members of the team. The villagers had a way of knowing when the Vietcong were around, and the villagers were making themselves conspicuously absent. Kepler knew that he was reaching but it was just possible that if the villagers were staying away, the Vietcong might still be around. And if the VC were still around, it might be possible to capture one of them and pump the prisoner for information about Fetterman and the others. Kepler wanted some

answers. He knew that, if they were lucky enough to grab a human intelligence resource, his field interrogation technique might
leave a lot to be desired as far as the Geneva Convention was concerned, but that was just going to be tough. He didn't have time
to fool around. Wherever they were, time had to be running out
for the others.

As HE CREPT CAUTIOUSLY along the trail with agonizing slowness, keeping first to one side, then the other, Private Lim of the
National Liberation Front could feel the fear twisting his intestines like a bad case of dysentery. The sweat ran down his face and
sides in rivulets, and the ancient, heavy Mosin-Nagant bolt action rifle felt slippery in his hands. For a moment he considered
that it might have been better to have been killed with the others
than to know such fear, but he immediately dismissed such an
idea. As bad as his situation might now be, there was, he knew,
no such thing as a fate worse than death. Death was the final ul-
timate insult to the body. Once you were dead, there was no means
of escape, no more *nouc-mam* or rare letters from your family.
There was only the long silence of the grave.

Lim considered ideas such as heroism and bravery foolhardy
notions that had little practical application in life and were best
left to the philosophizing of political cadres. What good did it do
to say that a man was brave when he was dead and there was no
one to earn a living and build a house for his family? Bravery did
not feed or shelter the family, and the man who was dead was beyond caring whether others thought him brave or a coward. Was
it not better to be a live coward than a dead hero? Evidently Lieutenant Lap did not think so. Or perhaps he did in his own way.
After all, had he not sent Lim to walk the point while he stayed
back, safe with the main group?

Lim had been a Vietcong soldier for a little more than a year.
In all that time he had never seen anyone die until today. He had
seen people who were dead, of course—casualties brought back
to their camp in Cambodia following raids on the ARVN and their
American advisors. He had seen the bodies of the dead police-
men following the raid on the South Vietnamese Nation Police
outpost at Tan Chau, a raid in which he had participated and actually fired his rifle a few times, although not actually *at* any-

body. But he had never really seen anybody *being* killed until the Tai striker had suddenly materialized out of the jungle growth alongside the trail and killed Chi and Rho with his big knife. Lim had stood momentarily frozen at the horror of witnessing death at such close proximity as Rho died before his very eyes. Only a low grunt had escaped his friend's mouth. Then Lim had run away, moaning in terror.

Lim would have liked to have helped his fallen comrades. But in that one brief moment he had discovered an inner truth about himself. He lacked the emotional strength, the inner resolve, to take another man's life. There are some people who simply cannot bring themselves to take another's life, and Lim was one of them. He did not know if that made him a better human being than someone who could kill or a worse one, but he did know that it was a poor survival trait for a soldier to possess. He wished that Lieutenant Lap could understand that as he himself did.

There was a hissing sound behind him, and Lim spun about, his heart pounding in his chest, nearly stumbling and falling in the process.

A short distance back along the trail, he could see Sergeant Nguyen, annoyingly motioning for him to continue. With the utmost reluctance Lim moved along the trail to the accompaniment of Sergeant Nguyen's frantic gestures for him to hurry up. Nguyen's vigorous exercising of his hands and arms were, for the most part, lost on Lim, who couldn't see much sense in hurrying to catch up to someone who was likely to kill you.

It was near midday and insufferably hot, as were all middays in the delta region. Even the animals had enough sense to rest during that time of the day. The only things foolish enough to be moving around in such heat were Americans and Tai and Lieutenant Lap, who was chasing them with his patrol. Perhaps Lap dreamed of promotion or of a decoration. Hero of the Revolution Second Class or whatever it was that the big shots in Hanoi handed out these days. Or perhaps he merely feared the wrath of Major Vo should they fail in their mission to capture the American.

Whatever his reasoning, it made little difference to Private Lim as he walked the point for the patrol. If he found the enemy, it seemed reasonable to suspect that he would die as his friends had, and if he did not, it also seemed reasonable to suspect that Lieutenant Lap would shoot him for cowardice and insubordination. The intricacies of the dilemma would have appealed to Lim's sense of humor had he not been the object of the dilemma.

Ahead the trail broadened, and Lim approached the wider pathway as though it were the most dangerous piece of real estate in all of Indochina. The sound of a startled bird suddenly taking flight with a great flapping of wings caused him to feel as though an invisible hand had closed about his heart and was squeezing it within his chest. When that was followed by a loud grunt and the sound of some animal, probably a wild boar, crashing through the underbrush after being disturbed by the bird, Lim nearly fell to his knees as his legs became rubbery and unwilling to support his weight. And then he saw it.

As his gaze swept along the trees lining one side of the trail, then darted across to sweep down the other side, a glint of light caught his eye. It was there for only a fraction of a second and then gone, but it brought his focus back to the center of the trail, and there, a few dozen meters ahead of him in the middle of the pathway, lay a familiar bundle. A few yards beyond it was a pile of something. It might have been cans or it might have been grenades, that and some kind of box. And above it, again, that brief glinting flash of sunlight.

Lim squatted on his haunches along the side of the trail, and slowly brought his rifle across his knees and would go no further. He waited for what seemed an eternity, feeling the sweat roll down his body. His bladder was full and felt as though it might burst at any second, but still he did not move. At long last he heard the voice of Sergeant Nguyen behind him.

"Private Lim! What do you think you are doing? You are holding up the entire patrol."

Lim inclined his head toward the objects lying in the trail by way of answer. His mouth was too dry to speak.

Nguyen followed Lim's gaze until he, too, saw the objects. He immediately brought his rifle into the ready position and scanned the sides of the trail for any sign of a trap.

"What is the problem, Sergeant?" asked Lap, coming forward.

"There is something on the trail, Comrade Lieutenant," Nguyen answered.

"I can see that, Sergeant. What is it?"

"I do not know, sir," replied Nguyen. "It appears to be a bundle of some sort."

"It is death," whispered Lim softly.

"What? What did you say, Private?" Lap demanded.

"It is death," Lim repeated. "All those who touch it die. I have touched it, and now it has come back to tell me that it is my time to die."

Lap stared down the trail at the object.

"What utter nonsense. It's nothing more than a poncho. It must be the one you spoke of, the one belonging to the American. Perhaps you will yet redeem yourself if you desist from making these fatalistic statements, Private Lim. Go and fetch it. I want to examine it."

"No," said Lim softly.

"Are you refusing to obey my order?" Lap spoke sternly. "Go and bring it to me at once!"

"No, sir," said Lim. "I will not go and fetch it."

"Bah! You cowardly fool. Sergeant Nguyen, go and bring me that poncho."

Nguyen looked dubious. "Comrade Lieutenant, do you think it wise? Perhaps it is a trap of some sort."

Lap exploded. He had already been irritated by Lim's continual delays in pursuing the enemy, and he was in no mood to put up with such nonsense now, further delaying them while the enemy slipped through their fingers.

"Am I surrounded by incompetents? Are all my men afraid of just one American and one filthy little Tai? I shall inspect it myself. Sergeant Nguyen, bring the men. Now, Sergeant."

"Yes, sir," said Nguyen reluctantly.

Lap strode boldly up the trail, his eyes fixed on the poncho, his gait almost swaggering. He knelt next to the bundle and stared at it curiously, tilting his head first one way, then another, to view it from different angles. It was a rolled-up poncho, all right, although a bit thick as though there might be something else rolled up inside it. A blanket perhaps. Lap examined it carefully. He could see no wires or strings that might lead to a booby trap. Gingerly he lifted the poncho and turned it in his hands. There was writing on it. The strange American name that Lim had spoken of. He read it carefully. These Americans had very long names apparently. There was even more to it than what Lim had sketched.

Lap stood, holding the poncho in his hand and waving the men forward to show that there was no danger. It was at that moment that a brief flash of light caught his eye. He turned and looked up the trail, seeing the items in the middle of it for the first time. Lap recognized the containers as American food. He had seen such items before, once in the field and once for sale on the black market in Saigon. If they had disturbed the enemy at his meal in such a fashion that he had not had time to take it with him, then they could not be far behind, he reasoned.

Lap started forward, and the glint of light caught his eye once more. He could almost smell the success. They had surprised the enemy at his meal, and now they would capture him, but they must hurry before the enemy could escape. He called to the men, urging them forward, then strained his eyes to see what had caused the flash. There! Something was hanging over the trail, a little bit to one side. As he approached it, Lap could see that it was a small metallic object hung on a cord that allowed it to swing freely beneath an overhanging branch. As he neared it, he stretched out his hand to touch it, allowing his grip on the poncho to relax. The poncho slipped in his fingers, and he partially dropped it, allowing it to unroll. As it did so, a small, olive drab can-shaped object dropped out of it and onto the trail next to him. Lap heard the *spoing* as the safety lever flew from the grenade.

"Cover!" yelled Lap.

He attempted to take one quick step away from the grenade before throwing himself to the ground. As he moved, he felt his foot snag on the thin, almost invisible wire strung an inch-and-a-half above the trail. Then his world exploded.

A huge geyser of dirt and stones erupted before Lap's face, and almost simultaneously a second explosion rippled back down the trail beneath him, hurling him into the air and setting off a second shattering explosion in the midst of the lead squad, flinging men and pieces of men in all directions. As the second squad dived for cover in the ditches alongside the trail, two more explosions filled the air with whining steel as the claymores were tripped, their hundreds of steel balls cutting men off at the knees, the waist, the neck, and giving the more distant Vietcong a fatal case of measles.

For just a moment all was quiet. Then, up ahead on the trail, a machine gun opened fire, spraying a long stream of bullets down the packed dirt pathway. The men in the fourth squad panicked and ran back in the direction they had come from, just in time to be met with a barrage of rocks propelled at supersonic speed by the third charge of plastic explosive.

The men from the third squad, caught between the explosions, took the only route of escape left open to them—down the side trail. Their squad leader died screaming in the white-hot glare of Smith's WP grenade as burning bits of phosphorus inexorably ate through the skin and muscle tissue of his face, shoulders, arms and chest, searching for the bone beneath. Those not killed or injured with the leader ran back toward the main trail and were shredded by the two fragmentation grenades dropping abruptly in their midst.

For less than a minute absolute pandemonium reigned in the jungle. The air was filled with explosions, shouts, the yelling of contradictory commands, screams of pain and shrieks of unreasoning terror. The cough and clatter of several hundred rounds of ammunition fired blindly at an unseen, unpresent enemy overshadowed the crashing flight of panicked jungle animals, drowning out even the startled screech of the ubiquitous monkeys. Then, as suddenly as the cacophony had begun, there came perhaps thirty seconds of absolute silence.

Private Lim picked himself up from the dirt of the trail, where he had been knocked by the flying body of a fellow VC soldier, and stared in numb silence at the incredible scene of mass carnage before him. Scattered over nearly a hundred meters of jungle terrain were dead bodies, dying bodies and bits and pieces of bodies. Hanging like a pall over this vast open-air charnel house was a sickly shroud of yellow smoke.

For a moment Lim thought that he had been struck deaf, so utterly complete was the silence. A sound even more dreadful began. The cries and moans of the wounded rose from the jungle floor in a climbing, tortured wail that crescendoed until it became a shrieking howl, like the demented cry of some lost dweller of the spirit world. Lim clapped his hands over his ears to shut out the sound, but it was useless. When the noise finally subsided to a sonorous lamentation, he dropped his hands. The left one came away red and wet. Part of his left ear was missing.

Lim shuffled through the maze of broken, twisted humanity, his expression the blank, unseeing countenance of a zombie, yet he saw. Here was a man whose life blood pumped out onto the ground from a severed leg, his eyes glassy, unfocused. Beside him lay a man with no face, yet the rising and falling of his chest indicated that he was not quite dead. Over there was a man with a hole in his side the size of a sun helmet, his intestines strung out for half a dozen meters among the bushes lining the side of the trail. He was sitting upright with his back against a tree, and as he looked at Lim, he smiled and winked incongruously before he died. Hands, fingers, sneakers with feet still in them that were no longer attached to a body, were strewn over the ground. A torn and shredded pair of lungs was draped limply over a tree branch, and a human heart lay in the dusty trail beneath them, still beating with a curiously quivering rhythm. Nearby lay the unmoving figure of a young soldier, the jagged end of a shattered femur driven through his throat by the force of one of the explosions.

Lim did not venture down the side trail, but he did cast a look down it. He could see the blood-soaked, sodden uniforms of several men, a few of them still moving. Beyond them were the still smoking bodies of the men who had been hit by the white phosphorus grenade. One of them screamed as the phosphorus continued to burn inside his body.

Lim turned his attention back to the main trail. A few of the men were sitting up now. Some were trying to help the more seriously wounded while others tried with equal futility to stanch the flow of blood from mangled stumps that had once been their own arms or legs.

As Lim walked among the bodies and the wounded, he found the still form of Sergeant Nguyen. The Sergeant's face was set in an expression of outrage and accusation. Lim wondered who he had been angry at during the moment of death. There was a hole the size of a beer can in the center of his chest and an exit wound the size of a melon in his back.

Lim searched through the carnage for several minutes before locating the remains of Lieutenant Lap. It was not an easy process. In the end he succeeded in matching the lieutenant's severed head with his crushed and mutilated body on the evidence of his leather pistol belt. Lying next to it were the tattered remains of a familiar object. The largest piece of it was about a forearm's length square and contained the strange writing that Lim had seen earlier. He stared down at the odd words, wondering once again at the profoundness of their meaning. MANUFACTURED BY THE IRVING AIR CHUTE COMPANY, INC. CEDAR RAPIDS, IA. Above that, in a slightly different lettering, was F.G.S. Smith, S/Sgt., R.A. 438/02/4551.

Lim did not know what the words meant, but he understood their meaning and marveled at the complexity of the American language.

"It is a very long name for death," he said.

It was only then that he noticed that, at some time during the ambush, he had pissed in his pants.

SMITH AND KRUNG HAD no trouble hearing the explosions when they occurred, even though they were over a kilometer away. The jungle muffled the dull crump of the grenades, but there was nothing dull about the sound of the C-4 or the det cord.

"I think we just bagged ourselves a few Cong," Smith gasped to Krung as he pulled up panting beside the Tai at the entrance to a side trail.

Krung, who wasn't even breathing hard after their three-quarter-mile run, smiled brightly at Smith and gave a quick nod of his head. "Cong blow up real good, Sergeant Sully."

Smith nodded in reply. "Real good," he agreed. "How come we stopped?"

Krung indicated the side trail.

"This come out near An Minh. We take, mean we have to cross couple hundred meters elephant grass near backside of village, but save maybe two, maybe three klicks we get back Camp A-Triple Nickel. What you think? Okay fine?"

Smith considered the trail. It would be a dangerous crossing. The swaying of the high, tough grass was sure to give their position away to any observer. Further, the trail that Krung had indicated wasn't on Smith's map, but then the map had been made by the French over twenty years ago. It might be worth the risk if it would save them a couple of hours getting back to camp.

"Are you sure this comes out near An Minh?" Smith asked dubiously.

Krung looked hurt. "Sergeant Sully, Krung no give bum steer. This the straight poop. No shit."

"Okay," said Smith with a shrug of his shoulders. "We'll give it a try. Only I'll take the point this time. The pace you're setting is killing me."

The Tai sergeant looked puzzled. "Krung no hurt Sergeant Sully. You okay fine? Krung not understand."

"It's an expression, Krung, that's all. It means you're going too fast for me. I can't keep up with you so I want to take the point for a while. You cover our tail, okay?"

Krung nodded and they moved down the trail. Forty-five minutes later they came to the edge of the tree line. Spread out before them, at the foot of a small, gentle slope, was a veritable sea of elephant grass. In the distance off to the right, Smith could see a cluster of huts and part of a mud and bamboo fence. To the left of the fence were a series of paddy field dikes.

"An Minh," said Krung authoritatively.

It didn't look like An Minh to Smith, but then he'd only seen the village once before and that had been from the other side.

"We cross that way," said Krung, pointing to their left. "Beyond second paddy dike is shallow canal, and we follow to trees way over there. Trail start again there, head toward camp."

Smith got out his compass and shot an azimuth on the distant paddy dike. He estimated the distance to be just under three hundred yards.

"Okay," he decided. "We'll crawl it. We don't want to stir the grass up any more than absolutely necessary. And that way at least we'll be low if we run into trouble."

They slipped down the hill and into the grass, Smith in the lead, Krung barely in sight to his left rear. They were about halfway through the grass when Smith thought he heard a rustling ahead of them. He held up his hand. Krung saw it and both men froze.

For a moment there was nothing, and then it came again, directly ahead of them. Smith motioned Krung farther to the left, but the sound shifted with them, getting slightly closer as it did so. Disgustedly Smith tried to flank whatever or whoever was ahead of them to the right, but again the sound shifted to match their direction. It had to be VC. Nothing else made any sense.

Slipping his last fragmentation grenade from his web gear, Smith showed it to Krung, then pulled the pin and held the grenade ready, the spoon trapped in the web of his hand. He was just about to throw it when he heard a voice not three feet away from him.

"You know, Sully, Derek's gonna be awfully pissed if you throw that thing at him."

The nearness of the voice startled Smith so much that he nearly dropped the grenade.

"Anderson? Cat, is that you?" Smith was incredulous.

"Unless there's two of me and I'm somewhere else."

"Where the hell are you? What the hell are you guys doing out here?"

Anderson pushed forward out of the grass slightly to Smith's right. "Right here. Sorry about sneaking up on you. We been stalking you for the last twenty minutes. Thought you were VC. Don't you think you ought to put a pin back in that thing before somebody gets hurt?" he added, nodding toward the grenade.

Smith glanced down at the grenade absently as though he had forgotten about it. He reinserted the pin, then grinned sheepishly at Anderson.

"Christ, Cat, it sure is good to see your ugly face again. Just what the fuck *are* you guys doing out here?"

"That should be obvious, even to a dumb bastard like you, Sully," said Kepler, pushing through the grass directly in front of him. "We came to take you guys home."

"Well, it's about fucking time you got here," said Smith, aiming a good-natured jab at Kepler's shoulder.

"Fucking-A time," agreed Krung. "We out here fighting whole fucking war by selfs."

"Is that Krung with you? How many men have you got?"

"That's it, Derek," answered Smith solemnly. "We're all there is. Kittredge and the others didn't make it."

Kepler nodded. "I know about Steve. We checked the hillock out in the swamp. Sorry, Sully. Have you heard anything from Fetterman's bunch?"

"Fetterman? Is he missing?"

"Afraid so," said Kepler. "Washington and Tyme with him. The captain got on to Colonel Bates, who got on to General Hull, and the two of them have got about a battalion out looking for all you guys along the border."

"Along the border? Why would they look along the... Oh! You figure maybe they've been..." Smith didn't want to say it.

"Captured. I'm afraid it kind of looks that way. Captain Gerber figured the VC would take them across the border into Cambodia as soon as possible."

"Oh, man. They are really in some deep shit."

"You don't know the half of it. Saigon shot three VC suspects up in Da Nang the other night, and Radio Hanoi had been promising to shoot a couple of American P.O.W.s if Saigon followed through with the executions. I guess I don't need to tell you Green Berets aren't likely to be invited in for tea and crumpets by the VC. They shot three Victor Charlies in Da Nang, and we're missing three Green Berets."

"You don't have to draw me a picture." Smith frowned at Kepler for a moment. "Say, do you suppose we could get the hell out of this Goddamned grass before Charlie comes along and puts the bag on the rest of us?"

"I thought you'd never ask." Kepler grinned, trying to break the tension. "Stick with me, old buddy, and we'll have you home in about twenty minutes."

"Twenty minutes," Smith snorted. "Unless I've seriously miscounted, we're still several klicks from camp. You got a pair of seven league boots in your backpack?"

"Nope, but Anderson does. Show him your boots, Cat."

Anderson produced the handset of an PRC-25 radio and keyed the transmit button on the handset.

"Zulu Six, this is Zulu Two, over."

"Zulu Six," the radio crackled faintly with Gerber's reply.

"The recon has born fruit. We have located the mad bomber and his trophy-collecting friend. They say their feet hurt. Can you send us a ride, over?"

There was a long pause, then the radio crackled again.

"Roger Two, the ride is on the way. Give coordinates. Over."

Kepler looked at Smith and grinned. "See. Seven league boots."

Twenty minutes later they were all laughing and downing Carling Black Label beer in the team house.

15

VC P.O.W. CAMP
NEAR HONG NGU

Fetterman could have used a beer, but he would have happily settled for a glass of water. In fact, a gallon of water would have been just about right, he decided. Two or three gallons and a couple of hamburgers would have been even better. Even ham and lima beans was beginning to sound good to him.

Anything sounded better than the occasional screams coming from the direction of Vo's hootch. By Fetterman's reckoning, which could have been off by a couple of hours or more due to his lapses of consciousness, Major Vo had been entertaining Washington since around 1500. It didn't sound as though Vo's new guest was enjoying the entertainment much.

It was oppressively hot in the cage. The hottest afternoon that Fetterman could remember experiencing in the Land of Eternal Summer, but then, in Vietnam, you swore that each afternoon was the hottest that you could remember. This one was like being in an oven. It was too hot even for the mosquitoes, who had abated their banquet, except for a few dozen grimly determined diners still droning languidly about his head. Fetterman wondered idly how many thousands of mosquitoes it would take to make a meal. There'd be enough of them after the sun went down if he could figure out a way to catch them.

Another scream brought Fetterman's mind back to Washington. It didn't have the same rhythmic quality to it as the beating that Fetterman had taken this morning. Was it only this morning? But whatever they were doing to him, it must have been pretty rough to get that kind of noise out of the big, ex-junior college football tackle. Washington was known as a man of few words, a man who entertained the striker's kids around Camp A-555 by putting out candle flames with the palm of his hand. He had once walked five miles on a broken leg without mentioning it to anybody. Then, on his return to camp, he had strolled calmly down to the infirmary and said to McMillan, "Hey, Doc. Take an X ray of this thing, will ya? I think I busted the distal end of my fibula." He had.

Fetterman tested his relocated shoulder joint gingerly. It still hurt but then so did almost everything else. It worked and that was all that mattered.

He tried to talk to Tyme again but could get only a moan or two and a bit of incoherent babbling out of the young soldier. After fifteen minutes, he gave up trying.

Then there was nothing to do but lie on the floor of the cage and wait for nightfall, moving as little as possible to try to conserve whatever body fluids that he might have left. Everything would depend on what kind of security arrangements the VC made at dusk. If they decided to hang a lantern over his cage and place a guard outside the door, that would be the end of it. But Fetterman didn't think that they'd do that. There'd been a lot of air traffic in the area during the day, most of it a bit to the south of the prison camp, and a light in the jungle at night stuck out like a wart on the end of a beauty queen's nose. Even with all the tree cover, Fetterman didn't think that they'd risk giving away the location of the camp like that. Not this close to the Special Forces camp and not this soon after the capture. Captain Gerber would have mobilized some kind of search party, and Vo wouldn't want to risk being deprived of his entertainment so soon. Not while he was enjoying himself. It wasn't as if the prisoners might actually be rescued, Fetterman knew. It was simply that Vo would execute them if there was any danger of a rescue attempt being successful. It wouldn't do to leave behind prisoners who could testify that they were tortured by the Vietcong.

Washington screamed again.

Fetterman lay listening to the scream, feeling a cold rage growing inside him. It wasn't hatred. Hatred was a hot, violent, unreasoning emotion. This one could be better described as a thirst for revenge.

"Some people in this world simply need to be killed," Fetterman muttered to himself. "And two of them are in this camp. Every time we've gotten our tails twisted in the last year, that Chinese bastard has been behind it, and Vo is a psychopathic sadist. I don't know exactly how I'm going to do it, but I'm going to get out of this hellhole, and when I do, I'm going to come back and kill both of those mothers."

For the rest of the day, Fetterman lay quietly, conserving his strength and developing various contingency plans. He still had a few tricks up his sleeve. Literally. His situation might be far from ideal, but he wasn't beaten yet. Not by a long shot.

At midnight he made his move.

It was a beautiful morning when Vo awakened and pushed aside the mosquito netting over his sleeping platform. At least it was as beautiful as any morning can be in the Delta. There was a faint breeze coming through the open window of the hut, and while it was not exactly cool, neither did it carry with it the stifling heat that would come later in the day.

Vo rose and took his shirt and trousers from the back of the lashed bamboo chair, slipping them on and buckling his Sam Browne pistol belt and holster about his waist before pulling on his boots. Then he walked over to a corner of the hut and fired up the tiny single-burner kerosene stove, putting the kettle on to make tea.

Looking through the window, Vo could see that it had only just begun to get light. He decided that he would go for a short walk through the camp while he waited for the water to boil, perhaps check on his guests and see if they were resting comfortably this morning.

Vo chuckled to himself at the thought of that. Resting comfortably. Soon they would rest in peace. But not just yet. Not for a week or two. Not until he had a few new guests to take their place. After that they could join the other two Americans, Versace and Roraback, who had been brought in three nights ago.

The PLA advisor had not been pleased with that development. He had argued that their presence here jeopardized the security of the operation in progress against Camp A-555, but the orders had come from Hanoi, and there was nothing that he could do about it.

Vo had agreed with him that it was a stupid thing to do, but then Hanoi often ordered stupid things to be done. So what if it would have been simpler to shoot them at the camps where they had been held? They had provided Vo with two days of entertainment before the arrival of the other three Americans. If Hanoi wanted Vo to shoot them, that was fine with him. He would have preferred a slower means of execution, but perhaps if the firing squad was careful, the two might not die at once. And they had been most entertaining while they had been Vo's guests.

The order had come from Hanoi last night: proceed with the executions at the date and time specified. At ten o'clock this morning Versace and Roraback were to be shot.

As Vo was leaving the hut, he met the camp's duty radio operator coming up the steps.

"Good morning, Major Vo. I have received an urgent signal for you from Hanoi," the man said, handing over a small scrap of paper. "Will there be any reply?"

"Permit me to read it first, Corporal. Then I will be able to tell you whether or not there will be any reply."

"Yes, sir. I'm sorry, sir."

Vo unfolded the scrap of paper and read the message with a combination of disbelief and anger. It instructed him to delay the executions until the morning of the 26th of September and at that time to execute all prisoners under his control.

"Have you read this message, Corporal?"

"Yes. Of course, Major Vo. I received it and copied it down myself."

"Has anyone else seen this?"

"No, sir."

"Good. Did you acknowledge receipt of it?"

"Yes, Major Vo. That is standard procedure."

"That is not so good. Did you repeat the message back?"

"No, sir. That was not requested."

"Excellent. Now listen to me. This message was garbled in transmission. Further, I was in the field at the time and never received it. Do you understand?"

The duty radio operator looked extremely puzzled. "No, Major Vo, I do not understand. The message seems perfectly clear to me, and you are standing right here."

"You do not understand because you are not meant to understand. This message does not say what it appears to say. It is a special code intended only for me. Now do you understand?"

"No, sir. I mean, yes, sir." The doubtful expression on the corporal's face made it plain that he, in fact, did not understand.

Vo tried again. "This is a special code which only I know. It informs me that the executions of the two Americans will proceed as planned. The others will be retained for a time until we have completed the questioning. It was sent to me in code because we have a traitor in our midst who would thwart our plans if he knew what they really were."

"If you say so, Major Vo."

"I do say so, Corporal. And I further say that, if you mention one word of our conversation or say anything about this message to anyone, you may very well be joining the Americans before the firing squad as a traitor to the Front. Now do you understand?"

The corporal understood that all right. "Yes, sir!" he replied crisply.

"Very well, Sergeant. Thank you. You may carry on."

"Sergeant? No, sir. I'm a—"

"I said you may carry on, Sergeant. Thank you, that will be all."

"Thank *you*, Major Vo."

The duty radio operator hurried away to ponder the meaning of his new promotion.

Vo stood on the porch until the man had disappeared from sight. Then he took a Zippo lighter from his pocket and put the flame to a corner of the paper. When the fire had burned almost to his fingertips, he dropped the paper to the ground. After the fire had burned itself out, he crushed the ashes beneath his boot and watched them blow away on the faint morning breeze.

It was the first order of the Front that Vo had disobeyed. At least, it was the first order of any significance, and if it was found out, the consequences would be most severe. Yet Vo had taken the risk because he was unwilling to let Hanoi deprive him of his entertainment. What difference could it make if the Americans were executed tomorrow or a week from tomorrow after he had had his fun with them? It was unfair of Hanoi to take away his entertainment in this fashion, and he would not permit it. He would execute the two prisoners according to his original orders, but he would not execute the three new ones until he had completed his entertainment. The two prisoners who had been transferred to his control were burned-out shells of men who had already served their purpose, and the Front could do with them as it pleased. But not the three new ones. They were his guests, his prisoners, and he would do with them as he pleased and to hell with the Front. The Front could have them when he was done with them, not before.

I think I shall start with this small older one, this Master Sergeant Fetterman, again today, thought Vo. I must not overtax any of them right away. The black soldier will need a chance to regain his strength before I have him entertain me again, but he is big and strong. I think that perhaps by this evening he will be sufficiently recovered. And this other one, the wounded one, he is not yet strong enough. Perhaps I will even have to feed him. We must not let him expire before he has amused us. So it must be this little man with the balding head. He interests me anyway. He always says that he is willing to talk, yet it does not seem to arise out of fear. He withstands pain even better than the big black. I wonder what his game could be? Well, this morning perhaps I shall ask him why he pretends to be willing to cooperate with us. That will be very good because it is not the sort of question that he will be expecting.

Vo walked down the trail to the cages and inspected the prisoners. He came first to Versace and Roraback. They were asleep or unconscious. It did not matter. By lunchtime they would be dead. Then he walked the trail in the opposite direction. The black soldier did not look well this morning. The burns covering his thighs and groin had a nasty, oozing, pustulant appearance, and his burned eyelids were nearly swollen shut. And the young wounded soldier was a pale, ashen, gray color. Vo might have thought him dead already if it were not for the erratic rise and fall of his chest.

Vo turned away from Tyme's cage and walked toward Fetterman's. He stared down at the small figure, wondering if today he should try the field telephone connected to the genitals or the bamboo shoots beneath the finger and toenails. He stared again. This could not be. The body in the cell, although turned face-down and partially covered with the many pocketed, tiger-striped jungle jacket, was a Vietnamese! Master Sergeant Anthony B. Fetterman had vanished!

A cry of anger arose in Vo's throat, climbing in pitch and volume until it became an animalistic howl of fury that awakened the rest of the camp and sent men running to the cage to see what the trouble was. A roll call revealed three men dead.

One of the inner perimeter guards had a dark discoloration about the eyes, a broken, swollen nose and a thin trickle of frothy pink fluid, now mostly dried, leaking out of one ear. A member of the outer perimeter patrol had had his throat expertly cut, severing both carotid arteries, the jugular vein and the trachea. They had to unwire the door to the cage to check the body of the third man. Except for a large purplish bruise on his throat, there was not a mark on him.

A check of the possessions of the dead men revealed that all three had been stripped of their M-1 carbines and ammunition, although two of the weapons were later found, their barrels bent at ninety-degree angles, bolts and firing pins, springs and operating rods missing.

Also missing from the guards' barracks was an M-14 rifle that had been captured from one of the prisoners, three magazines of ammunition and a couple of grenades.

Screaming at the top of his lungs, Vo pushed, prodded and kicked his men into action until he had dispatched nearly two hundred soldiers into the bush to look for the escaped prisoner. Only then did he turn to glare at the PLA advisor.

"Well, Comrade Major," Vo demanded of the Chinese officer, "what is your assessment of the situation?"

The Chinese officer gave Vo a thin smile and very calmly lighted a cigarette, his first of many for the day.

"It is my assessment, Major Vo," said the PLA advisor, "that Master Sergeant Fetterman is an extremely resourceful man. I have the feeling that I have met him before. I also have the feeling that eventually he will come back, although not, I think, in the company of your men."

"And your advice in this matter, Comrade Advisor?" asked Vo sourly.

The Chinese officer puffed languidly on his cigarette.

"That's easy," he said. "Pray to Buddha that he does not."

16

SPECIAL FORCES CAMP
A-555

Captain MacKenzie K. Gerber sat in the folding steel chair behind his desk and rubbed at his puffy, reddened eyes. A heavy china mug of steaming black coffee rested between his elbows, and his head, leaning forward, rested between his hands. The skin of his face looked pale and drawn, and the lines around his eyes and mouth were deeply etched.

For the third straight night Gerber had not slept. Despite the minor celebration caused by the return of Sully Smith and Krung, he still had too much on his mind to sleep despite his exhaustion.

Fetterman, Tyme and Washington were still in the field and unaccounted for.

Steve Kittredge was gone. What could be found of his remains had been flown away in an olive drab body bag in the back of the mail run Huey. Gerber hadn't yet been able to bring himself to sort through Kittredge's belongings and package them up for shipment back to his family or to write the requisite letter expressing his sorrow at their great loss. He didn't know if that would mean much to Kittredge's young wife and daughter. He hoped that the Medal of Honor would. Gerber had written the recommendation last night, and General Hull had already affixed his signature to second it.

Sully Smith had been recommended for the Silver Star. He had probably done as much, if not more than Kittredge, to deserve the MOH, but regulations required that a recommendation for the Congressional medal be accompanied by a witness statement of the action, and Smith didn't have a witness. His witness had called artillery fire in on himself as he was being overrun. In the infinite wisdom of the U.S. Army, it was easier to get a Medal of Honor for a dead hero than it was for a live one.

And then there was the problem of what to do about Robin Morrow. Robin had made it very apparent that she had fallen in love with Gerber, but until yesterday Gerber still nurtured feelings for her sister Karen, despite Karen's final rejection of him and her return to the States. Hell, maybe he was in love with both women. Logically it should have been an easy choice to make. Robin was here, loved him, and he loved her. Karen had gone home to her husband. It was enough to drive a man crazy, he thought.

"Good morning, Mack," said Hull, coming into Gerber's hootch. "You look like shit this morning. Get any sleep?"

Gerber gave him a lopsided smile and pushed himself up from the desk with some difficulty, listening to the joints in his knees crack. He felt like an arthritic septuagenarian. "No," he answered truthfully. "Did you?"

"Not as much as I like," Hull confessed, "but enough to get by on. What's the game plan for today? We going to go over the same ground again?"

"I thought we'd try a bit farther to the southwest, today, General. Check the area between Nha Bang and Chau Phu."

"You think the VC could have taken them that far by now?"

Gerber shrugged. "Who knows? I just don't know what else to try. They could have gone northeast toward Moc Hoa and crossed near Kompong Rau, or due north toward Svay Rieng. If they did either of those, they're probably already in Cambodia by now. You got any other ideas? I'm open to suggestions."

"Nothing that sounds any better, I'm afraid. Choppers should be here in about twenty minutes. You had breakfeast yet?"

Gerber shook his head. "Didn't feel like eating."

"Well, you're going to. Come on along and I'll buy you some pancakes. Sergeant Kepler says they're about as light and fluffy as a manhole cover this morning, but we got sausage from the World via Saigon to go with them."

"Excuse me, Captain, General," said Bocker, poking his head in the doorway. "Fire control tower reports green smoke south-west of camp. Thought you'd want to know."

"I don't understand," Gerber said. "We don't have anybody still in the field, do we? Outposts should have come in just after dawn."

"That's right, sir. LPs came in just after first light. We don't have anybody in the field. Except," he added, "Fetterman's bunch. They're still in the field, sir."

Gerber grabbed his helmet and snatched up his rifle. "Keep the men on the wall, Galvin, but have them stand down from their weapons. We don't want some nervous striker firing off a round and everybody letting loose. General Hull and I will be at the south gate immediately."

"Yes, sir." Bocker vanished.

"Do you suppose it's possible?" asked Hull, slinging his carbine.

"Possible? Hell, yes, it's possible. Where Fetterman is concerned, anything is possible. Let's go."

Bromhead met them at the gate, binoculars hung around his neck.

"What's happening? Can you see them yet?" asked Hull.

"Nothing yet, sir. So far just the smoke." He trained his binoculars on the distant tree line. "Movement to the right, Captain. Black pajamas. Must be a Vietcong."

"Why would he show himself? What's he doing?" Gerber demanded.

"It looks like he's surrendering, sir. He's taking off his shirt and waving it over his head, and now he's holding something out to one side in his left hand. Looks like a couple of rifles."

"All right," said Gerber. "Everybody just stand easy till we find out what this is all about. Don't anybody shoot."

"He's walking toward the camp," reported Bromhead. "Now he's waving something white. He seems to be having difficulty.... He just fell. Now he's getting back up and waving the white thing again. He keeps stumbling around. It looks like he's hurt or something. Now he's... Good Christ, it's Fetterman!"

"What? Are you sure?"

"Here, Captain. Take a look for yourself. I'd know that chrome dome of his anywhere."

Gerber snatched the field glasses and stared hard through the eyepieces. "All right. Stand down! Everybody get off the wall! Johnny, get a squad together and go get him. Where's Doc McMillan?"

"Right here," said a soft voice behind him. "Saw all the excitement and thought I'd come have a look. I brought my bag."

"All right, Doc, you go with them." Gerber glanced around. "Goddamn it! NCOs, get your people down off that fucking wall. Now!"

"WELL, DOC, HOW IS HE?" asked Gerber.

"Surprisingly well, considering what he's been through. He's got contusions and abrasions over forty percent of his body, along with one broken and three cracked ribs. He's suffering from severe dehydration and a dislocation of his left shoulder that he reduced himself while in the field, fortunately without doing any further damage as far as I can tell. His feet look like raw hamburger, and he's got a fever from a low-grade infection. And there are about a billion mosquito bites over eighty percent of his body."

"Anything else?" asked Gerber quietly.

"Yes," said McMillan, cracking a smile. "He's hungry and he wants a beer."

"He'll live, then?"

McMillan laughed. "He'll live, all right. Although right now he needs rest and fluid replacement. I've got two IVs running, but I think that, when they're through we can let him have that beer. Sometimes I think Fetterman could live through a B-52 strike." Then he turned serious. "He wants to talk to you, Captain. I don't think you're going to like what he has to tell you."

"What is it? What's the matter? The others . . . ?"

"They're alive, sir. At least they were the last time he saw them. I think I'll let him tell you. I don't believe I care to hear the story again."

Filled with a mixture of curiosity and foreboding, Gerber pushed through the doorway into the tiny, twelve-bed ward of the dispensary. The only other patient, a Tai striker recovering from an appendix operation, was at the far end.

"Christ! Master Sergeant, you look like death warmed over."

"Damned glad to see you, too, sir," Fetterman answered cheerfully, although his voice was a bit harsh. The sound reminded Gerber of the rattle of an old piece of paper that had been left lying out in the sun too long.

"The doc says you got something you want to tell me."

"Yes, sir. It's about Tyme and Washington."

"Where are they, Tony?"

"VC prison camp near Hong Ngu."

"Hong Ngu? You mean they're still in South Vietnam?"

"Yes, sir. We were captured just about the time Kittredge and the lieutenant stepped into it. When we sprung the ambush, the enemy counterattacked. Must have had seven or eight times as many guys as we did. We had to break contact and escape and evade. We got separated from the main group, and Justin was wounded. I was bandaging him up when the VC put the bag on us."

"You were all captured together?"

"More or less. Washington was trying to help some wounded strikers when they got him. The VC executed the strikers, sir."

"I know," said Gerber. "We found the bodies."

"Captain, Sergeant Krung, was he . . . ?"

"Krung made it okay. He found Sully and brought him in."

Fetterman leaned back and gave a sigh of relief. "Good. I'm glad to hear that." Then he noticed that Gerber had not mentioned the others. "What about Kittredge and the lieutenant's bunch?"

"Steve didn't make it, Tony. I'm sorry. Bromhead came through okay, though. His group took a real beating, but they were able to break contact and get back to camp. He was with the squad that came out to pick you up."

"Sorry, sir. I don't remember that too well. Thank him for me, will you?"

"Consider it done."

"I'm sorry about Kittredge, too. He was a good man. Never saw a man who could lay a mortar tube like he could. Best heavy weapons man I've seen in ten years with the Special Forces."

Gerber merely nodded. He couldn't see any point just now in telling Fetterman how Kittredge had died. "I'll tell you about it later when I bring you your beer. McMillan says you can have one as soon as you've finished your IVs.''

"Damned nuisance, if you ask me," snorted Fetterman, shrugging both arms. "Wouldn't be so bad if he could figure out how to put a couple of beers in the damned things.''

"Sorry," said Gerber. "Doc says you'll have to wait." There was a pause, and then Gerber said, "Tony, about Washington and Tyme . . .''

"Yes, sir. Like I said, they marched us all night through the jungle. We were blindfolded most of the time, but I counted pace and had a pretty good idea of where we were. They took us to a camp just a little north and east of Hong Ngu. I confirmed the location when I escaped.''

"You escaped? How?" Gerber felt like an idiot. Of course the man had escaped. That was obvious. But for some reason or other it seemed so unlikely that it hadn't fully sunk in yet.

"I had one of those new, plastic-coated escape and evasion maps, a button compass and a small survival kit sewn into the lining of my jungle jacket. The VC missed it when they searched us. There was a time or two when I could have slipped away before we got to the camp, but of course I couldn't do that, sir.''

Gerber was confused. "You could have escaped before you got there, but you didn't try? Why in God's name not?''

"I could have slipped away, sir, but not with the others. I had to wait until we got to the camp to find out where it was if we were going to have any chance of rescuing Washington and Tyme.''

"You allowed yourself to be taken to the camp so that you could help the others escape?''

"No, sir. So we could go back and rescue them. Tyme would never have made it in an escape attempt, sir. He's too weak. He took a hit in the shoulder and lost a lot of blood. I was hit in practically the same place once, and his was worse. I figured the only thing to do was let them take all of us to the camp so I could pinpoint its location and then bring back help. It's a big camp, sir. Looks like Charlie was figuring on doing a lot of business in the P.O.W. area. They had a lot of cages. I didn't see them, but Tyme said there were two other Americans already there, Rockford or Rock somebody, and a guy named Corbett. Ever hear of them?''

"Don't think so. Did Tyme actually see the other prisoners?''

"No. He overheard the VC talking about them. He said the VC talked like they were planning to shoot them."

"Did they?"

"I don't think so. At least I didn't hear any shots before I left. Tyme thought the camp commander was waiting for word from Hanoi. Boom-Boom was pretty incoherent, but from what I could gather, the executions weren't supposed to take place until today or tomorrow."

Gerber felt sick. The men could already be dead. They might all be dead by now.

"Captain," said Fetterman, "there's something else. The Chinese guy was there."

Gerber stared at him in disbelief. "Come on, Tony. For Christ's sake. The man can't be everywhere. You're becoming obsessed with him. The Chinese probably pulled him out of the area right after that little hunting trip you and Tyme took into Cambodia. We haven't had any reported sightings of Chinese advisors in the last two months. Anywhere in Vietnam."

"Captain, I tell you he was there. I recognized him, and he seemed to recognize me. It was the same man. What's more, they knew everything about us, our names, our ranks, who you were. I'm telling you, sir, it *was* him. And I'll tell you something else. We were set up, and he's the bastard who did it. I don't know how. He must have a spy in the camp or something."

"Only one?" said Gerber cynically. It was well known that the Vietnamese component of the Strike Force was infiltrated with Vietcong agents. Knowing who and proving it was another matter.

Fetterman ignored the comment.

"Captain, the guy was there. He knew me. He knew all about us. We were set up, and he did it. The SOB knows we were after him on the Cambodian raid, and this is his way of getting even. Call me paranoid if you like, but I know what I'm telling you. I can't prove it, but I *know*."

It seemed a pretty farfetched idea, almost as farfetched as the idea they'd put into practice a few months ago when Gerber had sent a hit team into Cambodia to assassinate the Chinese advisor to a group of VC who had been causing them a lot of trouble. Maybe Fetterman was right.

"How did you escape, Tony?"

"It wasn't easy, sir. Like I said, I had the little E and E kit sewn into my jungle jacket. When it got dark and I realized the guards weren't paying any particular attention to us, I sawed my way out of the cage with this."

Fetterman reached over to the tiny nightstand next to his cot and picked up a small knife. It was a piece of electric hacksaw blade that had been ground and sharpened into a small knife blade, with the hacksaw teeth still on the top edge, and a handle of split bamboo, wrapped with wire.

"I made the handle out of one of the bars I cut out of the cage and used part of the wire from the leg irons. Of course, once I got out, I had to find a body to put in the cage, and I had to fix the bamboo bar so they wouldn't notice I was missing."

Gerber stared at Fetterman in amazement. "Of course," he said. "What's this about leg irons?"

Fetterman explained the arrangement of U-shaped pieces and rod and how he had gotten out of them by sliding the U-shaped shackles along the rod, once he could squeeze out of the cage, until he was able to unwire the rod from the stake and slip the shackles off over the end.

"After that I found myself a passing VC and traded places with him," Fetterman concluded matter-of-factly. "With any luck at all, they didn't discover I was missing until this morning. I had to kill two other sentries on the way out, and I suppose they might have noticed that one of them was missing before morning, but I doubt it. Anyway, after I got through their perimeter patrols, I made my way into Hong Ngu and stole some fisherman's boat. I figured that, if the VC did notice I was missing, they'd expect me to make straight for the camp through the jungle so I headed away from camp, and came down the Song Tien Giang to just north of Cho Moi. Then I came overland to the camp, approaching from the southwest rather than the northwest. We've worked that area a lot, and I know the trails. Also figured the VC would be less likely to look for me there."

Gerber shook his head in amazement, then snapped it up suddenly. "Where'd you get the smoke grenade?"

"Oh, that. It was nothing. Slipped into the guards' barracks before I left and took it back from the VC who took it from me.

Got my rifle back, too, but I couldn't find Boom-Boom's or Washington's. Picked up three carbines on the way out, but I couldn't carry it all so I destroyed two of them."

"Ah, now, Tony, that's just too much. How could you possibly have known it was your rifle?" said Gerber, grinning.

"I checked the serial number." He paused. "Captain, I wish I had a photograph of your face right now."

Gerber gave a long snort, then both men broke into laughter. When it finally subsided, the conversation turned serious again.

"Tony, I've got about a battalion of men waiting to go get T.J. and Boom-Boom. Can you pinpoint that camp for us on the map?"

"Can but won't," said Fetterman. "Not if you're going in there with a battalion."

"What! Why?"

"Captain, that camp is run by a VC major named Vo. The guy is a real sadist and absolutely loony tunes besides. He talks like a hotel manager, calls the prisoners his guests and refers to torturing them as entertainment. I'm telling you, the guy is as crazy as a March hare. You go trying to put a big-assed air assault into that place, and he'll kill Boom-Boom and Washington for sure. Besides, he's got a couple of hundred men in there with him. Got to have, given the size of the force that hit us and what I could see of the size of the camp. You go in there making noise with a bunch of choppers, and your battalion is likely to find itself up against his battalion. While the two of you are slugging it out, he'll either off the prisoners or slip across the border into Cambodia. It's not all that far away, you know."

"Tony, be reasonable, will you. They'll damned sure hear us coming if we try to walk in with a battalion."

"Yes, sir, that's true. But I don't think they'll hear anything at all until it's too late if you let me take a squad of men in first, say about ten minutes before the helicopters, and spring our boys."

"Master Sergeant, are you out of your mind? You were captured by the Vietcong and escaped. That's your ticket out of here. We're sending you home, man. Back to Mrs. Fetterman and the kids. Your war is over."

"Not yet it's not. Not until I get Boom-Boom out and take care of the Chinese and that bastard Vo."

"You don't seem to understand me, Tony. You are going home."

"And you don't seem to understand me, Captain. I can lead a patrol in there and spring them. I can get them out if they're still alive. Your way, they're dead for sure."

In exasperation Gerber yanked back the sheet and pointed to Fetterman's feet. They had so many bandages wrapped around them that they looked like a poor imitation of Mickey Mouse's feet.

"And just how are you going to do it? How, Sergeant? Answer me that one, will you? How are you going to take a patrol in there with your feet looking like that? In a wheelchair?"

Before Gerber could stop him, Fetterman yanked the IV catheters out of his arms, swung his legs over the side of the cot and stood facing Gerber. The master sergeant's face was etched with pain, but his voice was icily calm when he spoke.

"Are there any more questions, sir?"

"Tony, please," begged Gerber. "Lie down."

"I walked on them this far, sir, and I can walk on them all the way back. Just get me as far as Hong Ngu, and I'll crawl if I have to. I can do it, sir, and I want this one. Please, Mack."

Gerber ran his left hand down the side of his face. His eyes felt as if they were full of sand, and he wanted to cry. He could tell that Fetterman was in pain, but the man was determined not to let it stop him. And he realized something else. It was the first time ever, in their nearly full year together in Vietnam, that Fetterman had called him Mack, despite Gerber's continual assurances that it was okay to do so.

"All right, Master Sergeant," said Gerber. "We'll see what can be done, but that's all I'm promising. It depends on what McMillan says about your fitness for duty. Damn it, Fetterman, at least sit down, will you?"

"Yes, sir. Thank you very much, sir." Fetterman eased himself back down on the edge of the cot.

"What's all the yelling about in here?" asked McMillan, sticking his head in the doorway.

"The captain and I were just having a little discussion," said Fetterman breezily. "He was trying to convince me that my feet hurt, and I was trying to convince him that they're my feet."

"He wants to lead the rescue party going after the others," said Gerber.

"What! Fetterman, you can't be serious!" McMillan exclaimed.

"That's what I told him," Gerber continued. "But he's too much of a bullheaded Apache to listen to reason."

"Aztec, sir. Aztec. Not Apache. We Fettermans have been Aztecs for centuries."

"I give up," said Gerber, throwing up his hands. "You try to talk some sense into him, Doc. I'm going to go out and get that beer for him, and then I'm going to sit down and drink the damned thing myself."

Gerber got up to leave.

"Well, if you two are done *discussing*, the patient has a couple of other visitors. And then the patient's doctor thinks he needs some rest."

"Tell him he's in no shape to be running around the jungle, will you, Doc?" Gerber persisted.

"Fetterman, you're in no shape to go running around the jungle," said McMillan sternly. Then he turned to Gerber. "See how easy it is?"

"Say, Doc," said Fetterman, "remember that time you and I went into Saigon to pick up some medical supplies and you said, 'First let's stop over at the Blue Parrot and see that dancer and have a quick . . .' Say, Doc, what was her name? I've kind of forgotten, but I think it's all starting to come back to me now. Co Bang, that was it, wasn't it, Doc?"

McMillan cleared his throat noisily. "No, that was not her name. I've never been in the Blue Parrot in my life—it's an off-limits bar as you well know—and anyway, there was plenty of penicillin to spare that month. And so help me, Fetterman, if you ever mention it again and word gets back to Louise Denton, I'll fill your IV bottles full of formaldehyde and saltpeter, and you'll wind up with a limp prick that will last forever."

"Does that mean I can go?" asked Fetterman.

McMillan turned to Gerber and shrugged. "Like he says, Captain, they are his feet."

"I'll be back with the maps," said Gerber sourly. "Then you can show me this great, harebrained scheme of yours."

"Thank you, sir. I knew you'd understand once you realized I have the highest enthusiasm for the mission."

"The highest enthusiasm. Why I ought . . ." Gerber shut up. He could tell that he'd lost the argument, and he decided that he'd better get out before he lost another one.

"Now, can I show in the other guests?" asked McMillan.

"I'd appreciate it, Doc, if you wouldn't use that term."

McMillan looked puzzled. "All right, visitors, then."

"Male or female?" joked Fetterman.

"One of each, actually."

Now Fetterman looked puzzled.

"Miss Morrow is outside with her camera and notepad in hand," McMillan said with a laugh. "She wants to ask you all sorts of questions about your miraculous escape."

"Oh, no!" groaned Fetterman in mock horror. "The insatiable curiosity of the press. Will they never leave me alone?"

"But first there's someone else."

"Has she got better legs than Morrow? If she has, send her in," quipped Fetterman.

"My guess is that he's got really ugly legs, but I'll bet they're a lot stronger than Morrow's." He turned to shout at the door. "You can come in, now, General."

"Hello, Master Sergeant," said Hull, stepping into the room. "I guess I can't call you corporal anymore, can I?"

The face was older, more creased and gaunt, the head balding like Fetterman's own, but Fetterman would have known the man if he'd bumped into him wearing a disguise on a New York subway.

Fetterman half rose from the cot.

McMillan pushed him back down. "You want to go back out into the field, you stay off your feet for now. Doctor's orders."

"Captain—I mean, General Hull. It's an extreme pleasure to see you again after all these years, sir."

McMillan looked at the two men and was surprised to see that both had wet eyes. He cleared his throat again.

"I've got lots of other patients to tend to," McMillan lied. "So if you two gentlemen will excuse me, I'll leave you alone to talk over old times."

As he went out, he closed the door softly.

17

THE JUNGLE NEAR
HONG NGU

The Huey UH-1D made five landings in five widely spaced LZs west and northwest of Tan Chau shortly before dark. Four of the passengers were dressed in gray-and-black-striped tiger suits. The fifth wore a many pocketed, sleeveless vest of black material over an all-black ninja costume that covered him from head to toe. All five got off at the second LZ, just northwest of Tan Chau, a few hundred yards from the Mekong River.

The men's faces, covered by camouflage makeup paint or the close fitting hood of the ninja suit, were invisible in the darkness, except when one of them smiled briefly, showing a quick glimpse of teeth filed sharply into points.

The men carried a wide variety of unusual weapons with them as they moved quickly into the trees lining the edge of the landing zone. Three Karl Gustav Model 45-B 9 mm submachine guns, widely known as Swedish Ks, with large sound suppressors fitted to the barrels, were augmented by a similarly silenced .45-caliber M-3A1 grease gun, and a likewise quieted Mk IIS Sten gun of Second World War vintage. The man in the ninja suit wore a Czechoslovakian-manufactured Skorpion machine pistol, also suppressed, in a shoulder holster beneath his left armpit. Two of the other men carried silencer-equipped .380-caliber Beretta semiautomatic pistols, the squat 1934 model. A much noisier U.S.-made M-79 40 mm grenade launcher, a locally made crossbow and a Soviet-made RPD light machine gun, captured a few months earlier from the Vietcong, along with a varied collection of fragmentation, white phosphorus and concussion grenades, rounded out the collection of military oddities.

The ninja carried a few other items familiar only to followers of the martial arts, all of them with the potential to kill silently. He had begun his study of the martial arts in the United States shortly after the Second World War when he was twenty years old and stationed in California with the U.S. Army. Later he had continued his interest in unarmed combat and the arts of kendo, akido, kenjutsu, kung fu, jujitsu, tae kwon do and finally ninjitsu during overseas duty tours with the Army in Honolulu, Korea, Thailand, Okinawa and Japan. At one time he taught hand-to-hand combat to students at the Ranger School in Fort Benning, Georgia. A member of no orthodox martial arts school, he blended his skills and knowledge of pressure points and nerve pathways into a no-nonsense killing art devoid of the formalized postures and flowery movements that characterized traditional forms and Hong Kong karate movies. He had learned to kill with the pressure of a single finger, and to control his own pain through willpower and Zen philosophy. He was an unlikely-looking karate killer and quite possibly, at that moment, the deadliest man in Southeast Asia. His name was Master Sergeant Anthony B. Fetterman.

No words were spoken by the five men. There was an occasional tap on the shoulder or a nearly invisible gesture of the hand to indicate that someone should go a certain direction or perform a certain task. But as far as speech was concerned, the men might never have realized that language had been invented. They hid, unmoving, just inside the tree line until it was completely dark, then the owner of the crossbow and sharply filed teeth, Sergeant Krung, led them through the woods to a place where they could observe the fishing boats working the evening catch out of the Tan Chau docks.

By 2200 the boats had all been brought in and the fishermen had gone home, except for one elderly gentleman who insisted on remaining to fish off the dock when everyone else had sense enough to go home to bed. It appeared as though he intended to make a night of it.

The old fisherman might perhaps have simply been a dedicated angler or a henpecked husband seeking to escape from his nagging mama-san for the night. Or he might have been a Vietcong agent, set to watch the river for interesting traffic. Fetterman could neither afford to take the chance nor wait for the old man to leave. With Krung and Kepler covering, he silently stalked the man, taking nearly fifteen minutes to cross the open dock area behind the fisherman without making the slightest noise to betray his presence.

When he was directly behind the old man, Fetterman waited patiently for him to bend down, extract a grub from a tin can and rebait his hook. Then, as he straightened to cast the line back into the water, Fetterman snaked an arm around the old man's neck and squeezed, putting pressure on both carotid arteries.

When he felt the man slump into unconsciousness, Fetterman immediately relaxed the pressure of his judo choke. Another few moments of continued pressure, Fetterman knew, would have caused brain damage followed rapidly by respiratory and cardiac arrest. It was not Fetterman's intention to kill an old man who might be nothing more than what he appeared to be. He left the man tied to a corner post of the dock, his hands bound behind him with nylon parachute cord and his shirt stuffed into his mouth for a gag. He would regain consciousness in a few minutes and spend an uncomfortable night, but he would be alive to be found when others came to fish in the morning. Fetterman and his men would be long gone.

When he had satisfied himself that the activity on the dock had not been observed by any late-night passersby, Fetterman signaled the others, who came down to the dock. They searched through the boats tied up there until they found one suitable for their purpose and then helped themselves.

It took nearly two hours to travel the eight miles to Hong Ngu, mainly because they kept in the shadows along the bank on the Tan Chau side until they had passed the island separating the two cities. When they were south of the point of the island, they poled their way across to the Hong Ngu side and hid the boat in a patch of reeds just below the town. After checking their equipment, primarily to make sure that the radios were still operating after the water crossing, they moved into the swamps and jungle to the northeast, heading for the area where Fetterman believed the P.O.W. camp to be located. It would have been a great deal simpler to have had the helicopter insert them below Hong Ngu. It also would have been a great deal noisier.

Almost immediately they encountered a Vietcong patrol but were able to avoid detection by quick action and the use of available tree roots as a backdrop. Twenty minutes later they encountered a second patrol, and a short time after that a third.

"Jesus!" Kepler whispered in Fetterman's ear after the third patrol had passed them by. "I didn't realize there were this many VC in all of Vietnam. Where the hell did all these guys come from?"

"A few may be local guerrillas," Fetterman told him, "but most of these guys are all wearing some sort of uniform. They're Main Force. I would guess that they are from the camp."

"So what are they all doing out here wandering around in the swamps?"

"I would guess," Fetterman answered, "that they are looking for me. They've had time by now to discover I'm gone, try the direct route between here and Triple Nickel and figure out I didn't go that way. Now they're looking for clues closer to home."

"That's a lousy break," whispered Kepler. "The woods are full of them. I don't see how we'll ever get in and out undetected."

"On the contrary," Fetterman replied, "it's an excellent break. It means the camp is still here. They didn't get excited and move the prisoners after I escaped. Watch and learn, Derek, and I'll show you how to become invisible before your enemies' very eyes."

"Great. 'Cause otherwise I don't see how we're going to get in there without being spotted."

"Relax," Fetterman reassured him. "Prison camps are designed to keep people in, not out. You'll see."

In all they encountered six patrols before finally reaching the outer perimeter of the camp. But those patrols were looking for a lone, injured, escaped prisoner, not a well-equipped, well-concealed five-man raiding party. Each time Fetterman's little group was offered ample warning by the noisy approach of the Vietcong patrols. They succeeded in remaining undetected.

At 0200 Kepler used the primary radio to signal the precise location of the P.O.W. camp to Gerber and the main assault force. Then he switched the PRC-10 off. The radios would now be used for communication only in an extreme emergency. They didn't want a stray burst of static giving their position away once they were inside the camp.

Getting in was fairly easy, as Fetterman had predicted. The VC guards, for the most part, were alert for another escaping prisoner, not an infiltrating assault. Two were encountered whose positions made the party's advance awkward, but they were conveniently killed by Anderson and Krung and offered no more problems. The bodies were carefully hidden by submerging them in one of the punji moats, all the stakes of which faced inward, and then they quickly crossed the moat on a hinged plank that Fetterman had assembled and brought along for that purpose.

By 0330 they were in position. They had completed their reconnaissance of the camp, pinpointing Vo's hut, the radio shack with its hand-cranked generator, the one longhouse, which still seemed to contain a few sleeping men, and the prisoner cages. It wasn't hard locating Washington and Tyme. The cells were where Fetterman remembered, and each now had a small kerosene lantern with a leaf shade hung inside the enclosure. An armed guard, who seemed reasonably awake and alert, stood outside each door. While they found many other cages designed to hold prisoners, they found no others that were occupied. Of the other two Americans that Tyme had mentioned to Fetterman there was no sign.

At precisely 0445, Krung shot the guard in front of Washington's cage through the throat with his crossbow.

At the same instant Fetterman snapped a piano wire garrote down over the head of the second guard, crossed the wooden handles over each other as he turned his back toward the guard's and pulled the wire taut, bending forward at the waist to lift the man off his feet as the piano wire cut into the man's throat from bottom to top, front to back. The only sounds were a short clatter as the man dropped his burp gun and a low, burbling noise as his blood flowed out.

Krung and McMillan immediately came forward and opened the cells by using a combination of end and side cutters on the wire closure.

The shackles were quickly cut away with a large set of bolt cutters, and McMillan made a quick assessment of each of the patients, making sure that they were still alive and could be safely moved.

"Fetterman?" Tyme whispered the question hoarsely and with obvious disbelief. "They said you'd been shot."

"Then they're either lousy shots or lousy liars. Be quiet, Boom-Boom. We've come to get you out."

Tyme nodded weakly. "I knew you'd be back."

"Listen, Boom-Boom, we can't find those other two Americans you told me about. Do you know where they are?"

Tyme shook his head. "Sorry. I never saw them. I heard some shots around midmorning. After that Vo came and told me you'd been shot trying to escape. Didn't really believe him because he had too many guys still out looking for you."

"They still are. Come on. Let's get you out of here."

As they loaded Tyme and Washington onto two folding stretchers, Anderson suddenly appeared out of the shadows, the sling of the RPD draped over his mammoth shoulders so that it hung in front of him, a Swedish K in his hands.

"All set on the claymores. Ready anytime you are, Master Sergeant."

Fetterman nodded and glanced at the plastic wristwatch he'd picked up back at camp. The time was exactly 0450. In the distance he could faintly hear the sound of approaching helicopters.

They carried Tyme and Washington to the edge of the small clearing that Fetterman had seen when he had first arrived at the camp, pausing only long enough to permanently ensure the quiet of the two guards in the well-camouflaged hut near it.

Anderson set up the RPD to provide covering fire, should it be necessary.

"Derek, you still got the strobe unit?" asked Fetterman.

"Right here," answered Kepler, "although if it gets much lighter, a smoke grenade will probably work better."

"Okay. You're in charge. If I don't make it back in time for the evac chopper, you get everybody out of here. Don't worry about me. I'll catch a ride back with the main group."

"Just where in the hell do you think you're going?"

"Got a little unfinished business to attend to. I'll be back."

"Fetterman, for Christ's sake . . . Fetterman!"

But Fetterman was gone.

The sound of the helicopters was getting louder. Enough to be plainly heard by anyone who cared to listen. Fetterman moved quickly back into the camp and hurried down the trail. As he did, a VC stepped out into the pathway directly in front of him. Reacting instinctively, Fetterman pulled a shuriken from a pocket. The throw was only about five yards, and the heavy, razor-sharp throwing star embedded itself nicely in the VC's forehead. Fetterman hadn't even broken stride.

Fetterman moved past the guards' barracks and through the camp, past Vo's hut to the radio shack. He stepped quickly up the low step to the doorway. The suppressed M-3 made a low, guttural coughing as he hosed down the interior, killing the two men inside and riddling the radio equipment with bullets.

Fetterman didn't dawdle to admire his handiwork. He changed magazines on the grease gun, then raced back into camp toward Vo's hut. The sound of the helicopters was becoming quite loud now, and people were beginning to come out of their hootches to see what the noise was all about.

As he ran toward Vo's hut, Fetterman caught sight of a flash of familiar khaki and loosed a long burst at it. The Chinese dived back into a hut, and Fetterman tossed two grenades, one fragmentation and the other white phosphorus, in the open doorway behind him. Fetterman couldn't wait to check their effectiveness, but he heard both grenades go off and felt the heat of the WP. A moment later he heard two sharp explosions ahead of him as someone hit a trip wire outside the guards' barracks. The helicopters were beating the air into submission now, and Fetterman could hear the door gunners laying down suppressive fire along the edges of the LZ.

As he reached Vo's hut, Fetterman lobbed his second WP grenade inside, found cover and waited for the blast. The explosion seemed to lift the roof from the hut, setting the entire structure on fire.

A moment later a figure ran from the hut, his clothing aflame, screaming in pain as he beat ineffectually at the burning cloth and pieces of phosphorus with his hands. It was Major Vo. Fetterman watched the spectacle with an abstract detachment until the man fell to the ground and lay still. Then he walked over very calmly and emptied his grease gun into the smoldering corpse.

18

SPECIAL FORCES CAMP
A-555

A very tired Tony Fetterman sat in the team house, finally drinking the beer that McMillan had promised him. His feet were propped up on the table, and they hurt like hell, but he had a curiously warm feeling inside.

Tyme and Washington were on their way to a hospital in Saigon, and Doc McMillan was keeping them company on the trip. They both had a good chance of complete recovery.

Lieutenant Colonel Bates had arrived from B-Team Headquarters, and Gerber was regaling him with the tale of how General Hull had leaped out of the C and C ship when the air assault had inserted, fired twice at a fleeing Cong and had another pop up out of a spider hole directly in front of him only to discover that his carbine had jammed. The general, thinking quickly, had pulled off his own helmet and had beaten the VC to death with it.

"That's the way John Wayne would have done it." Bates laughed.

Gerber didn't bother to tell them that what made it such an excruciatingly funny story was that that was exactly the way that he had done it a month earlier when his M-14 had jammed.

Morrow was there, too, alternately snapping away with her motor-driven 35 mm camera and chugging down large gulps of beer. She paused occasionally to stare at Gerber with a look that made Fetterman feel happy for the captain but a little bit uneasy about the possible consequences.

The mop-up operation had taken the rest of the morning and most of the afternoon but had been a success. They had inflicted heavy casualties on the VC with a confirmed body count of forty-two and had suffered only light casualties themselves. The enemy had been scattered, unable to mobilize reserves or organize to fight effectively with their radio command center knocked out and their commanding officer dead. The VC plan to cut off the head of the American dragon had backfired.

There were only two dark notes. They had been unable to find the two Americans that Tyme had spoken of, and the Chinese had somehow escaped Fetterman once again. No body had been found in the smoking remains of the hut that Fetterman had seen him duck into.

Anderson had tuned in Radio Hanoi, which was blaring out rock tunes, and everybody seemed to be having a good time. Then the music was interrupted by the strains of *Vietnam muon nam*, and the announcer broke in with the evening propaganda newscast. His first story was the announcement that a Captain Humbert Rocque Versace and Sergeant Kenneth M. Roraback had been executed at ten o'clock in reprisal for the execution in Da Nang of three Vietcong suspects.

For a moment everyone was very quiet. Could they have come so close, yet been so far away? Then Fetterman heard the click-whir-click-whir of Morrow's camera as she photographed the stunned faces of the men around her.

For a moment everyone glared at her, then the tension was broken by an insane chuckle from Fetterman.

"Lady," he said, "I thought I was hard, but you are one tough cookie."

"Damn it, I feel for them and their families, too," Morrow protested. "It might have been any of you. But I'm still a reporter. I'm just doing my job."

"Miss Morrow, that's all any of us are doing," said Fetterman.

Then they all laughed.

Because it was good.

GLOSSARY

AC—Aircraft commander. The pilot in charge of the aircraft.

ACTUAL—The actual unit commander as opposed to the radio-telephone operator (RTO) for that unit.

AK-47—Soviet assault rifle used by the North Vietnamese and the Vietcong.

AO—Area of Operation.

AO DAI—Long dresslike garment, split up the sides and worn over pants.

AP ROUNDS—Armor-piercing ammunition.

ARTY—Artillery.

ARVN—Army of the Republic of Vietnam. A South Vietnamese soldier. Also known as Marvin Arvin.

BAR—Browning Automatic Rifle.

BEAUCOUP—Many.

BISCUIT—C-rations or combat rations.

BLOWER—See *Horn*.

BODY COUNT—The number of enemy killed, wounded or captured during an operation. Used by Saigon and Washington as a means of measuring the progress of the war.

BOOM-BOOM—Term used by Vietnamese prostitutes to sell their product.

BOONDOGGLE—Any military operation that hasn't been completely thought out. An operation that is ridiculous.

BUSHMASTER—Jungle warfare expert or soldier skilled in jungle navigation. Also a large deadly snake not common to Vietnam but mighty tasty.

C AND C—Command and control aircraft that circles overhead to direct the combined air and ground operations.

CARIBOU—Cargo transport plane.

CHICOM—Chinese communist.

CHINOOK—Army Aviation twin-engine helicopter. A CH-47. Also known as a shit hook.

CLAYMORE—Antipersonnel mine that fires 750 steel balls with a lethal range of 50 meters.

CLOSE AIR SUPPORT—Use of airplanes and helicopters to fire on enemy units near friendlies.

CO CONG—Female Vietcong.

DAI UY—Vietnamese Army rank equivalent to captain in the U.S. Army.

DAP LOI—Single-shell booby trap, sometimes a 50 mm round, with a nail for a firing pin. Small and virtually undetectable, it could put a round through a trooper's foot.

DCI—Director, Central Intelligence. The director of the Central Intelligence Agency.

DEROS—See *Short-timer*.

DI DI MAU—Vietnamese expression meaning "get the hell out."

DIEN CAI DAU—Vietnamese. Literally "off the wall." Used to refer to a person who is crazy."

DONG—Unit of North Vietnamese money equivalent to about a penny.

FIIGO—Fuck it, I've got my orders.

FIVE—Radio call sign for the executive officer of a unit.

FNG—Fucking new guy.

FRENCH FORT—Distinctive, triangular-shaped structure built by the hundreds by the French.

FUBAR—Fucked up beyond all recognition.

GARAND—M-1 rifle that was replaced by the M-14. Issued to the Vietnamese early in the war.

GARRET TROOPER—Rear-area pogue; a fat cat, someone who doesn't get out and fight in the war.

GUARD THE RADIO—Term that means to stand by in the commo bunker and listen for messages.

GUNSHIP—Armed helicopter or cargo plane that carries weapons instead of cargo.

HE—High-explosive ammunition.

HOOTCH—Almost any shelter, from temporary to long-term.

HORN—Term referring to a specific kind of radio operations that used satellites to rebroadcast messages.

HORSE—See *Biscuit.*

HOTEL THREE—A helicopter landing area at Saigon's Tan Son Nhut Air Force Base.

HUEY—A Bell UH-1D, or its successor, the UH-1H, helicopter, called a Huey because its original designation was HU, but later changed to UH. Also called a Slick.

IN-COUNTRY—Term used to refer to American troops operating in South Vietnam. They were all in-country.

INTELLIGENCE—Any information about the enemy operations. It can include troop movements, weapons capabilities, biographies of enemy commanders and general information about terrain features. It is any information that would be useful in planning a mission.

KABAR—A type of military combat knife.

KEMCHI—Korean foul-smelling cabbage delicacy.

KIA—Killed in action. (Since the U.S. was not engaged in a declared war, the use of the term KIA was not authorized. KIA came to mean enemy dead. Americans were KHA or killed in hostile action.)

KLICK—A thousand meters. A kilometer.

LBJ—Long Binh Jail.

LEGS—Derogatory term used by airborne qualified troops in talking about regular infantry.

LIMA LIMA—Land line. Refers to telephone communications between two points on the ground.

LLDB—Luc Luong Dac Biet. The South Vietnamese Special Forces. Sometimes referred to as the Look Long, Duck Back.

LP—Listening Post. A position outside the perimeter manned by a couple of soldiers to give advance warning of enemy activity.

LZ—Landing zone.

M-14—Standard rifle of the U.S., eventually replaced by the M-16. It fired the standard NATO 7.62 mm round.

M-16—Became the standard infantry weapon of the Vietnam War. It fired 5.56 mm ammunition.

M-79—Short-barreled, shoulder-fired weapon that fires a 40 mm grenade. These can be high explosive, white phosphorus or canister.

MACV—Military Assistance Command, Vietnam. Replaced MAAG in 1964.

MEDEVAC—Medical evacuation. Also called Dustoff. Helicopter used to take the wounded to medical facilities.

MEDCAP—Medical Civilian Assistance Program.

MIA—Missing in action.

NCO—Noncommissioned officer. A noncom. A sergeant.

NEXT—The man who says he's the next to be rotated home. See *Short-Timer.*

NINETEEN—Average age of the combat soldier in Vietnam, in contrast to age twenty-six in the Second World War.

NOUC-MAM—A foul-smelling (to the Americans, at least) fermented fish sauce used by the Vietnamese as a condiment. GIs nicknamed it ''armpit sauce.''

NVA—North Vietnamese Army. Also used to designate a soldier from North Vietnam.

O-1 BIRD DOG—Single-engine recon aircraft (usually a Cessna) used for forward air control and artillery observation. Their pilots were called FAC pilots.

OD—Olive drab; standard military color.

P-38—Military designation for the small, one-piece can opener supplied with C-rations.

PF—Popular Forces; Vietnamese soldiers drawn from the local population.

P.O.W.—Prisoner of war.

PRC-10—Portable radio.

PRC-25—Standard infantry radio used in Vietnam. Sometimes referred to as the "Prick 25," it was heavy and awkward.

PROGUES—Derogatory term used to describe fat, lazy people who inhabited rear areas, taking all the best supplies for themselves and leaving the rest for the men in the field.

PUFF—A prop plane carrying enough flares to floodlight a mile radius and capable of firing 6,000 rounds per minute. Also called Puff the Magic Dragon and Spooky.

PULL PITCH—Term used by helicopter pilots that means they are going to take off.

PUNGI STAKE—Sharpened bamboo hidden to penetrate the foot, sometimes dipped in feces.

R AND R—Rest and relaxation. The term came to mean a trip outside of Vietnam where the soldier could forget about the war.

RF STRIKERS—Local military forces recruited and employed inside a province. Known as Regional Forces.

RINGKNOCKER—Graduate of a military academy. It refers to the ring worn by all graduates.

RP—Rally point.

RPD—7.62 mm Soviet light machine gun.

RTO—Ratiotelephone operator. The radio man of a unit.

RULES OF ENGAGEMENT—The rules that told the American troops when they could fire and when they couldn't. Full Suppression meant that they could fire all the way in on a landing. Normal Rules meant that they could return fire for fire received. Negative Suppression meant that they weren't to shoot back.

SAPPER—Enemy soldier used in demolitions. Used explosives during attacks.

SIX—Radio call sign for the unit commander.

SHIT HOOK—Name applied by troops to the Chinook helicopter because of all the "shit" stirred up by the massive rotors.

SHORT—Term used by a GI in Vietnam to tell all who would listen that his tour was almost over.

SHORT-TIMER—Person who had been in Vietnam for nearly a year and who would be rotated back to the World soon. When the DEROS (Date of estimated return from overseas) was the shortest in the unit, the person was said to be "Next."

SKS—Simonov 7.62 mm semiautomatic carbine.

SMG—Submachine gun.

SOI—Signal Operating Instructions. The booklet that contained the call signs and radio frequencies of the units in Vietnam.

SOP—Standard operating procedure.

STEEL POT—Standard U.S. Army helmet. The steel pot was the outer metal cover.

1077—Police call code indicating negative contact.

TAI—Vietnamese ethnic group living in the mountainous regions.

THREE—Radio call sign of the operations officer.

THREE CORPS—Military area around Saigon. Vietnam was divided into four corps areas.

THE WORLD—The United States.

TOC—Tactical operations center.

TWO—Radio call sign of the intelligence officer.

VC—Vietcong. Also called Victor Charlie (phonetic alphabet) or just Charlie.

VIETCONG—Contraction of Vietnam Cong San. A guerrilla member of the Vietnamese Communist movement.

VIETCONG SAN—Vietnamese Communists. A term in use since 1956.

VIETMINH—Vietnamese who fought the French; forerunner of the Vietcong.

VNAF—South Vietnamese Air Force.

WIA—Wounded in action.

WILLIE PETE—WP, white phosphorus. Called smoke rounds.
Also used as antipersonnel weapons.

XO—Executive officer of a unit.

ZAP—To ding, pop caps or shoot.

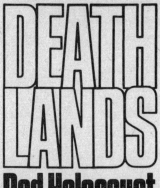

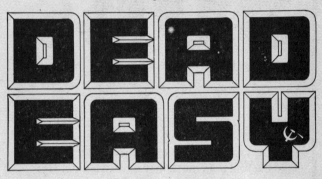

**Nile Barrabas and the
Soldiers of Barrabas are the**

SOBs

by Jack Hild

Nile Barrabas is a nervy son of a bitch who
was the last American soldier out of Vietnam
and the first man into a new kind of action. His
warriors, called the Soldiers of Barrabas, have
one very simple ambition: to do what the
Marines can't or won't do. Join the Barrabas
blitz! Each book hits new heights—this is
brawling at its best!

"Nile Barrabas is one tough SOB himself. . . .
A wealth of detail. . . . SOBs does the job!"
—*West Coast Review of Books*

**GOLD
EAGLE**

Available wherever paperbacks are sold.

SOBs-1